from

016-3498

email -

haska131313@yahoo.com

Thanks for the review.
Jan

FAT FOX

Jan Franklin Tooke

All rights reserved. No part of this book shall be reproduced or transmitted in any form or by any means, electronic, mechanical, magnetic, photographic including photocopying, recording or by any information storage and retrieval system, without prior written permission of the publisher. No patent liability is assumed with respect to the use of the information contained herein. Although every precaution has been taken in the preparation of this book, the publisher and author assume no responsibility for errors or omissions. Neither is any liability assumed for damages resulting from the use of the information contained herein.

Copyright © 2010 by Jan Franklin Tooke

ISBN 0-7414-6056-4

Printed in the United States of America

This is a work of fiction, but was inspired by a few true and real happenings. Names, characters, places, and incidents either are the product of the author's imagination or are used fictitiously. Any resemblance to actual events or locales or persons, living or dead, is entirely coincidental.

Published October 2010

INFINITY PUBLISHING
1094 New DeHaven Street, Suite 100
West Conshohocken, PA 19428-2713
Toll-free (877) BUY BOOK
Local Phone (610) 941-9999
Fax (610) 941-9959
Info@buybooksontheweb.com
www.buybooksontheweb.com

Index of Chapters

Part One

1. Viet Nam 1967 — 1
2. After the War — 10
3. Trouble in East Los Angeles — 16
4. The Famous Doctor Savornin — 25
5. Home With Linda after Being Shot — 28
6. Three Months Later in Louisville — 30
7. The Lessons on How to Eat Right — 32
8. Sixteen Months Later — 36
9. Nearly Two Years After Narvelle Was Shot — 37
10. Charlotte, the Fat Fox — 43
11. Vel Trips Out — 46
12. Deadly Practice — 50
13. Evening at Narvelle's House — 53
14. Where Is Your Stomach? — 56
15. Vel Goes Fox Hunting — 58
16. The Strangest Christmas Gift — 61
17. A Church Full of Happiness — 66
18. Vel Boasts — 70

Part Two

19. Charlotte's Brother Mork, A Few Years Before She Was Shot — 75
20. The Dancers — 78

21. Mork's Wife Dixie	81
22. Robby at Home	85
23. Mork Gets Told	88
24. After Dixie Left Him	93

Part Three

25. Vel's Next Targets	97
26. Andy in Sturgis, Two Years Later	103
27. Ho, Ho, Ho, a Giant	110
28. Hot Rods	116
29. Richard Head, Nine Weeks after the State Fair	118
30. Physical Therapy	128
31. LAPD	130
32. The Pretty Moon-Eyed Reporter and Richard Head: A Year Later	132

Part Four

33. Vel Seeks Fame	137
34. Vel and Fragile Discuss His New Target	141
35. Not Enough Information	144
36. The Longest Day	153
37. The Police Department Again	158
38. Mary Lynn and Stephen Manson	160
39. Mary Lynn Goes Home	162
40. Hot Shot Cowboy	164
41. Nutty Narvelle	171
42. Chicago Air	178
43. Fragile Councel	181

44. The Cowboy Is Back In Town	183
45. Mad Mary	186
46. Andy, Lucretia and Joshua Meet	190
47. Repeat That Please, the Second Interview Continues	194
48. Vel Wants to Escape	199
49. A Bag Full of Nuts	201
50. Jackson Hole	203
51. Joshua Gets It	205
52. Mother Mary and God	213
53. What to Do, What to Do, What to Do	215
54. Bloody Mary	219
55. Bad Moon Rising	221
56. Bang, Bang, You're Dead!	231
57. A Wood Box	239
58. Johnny Cake	242

Mark Twain said,

"Everyone is a moon, we all have a dark side."

PART ONE

CHAPTER ONE
VIET NAM 1967

The air was hot and dank while threatening clouds of gray and white, patchworked the pale blue sky. It was suddenly silent; the soldiers knew it was a bad sign, they were quiet too. The bird calls and monkey cries that escorted them all morning long, were no longer heard.

Then, Bang! Bang! Boom! rat-a-tat-tat, zip, zip, zip, sizzle, kaboom! The air exploded dangerously in the humid gray Viet Nam jungle. Mysterious vapor and a billion green leaves hid the group of small, but mighty, North Vietnamese soldiers, from the platoon of Marines who waded towards them through an inch of water. Down into the muck, mire, and tall grass, the Marines fell, not from pain, but from the instinct and the will to stay alive. Rat-a-tat-tat, rat-a-tat-tat, the enemies machine gun opened up again, spraying bullets like hot bees into the water, the dense grass, overhead, and into the bodies of two teen-aged American boys. Later, their painful cries would make their mothers moan.

"Fuck this shit!" Narvelle yelled, and like hot toast, up he popped, alone in the killing field, machine gun blazing in his hands. He aimed in the general direction of the Viet Cong's machine gun flashes. Like John Wayne in a movie, he let it rip, bam, bam, bam, bam, rat-a-tat-tat, rat-a-tat-tat. He sprayed the Viet Cong with a hundred pieces of hot lead, while strangely, no one fired back. Then he hit the ground and the muddy grass as quickly as he had jumped up. His gun barrel was steaming hot. His heart was racing. Seconds later all hell broke loose. Bullets punctured the air, the grass, trees, and the soft tissues of young men fighting for their lives against young men that they could barely see. A surrealistic haze of gun smoke and fog engulfed them all. An eternal minute later, the shooting stopped again. Each side waited anxiously for the air to clear.

Sergeant Harold Glasscock grabbed his phone. He was the boss here. He quietly growled, "Send me a God damned gunship ASAP, you know where we are, this is Sgt. Glasscock, Operation Sky King!"

A voice crackled back, "Yes sir, it's on the way!"

Each Marine went to work, carefully, and methodically, retracing the puffs of smoke from the Viet Cong's guns, then took deadly aim. Gradually the exchange of flying lead decreased, and after ten minutes or so of precise Marine reaction, a welcomed silence appeared. The stillness now was only broken by the occasional "pop" of a single rifle shot. As they waited for reinforcements, a kind breeze daintily puffed the air clean, making the leaves rattle quietly in the dense jungle grove.

Then, out of nowhere, it arrived. A foreboding looking, black Apache helicopter, sprang from the hill behind the Marines and quickly opened fire with four fifty caliber machine guns. Its blazing guns pulverized the jungle in front of the Marines where the Viet Cong were nestled. Thousands of bullets from the gunship hit the Earth in a few seconds, literally blowing trees into toothpicks. Next, rockets zipped from the deadly Apache and exploded like the fourth of July, along the entire one hundred yards of jungle where the enemy hid. No return fire came from the Viet Cong. The chopper paused, curiously circled the area, and then drifted backwards over the hill from whence it came. Once more, an eerie silence returned to this wet gray place.

Suddenly, it was over.

The Viet Cong had disappeared. They took their dead and wounded with them into their tunnels and caves underground. The shell-shocked Marines didn't go after them. They tossed a dozen hand grenades and explosives into the holes in the ground, trying to kill as many of their enemies as they could, and to seal off the tunnels. All that was left by the enemy was a few rifles, hundreds of bullet casings, a few pieces of bloody clothing, a map full of holes, a dead dog, and a fire pit with the remains of a cooked pig.

A welcomed calm settled in the grove as the clouds broke loose overhead, allowing a heavenly funnel of God's light down on them. Two teenage Marines, fresh out of boot camp, on their very first patrol, lay dead; four men seriously wounded and the remaining nineteen soldiers left the area without a scratch or wound. It was June, 1967. Bug infested, humid, hell.

In the tent, Narvelle, Harold, Jake, and John had become blood brothers. Their nicknames stayed with them throughout their lives after the war. Narvelle Phelps was simply called Vel. Harold Glasscock appropriately answered to Fragile, Jake Smith went by Snake, and Johnny Anderson was called Johnny Cake, he was the calmest one of the bunch, everything was a piece of cake for him. Johnny had been to hell and back.

Now they stood silently over the bloody shattered meat of their dead companions. No tears, each in shock as they stared at the faces of death. None of them ever really expected to end up in this God forsaken place. The allure of being a Marine, with all the fancy clothes, the macho cadences, and the tough guy attitudes, had been stripped from them that day. They were all now seasoned killers. Life no longer seemed so precious or so difficult to extinguish to any of them.

Later that week, their tent filled lazily with marijuana smoke as a bong was passed around by the four young friends. Each slowly took a hit, breathed in deeply, then waited for the welcome numbing sensation to arrive. Creedence Clearwater Revival music filled the tent and pulsed into the dark night. Narvelle was relaxed and in a talkative mood, he bragged about his John Wayne stance in the fire fight with the gooks. They all laughed hysterically when he told them that as he jumped up and opened fire, he pooped his pants, literally.

The ancient Talmud says, "There is a friend that sticketh closer than a brother." Any one that has been in the military knows this to be true. True friends are hard to find. Military friendships are some of the strongest bonds ever made. Some friendships are so bonded that you would literally give your life to save your friends life. That night, in the smoke filled tent, the four red-eyed soldiers vowed that they would always be loyal friends.

Everyone who knew Narvelle Phelps, all of his life, agreed that he had always exhibited episodes of nervous behavior. His long history of quirks had been apparent, even when he was a little boy. Perhaps he was just born, "nervous."

As a young child, maybe five years old, he remembered that his unusual behavior bothered him, and his parents. Direct questions by his father, where he was put on the spot, often seemed to trigger what he described as, sweating, shaking, fits. His dad, on many occasions throughout his youth, mimicked him unmercifully, as he teased, "Don't have a fit and fall in it!" His father often laughed, while Narvelle shivered, and sometimes cried, when the nervous fits occurred.

His dad thought it was all funny, entertaining, harmless, and cute.

Often as a child when Narvelle "lost it" at home, he would just stand there, cry, and shake piteously until his mother would arrive to rescue him; her warm hugs always seemed to calm him down.

In eighth grade he struck back at society, and his peers, for the first time. One day in junior high school, he truly "lost it big-time," when he went into something just shy of a rage. A fat, arrogant, mean, bully, named Dutch, had teased him often for years, sometimes pushing him into the girl's restrooms, sometimes tripping him in the hall, sometimes smashing a drink of soda-pop into his face, or mimicking Narvelle's nervous behaviors.

Here's what happened. One day at noon, as Narvelle sat to eat lunch with his friends, Dutch brazenly approached their table. As he stood boldly at the end of the table with a "shit-eating grin," staring at Narvelle, he suddenly blurted out, "you are a skinny, nervous, chicken-shit!" Narvelle felt a switch flip inside that he had never felt before. Magically, like an action hero, he leapt into action. The lunchroom filled with the scream of a banshee, as he jumped up onto the table, ran forward and kneed Dutch squarely in the face. Dutch spit his mouthful of peanuts and Coke, all over two screaming girls, sitting at the end of the table. Table food went flying in all directions as the table rocked sideways. Narvelle's buddies urged him on, yelling, "Kill the son-of-a-bitch!---fuck him up, dude!"

Narvelle almost did.

Dutch landed flat on his back on the floor, he was not unconscious, at that moment, but he was definitely stunned. The last thing that he saw before the ambulance carried him away, was Narvelle jumping through the air from the table, directly onto his head, like a starving panther after red meat.

He landed squarely, straddled Dutch's head and began to play basketball with the bully's skull, on the floor. Thud, thud, crack, bounce, thud and one more crack. After a half a dozen quick, hard, head smacks to the floor, two of Narvelle's friends tackled him, saving Dutch's life. Dutch had blood running freely from his ears, and was unconscious. He appeared to be dead, his eyes were rolled back up into his head.

Surprisingly, Narvelle was calm as a cucumber afterwards, big smile on his face, not even sweating, as he let go of his grip and stepped back from his prey. The peace of mind that followed him like a happy-puppy, stayed with him for a month; he liked it and spoke of it often.

Narvelle's second problem was that he sometimes stuttered, unexpectedly. Difficult questions by teachers or his parents could easily trigger his stuttering. In certain stressful situations, he would quickly go from normal, to his worst anxious jumpy appearance, where he would tremble and sweat, and finally, stutter. It was embarrassing, he hated it.

While in high school, he got into a few more fights with a few boys who dared to make fun of him. He quickly earned a reputation as someone not to mess around with. Once he had conquered "the school bully," he was no longer afraid to leap into action, any action, on his own. His best buddies would lightly joke with each other and respectfully say, "Don't go Narvelle Phelps on me!" Everyone in high school knew what that meant, especially Dutch, who fully recovered from his beating, quit his bullying profession, and became a good friend of Narvelle's. He enjoyed telling everyone that Narvelle had knocked some sense into his head.

Of note also, is the story of his greatest excitement while in high school. It happened his senior year.

Narvelle worked a paper route during his years in high school. After saving his money for quite a while, he bought something that he had dreamed about for a long time, a motorcycle. It was a used, 1953 Triumph. Stripped down, it had a single seat, no windshield, a gas tank that was deep cherry red and a bobbed cherry red fender over the fat rear tire. There were no mufflers on it, just short pipes that came from the engine, with no baffles; the mufflers had been removed by the previous owner. It was as beautifully loud and melodic as any Harley ever made, it just sang a different tune.

One day, on his way home from a friend's house, he sat at a red light waiting for it to change. The Triumph was making its deliciously loud, thump, thump, thump sounds. Then the nightmare from Hell showed up, a cop-car slowed down and carefully looked him over. On went the flashing red light and the siren, as Narvelle felt the adrenalin squirt in his veins.

Some decisions are made quickly when you're a teenager, he decided to escape.

Narvelle turned right and up the street he sped, full throttle, with the screaming cop-car in full pursuit. He ran the red light with the cop-car right behind him. Down the first street on the left he went, looking for his escape route at the end of the street, in the cul-de-sac. As he neared the end of the street he suddenly realized that he had taken the wrong street, it was the next one over that he needed to be on. He slowed down at the circle at the end of the street, with the cop-car still on his heels, screaming and blinking. Calmly he turned around and up the road he went, while the cop jumped out of his car, waved his pistol and yelled at him to stop. "He ain't going to shoot me," the kid thought. "He can see that I'm just a kid." Narvelle was wearing cut off Levi's, tennis shoes, no shirt, and sun-glasses.

Through the stop sign at the top of the street, onto the main street, and to the left he scurried. Down the next street and to the end of it, his thunderous Triumph raced, looking for the bicycle trail. The cop was on his way. Along the narrow bicycle path he scampered, his heart pounding. Close to an irrigation ditch, he steered the bike carefully for two hundred feet, then through three neighbor's yards. Finally, the cop car couldn't follow him, his escape was real. A wide grin cracked his cheeks.

Thankfully, a few minutes later, he pulled up behind his house, turned the key off, and laid the motorcycle on its side behind a large flowering lilac bush. He couldn't stop grinning.

While he hid there safely, the cop car whined and cried as it searched the neighborhood, fifteen minutes later the siren was no longer to be heard. The calm that accompanied his excitement during the chase, stayed with him as he ambled into the house, arms swinging, triumphant, in teenage-cocky stride.

Narvelle knew that he was a young man who could act on his decisions.

Another notable incident happened a year earlier, when he was in his junior year in high school. Narvelle and a friend named Freddy, slept overnight in the large janitor's supply room, in the girl's gym, next to the girls open shower. The next morning they spied on a bunch of girls showering together like mermaid nymphs. After three minutes of wide-eyed grinning and giggling, they boldly opened the door that they were hiding behind, then they whistled-a-happy-tune as they strolled casually through the running showers, between the shower nozzles, the water drops, and the girls. The walls resounded with the screams and shrieks of a dozen, naked, wet young ladies, and boisterous laughter. He and Freddy were world famous, in their own minds, after that.

All through school, Narvelle earnestly wanted to get over having nervous episodes and the stuttering nuisance. His observation of how he felt during the times that he did brave things, was, that most brave acts left him feeling calm, normal, at peace, and in control, most acts, not all.

When high school was over, he used his nervous history as his main reason for joining the Marines. The recruiter told him that the Marines would make a man out of him, for sure, 100% guaranteed, so he joined up two weeks after graduation.

Time passed quickly for the Marine, suddenly, the four years of active duty for Narvelle, ended abruptly. He was sent "back to the world" of Southern California, from whence he came.

Soon after Narvelle got home from the war, Vel landed a job delivering packages, as a delivery truck driver, in Long Beach, California. Piece of cake job. He rented an apartment, bought a dog and his life appeared to be good and normal. The dog was named "Ditty-bite." Narvelle loved to tease people when they asked the dog's name.

His best friend, Harold "Fragile" Glasscock, returned home four months after he did, and got a job as a house painter, north of San Diego. Jake became a plumber in Louisville, KY, and Johnny Anderson took the easy way out; he sold illegal drugs in Los Angeles. They called each other occasionally to discuss the war and to talk about how it was to be home. None of them ever truly got over the trauma that they had lived through in the killing fields of Viet Nam.

All four of them had vivid flashbacks and ghoulish nightmares that haunted them from time to time, for the rest of their lives.

CHAPTER TWO
AFTER THE WAR

A year after coming home from the war, Narvelle decided to go to night-school, he was twenty three years old. One evening, just before sundown, he drove slowly through the parking lot of Ransom Junior College, on his way to an English class, looking for a place to park. A car, a few feet ahead of him, with its tail lights on, was getting ready to back out of where it was parked. As Narvelle waited, he slowly lit a cigarette, then leaned over to find another good country music station on his radio. When he looked up, his parking spot was clear, but another car had come quickly from the next row over, and was pulling into it. After the car parked, immediately, a tall, skinny, white-boy, jumped out of it and headed for the campus.

Narvelle rolled the driver-side window down and yelled, "Hey dip-shit, I was waiting for that spot!" The boy flipped him 'the bird,' as he walked off, without looking back.

A pen and a notebook were handy, so Narvelle recorded everything. He put the notebook in his glove box and drove to the next parking lot, three hundred feet away. "I'll fix that rude idiot, someday," he muttered to himself.

Two weeks later, at the same time of day, he entered the same parking lot where the incident had occurred. As he found a spot to park, he looked up and there was the tall, skinny, white boy, parking his car, six stalls away. Narvelle opened his glove compartment and pulled out his notes, then he reached for a serious little tool that was hidden in the glove compartment. Payback was on its way.

He waited for a few minutes, then Vel took the valve stem remover, his tool for revenge, and got out of his car. No one was around, it was almost dark as he quickly removed the valve covers, then unscrewed the valve stems from all four tires. Like a bad case of gas, the air whooshed out. A few seconds later all four tires were totally, pancake, flat. He threw the valve stems far away, into the tall grass, as he laughed.

"I hope you're in a hurry to go somewhere, jackass!"

Six months of college convinced Narvelle that he was not good college material at that time of his life, so he quit school, and continued with his driving job, working with his delivery job.

Shortly after that was when he met Linda, the love of his life.

The doorbell rang, Linda smiled as she quickly opened the door. Standing there on her porch was Narvelle Phelps with a package, and a claim receipt to sign. She greeted him in a friendly manner, warmly, "Good morning. How are you doing?"

Speech escaped him for a moment, he said nothing, his mouth was unable to utter a word for a few seconds. She could see that he was smitten by her presence. She was impressed.

When she took the receipt form to sign it, he dropped the package, it tumbled down the five steps that led up to her porch. Narvelle whirled around quickly and hopped down the stairs after it. With a sheepish smile he trotted back up the stairs, both arms wrapped around it this time, like it was a precious football, "sorry about that," he whispered as he smiled, just a little.

Again, she was impressed.

Linda means beautiful in Spanish. She was that, with long dark hair, pretty blue eyes, and a gentle, sweet countenance. It was love at first sight for Narvelle.

"Don't worry; it's not breakable," she giggled as she let him off the hook, graciously, with a gentle smile of her own.

Linda Newbold was her name, she graduated from the University of Southern California, with a degree in Nursing in the summer of 1966, and worked as an ER Nurse. Life was good for her, she was brilliant, kind, nice looking, and loved to laugh. She also was a hell of a good cook. Narvelle asked her out the day that he met her, they were inseparable for the next few months. Linda grew to love him too, and consented to marry Narvelle, ten months later.

Two wonderful weeks in Hawaii was their wedding present to each other.

Three years after their marriage she gave birth to their only child, a daughter, named Olivia Jane, after the famous singer. Their attention and love showered down on Olivia, and everyone who knew the Phelps, knew that Olivia was their pride and joy.

Life appeared to be good and normal for them, but it wasn't totally, for him.

Narvelle continued to suffer from his dreadful war experiences, with terrible nightmares, visions, and vivid flashbacks. His favorite choices of escape and solace came through the use of Pot, and LSD. When Linda found out about his drug usage, she threw a complete fit. After many months of her constant pleading, Vel finally agreed to seek professional help.

The Veterans Hospital arranged for marriage counseling, drug counseling, and psychological help. So he attended counseling sessions and group therapy for ten months, with Linda faithfully by his side. The legal drugs that his shrink gave him, seemed to depress him, made him often think of suicide, gave him heartburn, and left him with an urge to gamble. He eventually quit taking the prescription drugs after he tried them for what he considered to be, a reasonable amount of time. Narvelle noticed that they left him tired beyond what he felt was normal for him; their many adverse effects, he didn't like.

Gradually, he went back to the forms of dope that his friend Johnny so easily provided. He liked his episodic escapes from life much better with the illegal stuff, than the prescription stuff.

Narvelle's favorite drug was "Pot," which was smoked fairly often during the next dozen years of his life.

After a year of marriage, Narvelle slowly started to gain weight. One of his favorite things to do was to get stoned and go with Johnny to an all-you-can-eat restaurant, and gorge himself. It was their time to laugh, tell brave war stories, and eat like pigs as they rehashed old times.

He loved it. Looked forward to it.

Narvelle's over-eating binges continued unabated for many years. He continued to steadily gain weight without any apparent concern. It was like he didn't care about how big he got or how he looked. He just kept buying newer and larger clothes.

Two years after his marriage to Linda, she began to comment loudly and often, about his eating binges and his increasing weight gains. She tried to tolerate his continually growing body size, but was openly angered and disappointed by his lack of control, lack of concern and the obvious changes in his physical appearance.

His obesity disgusted her, she told him so.

Narvelle's buddies began to tease him and tell him that he had come down with "dun lap disease." That is defined as when your belly "dun lap" over your belt. They also accused him of having "dickie do" disease. That means your belly sticks out farther than your "dickie do." His belly did for sure, he was getting blubbery fat.

"Hell, I could write a book about some of the strange stuff I have eaten while I was stoned," his friends had often heard him say.

Sadly, his indulgent eating habits continued.

Seven years after being discharged from the Marine Corp, because of his excessive eating binges, Narvelle, "Vel" Phelps weighed in one day at his doctors office, an ugly, unattractive, miserable, hefty, three hundred and seventy nine pounds. More than one hundred and seventy pounds, obese.

As an obese person he felt like hell, and found that every step he took was a major effort. His inner thighs rubbed together when he walked, chaffing his skin red.

He still delivered packages, but his manager was very upset about his slowed-down work performance and his physical handicap. Narvelle was formally warned that he might lose his job, if he continued to under perform. Linda continued to harp about his great size and about him not trying to lose weight, to no avail. One evening as they got ready for bed, she told him that he had become very unattractive and that sex with him was no longer an option.

Narvelle half-heartedly tried to go on a few diets, but they were all difficult to stay on for a long time, he would yo-yo up and down, thirty pounds this way, and thirty pounds that way.

His need of large amounts of food continued to amaze his friends; however, they did nothing constructive as they all stepped back politely, patiently, tolerating his behavior, using his war history as justification.

As life went on, he started to drink too much booze and continued to eat like a pig, slowly slipped farther and deeper into a severe and boring state of depression.

Narvelle's late night eating binges before going to bed, often gave him episodes of burning throat, "Reflux Disease." Nasty tasting hot stomach acid would shoot up his throat, out of his mouth and nostrils, as he tried to sleep. The anti-acids that he ate like candy, helped some, but didn't remedy the problem.

One night after a big fight with Linda about his weight, she called him a "lard ass" and threatened to divorce him if he didn't get help. He left her crying as he escaped the house.

Johnny and Harold befriended him at their favorite local pool hall named Vinnie's. They ate two large pizzas and had a beer (or twelve) as they shot pool until two AM. Later, when Narvelle returned home, he tiptoed quietly into the kitchen, where he quickly downed a couple shots of Jack Daniels whiskey, then went upstairs and slipped quietly into bed, still drunk, not knowing what to do with his life, still escaping.

Down deep, Narvelle craved some excitement in his life; little did he know that his life was going to change soon, dramatically.

CHAPTER THREE
TROUBLE IN EAST LOS ANGELES

The next day after his drinking binge, Narvelle sipped a beer as he rested on the couch, half watching television, nearly asleep. Ditty-Bite was curled up in his dog bed next to him, talking in his sleep and passing gas. It was late Saturday morning, and he had just finished the slow arduous task of mowing the grass. Linda was grocery shopping and Olivia was next door playing with the neighbor girls, as usual. The phone rang off the wall for him, seven times, before he finally pulled himself erect and answered it.

"Hey, Johnny, whass up my man?" Narvelle puffed into the phone, out of breath.

"Listen brother, I got a new batch of good shit. It's called Maui Wowie. If you want some, come on over and get yourself some, I'll be home for the rest of the day."

"O.K. that sounds good, I'll be over in a few hours."

A few minutes later Vel carefully wedged himself into his old station wagon and headed for John's house in East Los Angeles, a dangerous part of town.

Johnny lived in a small well-kept house on the outskirts in a rough part of the big city. His property boasted a generous two car garage and a yard that was nicely fenced to keep his two dogs in. A few homes nearby were protected by metal bars on their windows. Some of the local stores had their names and wares written in Spanish only. Trash littered the sidewalks and curbs of some streets, not all. There were many small, well-kept homes, amidst the run-down homes that signaled his area as a place of transition. A few old cars had died in some of the yards and on the streets, never to be moved again.

Narvelle drove by John's squared-away house at approximately 2:30 in the afternoon, then again ten minutes later to make sure that everything still looked calm. The street was lined with cars near John's place, no place to park close by, so he parked down the street about two blocks away, at a Seven-Eleven store. Narvelle figured that it was a safe place to park his wagon and that the walk to John's house would be good for him.

As he grudgingly lumbered up the sidewalk towards Johnny's house, he passed four young Mexican men that were raising hell, in public. Cussing, laughing, and yelling. They were sitting in the bed of an old, beat up, dark green Chevrolet pickup truck. It was dressed up with beautiful expensive rims, and tires that had halibut-bone white writing on them. Their obvious partying was stoked by a large whiskey bottle being passed freely in broad daylight. Happy Mexican music boomed from the radio in their truck, clear as a bell.

Narvelle avoided looking at them as he passed by.

"Dude, look at that fat-bastard!" one of them yelled loud enough for him and all the nearby neighbors to hear. They all laughed. Narvelle lowered his head and kept on walking as he pretended that he didn't hear what was said. A few feet after he passed the truck, he heard the angry squeal of tires and the sudden roar of an engine. Then he heard the old familiar war sound of guns being fired rapidly, bang, bang, POW, zip, bang. Narvelle turned towards the street, as a bullet hit his stomach, and saw the light blue car that the bullet came from. Inside the car, through the windows, were the outlines of three young men, their pistols silhouetted by the sun, yelling as they drove off.

Narvelle had never been shot before, but he immediately knew it when it happened, for sure; the bullet broke apart inside his gut. It felt like a hot sharp dinner fork had been poked and twisted through his skin. His stomach felt overfull, like too much, all-you-can-eat, gut pain. How strange he thought, "It doesn't hurt as much as I thought it would." He placed his hand over the small hole on the left side of his stomach, blood slowly oozed between his fingers. His head started to swim and he suddenly felt like he was going to throw up. Another pain began on the opposite side of his belly. Panic gripped his senses. Trying not to over-react, he took three slow deep breaths, they didn't help. Suddenly he started to sweat, his head began to swim as his vision blurred, and tears welled up in his eyes, he could barely see.

"What the hell?" Narvelle tried to shout. "Somebody help me, I've been shot!"

He stopped walking as he tried to think clearly. Beads of sweat ran freely from his forehead, burning his blurred eyes, his hands were trembling.

"I can't go to John's house, the cops will come there, I've got to get back to my wagon and get to a hospital," he thought out loud. Slowly, he turned around and headed for his car which suddenly seemed to be a mile away.

One of the young Mexicans was lying on his back on the sidewalk near him, shot in the eye. A trickle-river of blood was winding, snake-like, across the concrete. The other three Mexicans were screaming, yelling, and cussing loudly in Spanish. One of them had been shot in the leg and the crotch, his pants were covered with blood as he twisted about, moaning, in agony.

Within a minute, the street started to fill with curious children, women, and the sound of wailing voices. Then an old woman screamed and passed out in the middle of the street while a young Mexican girl ran to the house to call an ambulance.

Narvelle made it about 10 feet past the green pickup truck. There, he stopped to rest as blood ran through his fingers and down his shirt, on to his pants. His eyes darted around anxiously, looking for help but saw nothing. Then gray darkness overtook him. Soon he was out cold on the sidewalk, bleeding steadily, like a stuck pig.

Two ambulances screamed to the rescue a few minutes later. The young Mexican, shot in the eye, was on the ground, dead. The other gunshot victim was still alive, moaning loudly, from the bed of the truck, as he carefully cupped what was left of his privates.

A police car showed up just before a fire truck arrived. The street was mobbed by curious onlookers, a few minutes later a news truck appeared.

Narvelle was transported by ambulance to Los Angeles General Hospital. It took two young medics and two strong firemen to pick him up and put him on the stretcher, he was bleeding slowly but steadily, his face was pasty white, barely alive.

A three hour surgery saved his life, and put him back together. Six ribs were shattered and his liver was seriously damaged. The surgeon removed 70% of his liver, his stomach was almost completely destroyed. The doctor removed the damaged part of his stomach, then clamped the remaining portion, before he removed over a foot of Narvelle's small intestine.

The next day after his surgery, Narvelle woke in the early afternoon to the angelic voice of his wife Linda. She had been there in the room for hours, waiting for him to come alive.

"Hi there Marine," her melodic voice floated above him in the air, trance-like, perhaps real. He couldn't tell, at first. She held his hand as he squinted up at her from his drugged position, a hose in his nose. He felt like his head was in a bucket, and that someone had banged on the bucket for an hour, with a stick. Slowly and quietly, she explained what had happened to him.

"You were accidentally shot in a drive-by shooting. I guess you were in the wrong place at the wrong time. The doctor says you should recover nicely, he's not worried. He said the bullet broke apart, so he had to remove some of your small intestine and your liver, as well as more than 80% of your stomach. He also said that your stomach was damaged the most, so, he did a stapling procedure on it. Now, your stomach won't be able to hold as much as it could before." She paused for a few seconds as he digested what she said, smiled kindly and added, "This may all turn out to be a blessing in disguise."

Narvelle grinned weakly as he held her hand and spoke humbly, "I love you so much baby."

Linda leaned over and dutifully kissed him on the forehead, then she stood military erect as her eyes drifted coldly towards the window. She paused for five seconds and then she looked him directly in the eyes, her face was serious, as she said in a quiet, determined voice, "What is love, Narvelle?"

She waited. He looked at her staring deeply into his soul, as big crocodile tears slowly came to his eyes. "I have been thinking a lot about love recently." She continued, "I know love is a lot of things. I've read the Bible definitions and they are wonderful. You know, love is kind, patient, not quick to anger, forgives easily and so forth. I agree with all of that. However, I recently read a book that gives a modern, working, description of love, that I want you to know about.

After the initial infatuation has worn off, the chance for real love starts. It is a work that lasts a lifetime, it is---- "the willingness, desire, and commitment, to work at nourishing your spirit and/or someone else's spirit." She paused. "All of the words from this statement hit me like a sledge hammer, especially, work, and nourish." Linda stopped as she regained her momentum, then she continued. "If and when someone is no longer willing to work at a nourishing behavior, then the love is gone. This is the best definition that I have ever read; it really describes what happens when people truly love each other."

Narvelle said nothing, but listened patiently, her serious demeanor demanded it. It all made sense to him so far.

Then Linda went on. "Your spirit is housed in your body, right?" He nodded again. "If you defile your body you are messing with the house of your spirit. I believe that we can defile our body by taking too many drugs, legal or illegal. We can also defile our body by eating or drinking too much. When you allow your body to get grossly overweight or underweight, you have defiled it for sure. We both know that gluttony is one of the seven deadly sins. I have been thinking a lot about you and your weight problem; how can you love yourself and at the same time allow your body to become obese?"

Narvelle hung his head in shame, embarrassed, she was right and he knew it. This was the first time that he had allowed her words to penetrate his troubled mind, about his weight problem.

Linda ended with, "On the way over here, I thought that my new love definition could be altered a little to include; a willingness to work at nourishing your body or someone else's body. This strange thing that has just happened to you may end up becoming a real blessing. Lots of studies say that people who have had stomach stapling done, end up losing a heck of a lot of weight. If you will let me, I will help you find a better way to eat, and we can work on nourishing the temple of our spirits, together. I am willing to work with you and to work on myself, so that we can both get back into reasonable shape.

I want you to seriously think about it. O.K.?

We can talk about it more when you get home. And just in case you are curious, I do love you very much, you big lug."

He smiled from ear to ear.

Lovingly, Linda leaned over and kissed his hand, then promptly turned and left the room. As she walked down the hall she felt a sudden urge to stop. Ahead, she noticed a kind looking nurse at the nurse's station. Linda felt pushed by an unseen force as she walked up to the nurse and said, "Hi, my husband is in room 314. His name is Narvelle Phelps. My name is Linda Phelps. I am also an RN. This might be a strange thing to ask of you, but somehow I feel compelled to ask. Is it possible that you could guide me to an open minded nutritional counselor?"

The desk nurse smiled as Linda went on with, "I know that there are all sorts of opinions about diet and nutrition, I would like to get in touch with someone who is up to date in natural methods of diet, and is not so strongly influenced by the old fashioned diet information put out by the AMA."

The nurse at the desk continued smiling, then paused, leaned forward and carefully whispered, "that's the most interesting thing I've had asked of me lately." She added, "I know that you don't know me from Adam, but I don't like most doctors. I just work here to make a living, my heart is elsewhere when it comes to really being healthy.

A few years ago I went to an alternative health doctor that is truly excellent, she was raised in an Amish family. Her name is Martha Ledbetter. She is a real pistol, up to date, straight forward, smart as hell, and won't mislead anyone.

Martha is an RN, and has gone on and received a degree in Nutritional Counseling. After all that training she became a doctor, she is a Homeopath. She lives in New Albany, Indiana on a small farm."

The nurse continued, "People go to see her from all over the country. She is the only person that has changed my physical health for the better. I trust her. For many years I had constant heartburn, chronic fatigue, arthritis pain, and I was tired all the time. I tried the traditional medical prescriptions and ended up taking pills to counteract the pills that I was taking. When I finally read about the side-effects of all that prescription stuff, it seriously started to worry me.

I heard about Dr. Ledbetter and heard some really great success stories from people who had started using her natural ways, so I went to see her. Now I follow what she says to do, and I am doing really well, I feel so much better and I'm not tired all the time. You don't know this, I have lost over 40 pounds in the last three years, I no longer suffer from any of those symptoms that I used to have." She paused. "I don't take prescription medications anymore. Please don't read me wrong, there's a time and a place for everything."

With a kind smile, the nurse reached under the ledge between them and pulled out a picture of her when she was overweight. It was difficult to recognize that it was her. "That's what I looked like a few years ago," she laughed, "Let me get the good doctor's phone number for you."

She wrote the number on a piece of paper, handed it to Linda and smiled. "I hope that you find some help with Dr. Ledbetter. Please come by and let me know how it all works out for you. By the way, I'm Sherry Bryce and it was nice to meet you." She stuck out her hand and Linda replied, "Linda

Phelps. Thank you so much. I feel that God has directed me to come here today to meet you."

Tears of thanks spilled from Linda's eyes, as she lovingly gripped Sherry's hand.

CHAPTER FOUR
THE FAMOUS DOCTOR SAVORNIN

Six hours after Linda left the hospital, Narvelle turned on the television in his room. A special program was just beginning about Doyd Savornin, the famous Medical Doctor who believed in medically-assisted-death, euthanasia.

Narvelle listened carefully.

There are moments in our lives when we see, hear or experience things that permanently change our behaviors and thoughts forever, such was the effect of this television special on Vel. He never forgot what he heard that evening. From that moment on he started to think more about his "existence." Mesmerized, Narvelle hung on every word.

Pictures of the doctor, popped up on the screen. He was short, intelligent looking, and appeared to be normal. The deep gravely voice of the narrator began these words.

"Ladies and gentlemen, the subject of tonight's program may be unsuitable for children under the age of eighteen, we are going to talk about euthanasia, or mercy killing. The man we are going to discuss this evening is Doyd Savornin, MD. Doyd was born in 1930 in Oregon.

Dr. Savornin has openly voiced his opinions, and his disdain of those who have a closed mind to medical research. He presently is involved in a crusade to allow mercy killing or as he calls it, medically-assisted-death; on a wall at his home there is a sign that says, "it's not a crime to die without pain and suffering." He openly states that his new goal in life is to end the suffering of people who are terminally ill. He believes that our medical society has the obligation and responsibility of assisting terminally ill people through this natural process, just like being assisted through the natural process of being born. Many years ago Dr. Savornin visited Lithuania and saw, first hand, that medically-assisted-death was practiced there. He returned here to initiate a change in how terminally ill people are allowed to pass on.

He argues that we put our dogs, cats, and horses to sleep as a form of love for them, to help them escape their final misery. They can't do it by themselves, "Why shouldn't we do the same for our loved ones?" Other arguments in his literature discuss the financial strain and devastation on patients and their relatives, who do not have adequate health insurance or other financial reserves.

Dr. Savornin believes that a healthy sense of humor is essential to a happy and productive life, he also believes that we all should be careful about what and how much we eat. A book that he recently published is about diet. He says quite frankly that fat people appear to be jolly, but that they really are not, down deep they don't like being fat. He states that there is a public stigma about being overweight, that obese people are often viewed as being less intelligent than people of average weight, and that they suffer from much discrimination in our society.

He suggests that we should make a habit of leaving half of our food on our plate, servings of food in Europe are half the size of servings here in America. He states that we are the most overfed and under nourished country in the world. He reminds us that we have the highest rate of heart attacks and obesity related diseases.

Only those who are medically and legally diagnosed as terminally ill are eligible for this method of assisted death. The doctor claims to have assisted 16 people, thus far, with his procedure."

The announcer paused, "and now a word from our sponsor."

Narvelle reached over slowly and turned the television off, spellbound from what he just heard. He had listened carefully to every word and knew that what he heard would stay with him, forever. He was fascinated by the boldness of the doctor.

Life would never be the same for him.

His eyes drifted towards the clock, they stayed there, watching it tick, almost trance like, for a long minute. "Wow!" was all he could say.

He rehearsed and repeated it all, over and over in his mind for a few minutes, as he realized that he was in complete agreement with the concept of euthanasia, and with Doctor Savornin's views on obesity.

"Fat people don't like being fat, that's for damn sure; he nailed that right on the head! And I totally agree that folks who are terminal, need to have the right to die painlessly and gracefully. I really like that son-of-a-bitch; I wish that I was doing something cool with my life, like he is," Narvelle whispered secretly to himself. "Maybe someday I will."

CHAPTER FIVE
HOME WITH LINDA AFTER BEING SHOT

Four days after being hit by a stray bullet, Narvelle was home, recovering nicely. From his easy chair he blurted out, "Hey there, sweetheart! What do they call a young soldier in Viet Nam?"

Linda didn't answer from her side of the room.

"A youth-in-Asia."

They both laughed politely.

He added, "Here's some really funny crap. This is no shit, this really happened. As I was on the elevator going down to be released from the hospital, two ladies got on. This one lady said to the other one. "We got to get out of this hospital. They got fleas up there on the fourth ward. As I passed a room, up there on the ward, I saw a woman in a wheel chair, and her legs was all puffed up and bruised and nasty looking. I heard the doctor in the room tell the nurse that she done got the 'flea-bite-us,' all over her legs." He paused, watching Linda's facial expressions.

"I laughed so damn hard that I pissed my pants."

Linda smiled her tolerant nurse smile, then she said, "Speaking of euthanasia, I had a patient who was trying to be creative with names for her twin daughters. Honest to God, she told me that she named one girl Anastasia, and the other one Euthanasia," Linda added. "She called her girls Annie and Euthie."

They both laughed at that.

"Have you ever heard of Dr. Savornin?" Linda asked.

"Strange you should ask. I saw a special on him while I was in the hospital. He is a real honest to God pioneer, and I think he might be on to something good, what he's been doing makes perfect sense to me," Narvelle replied, then added, "If I ever get all messed up terminally sick, and am ready to go, please don't keep me around like a vegetable, O.K?"

"There is a time to die," Linda stated objectively. "It is a sad shame, and it is very depressing to go to the nursing homes and see patient's pictures of them, when they were in the prime of their life, then see them in a nearly vegetative state in their bed, waiting to die. I know that I couldn't work there; I would be depressed beyond repair. I've seen many patients that are so messed up that I have actually prayed for them to pass on, soon."

"Hey Linda, I'm looking at a map. New Albany, Indiana is just across the river from Louisville, Kentucky. We could go see my old Marine buddy Jake, and his wife and kids, and go see that lady doctor in Indiana, about how to eat right, and get it all done at the same time. I really am tired of being what you so graciously called me once, a "fat fuck."

I have two weeks off about three months from now. You've been raising hell with me about eating better, what do you think? I've already lost about ten pounds in the last two months since I got out of the hospital."

Linda smiled kindly and said, "That would be great honey, I'll put in to get some time off, and I'll get the airplane tickets."

CHAPTER SIX
THREE MONTHS LATER IN LOUISVILLE

Linda and Narvelle arrived in Louisville, Kentucky, a few months after he was shot. They visited Jake and Tara and their four children, rode the river on the big paddle boat with a million lights on it, drove by the Kentucky Derby, saw Colonel Sander's first restaurant, and went to the Kentucky State Fair.

Sensitized by Narvelle's experience, he and Linda both noticed the unusually large number of grossly obese people at the fair. They both commented on it, about how unattractive they are, yet how they appeared to not care about their abnormal size, many of them acted like they were proud of it as they strutted by.

Their trip to Dr. Ledbetter's office was an eye opener for both of them. In the doctor's large office were dozens of books on racks for sale, copious shelves of organic food, herbal medicines, and fresh vegetables. Varieties of organic meats were in a massive freezer. The office was bright, happy, clean, freshly painted, and had childish pictures here and there on the walls. The pictures looked like they were painted by school children, probably in the third or fourth grade.

Dr. Ledbetter was a stout woman in her early fifties. There were no wrinkles on her face and she didn't wear make up, her long hair was not colored. A few white and gray hairs appear easily among her dark brown hair. Her appearance was natural and healthy, without apology or pretense. She looked vastly intelligent with her glasses perched on the end of her nose, her beady brown eyes didn't miss a thing.

She apologized for not shaking their hands, "it spreads bugs," she said. The doctor listened carefully to Narvelle and Linda without saying much for about five minutes.

Once she got the history of Narvelle clear, she did blood pressure tests, and then asked them a litany of health related questions about family history, aches and pains, medications, illegal drugs, sex, what they ate, when they ate, how they slept, what they did for a living and for fun, and on and on.

The lady doctor wrote it all down, then she explained quickly and thoroughly about how the body works, how food is digested, what is good food, what are bad foods, and the natural things that can help them both to be healthier, her attention to detail was meticulous. She suggested a couple of good books for them to read from her arsenal of knowledge in the front office.

Suddenly Dr. Ledbetter stood up, looked at the clock on the wall, and said, "I must go. I have another new patient to see. Call me on any Sunday night between six to ten pm if you have questions. There is no charge for calling me. Good luck to you both. You can pay the young lady at the front desk. I would like to see you both in two years, unless you choose to see me sooner." She handed them a paper with her instructions summarized on it, smiled briefly, and promptly left the room.

An hour and a half had gone by like the finest of movies, Narvelle and Linda were mentally exhausted. They looked at each other and smiled, both of them were unusually happy as a rare look of peace spread across Narvelle's face.

CHAPTER SEVEN
THE LESSONS ON HOW TO EAT RIGHT

The next day at home, Linda sat quietly at her desk, pen in hand. Overwhelmed, and very impressed by what she had recently learned, she wrote on a yellow notebook pad as much as she could remember from the visit with Dr. Ledbetter.

What they had learned and what she wrote down was:

THE FOOD INDUSTRY IS NOT YOUR FRIEND!

Linda continued with: For ninety percent of American food companies, it is all about making money. Sugar has been substituted with high fructose corn syrup in many foods because it is cheaper. It is worse than sugar because it keeps your body from producing essential hormones that control and regulate energy---and inhibit hunger. Therefore you overeat, when food has high fructose corn syrup in it! Your stomach can't tell when it's full when foods contain high fructose corn syrup. Read all labels and avoid it.

There are good foods and bad foods. Bad foods provide empty calories. They are empty of nutritional chemicals that are needed for optimal health. Bad foods produce energy but make our bodies over-work or over-react in order to get the energy that they provide. White sugar, white rice, and white bread were given as examples of poor choices of things to eat.

Good foods are full of nutrition and of course provide energy easily. An example of a good food is a live food such as a raw apple. It is literally full of nutritional things like natural sugars, vitamins, minerals, and enzymes, and phyto-nutrients that keep us healthy.

Cooked foods have much less nutrition than raw foods because high heat destroys most of the vitamins. Don't use your microwave. Don't boil, bake, or heat to death everything you eat. Eat more raw natural foods. Make about one third of what we eat be raw fruits, nuts, and vegetables.

Organic foods are a better choice if you can afford them. Most organic foods contain from three to around thirty times more nutrition than non-organic foods.

Many obese people are obese because they eat the wrong things and too much of it. Many are overweight because quality food is more expensive than junk food. Obese people don't walk or exercise enough.

Shop for food in a HEALTH FOOD STORE. That's why it's called a health food store, healthier food selections.

80% of the food in a common grocery store is unhealthy due to how the food is processed and produced.

Read a good book about "food combining," and one on "insulin production cycles." - - - - - - - - - - -

Linda was done, for now.

A few weeks later as Narvelle walked in the house, after work, his sly smile indicated that he was up to no good. He thought he could stump Linda. "So, I've got a couple of questions," he said dryly. "What's a vitamin and what's an enzyme and what do they do?" Good questions he thought.

Linda responded without thinking, "Well according to the pamphlet that the doctor gave us, it says---Vitamins are not made by the body. We must eat food to get them. They don't give us energy. They enable energy sources to be used more efficiently by our body. Energy comes from proteins, carbohydrates, and fat as it is converted into sugar. Vitamins help our energy sources to work better and easier. Vitamins are like a hard working crew that takes care of growth and development, and they keep our bodies cells working smoothly. They prevent some things from going wrong, and can put other things right again."

Linda methodically added, "Enzymes are chemicals that are made by our body and are also found in uncooked vegetables, meats and so on. They speed up chemical reactions in our cells, which will lower the amount of energy that is needed for cellular reactions to occur. For example chewing your food really well stimulates digestive enzymes in your saliva, and these enzymes help things to digest better so you get more energy and benefits from the food you eat, and less chance for indigestion or non-digestion." Smiling cautiously, she stopped talking for a few seconds then added the bottom line.

"Fat is stored energy, when we take in more energy than we use. It's all about ENERGY, how we get it, and how it is used!"

After her excellent dissertation, Narvelle had a big surprised smile on his face and his eyes were laughing. He stared at her in amazement for a few seconds then shook his head.

"Damn, girl! I'm glad I asked, that was a hell of a dissertation!" he laughed. Then he jokingly added, "You're a real suppository of information aren't ya?"

"You're full of shit too honey," she quickly replied as she giggled. She was good with words.

"Accept it big boy, I got ya! I have studied this stuff and I've got it clear as a bell in my pretty little brain." Linda smiled beautifully and pointed at her head, like a pixie.

Narvelle confessed, "Truth is girl, I've eaten like a race horse from the time that I joined the Marines. I know that I don't chew my food enough and I eat too damned fast. It's all a bad habit. In basic training we would go into the chow hall, eat as fast as we could, then we had to be outside in formation, all in less than five minutes. The bad news is that slowing down and eating right is going to be a hard habit to change. The good news is this, I'm going to do my best to change my ways of eating, for me and for you." He looked sincere as he finished with, "I want to be serious for just a second, and I sincerely thank you for your concern about all of this."

"You're welcome my chubby ol' friend." She smile kindly and kissed his cheek, three times, ruffled up his hair, then kissed him again.

"I think that you have been given a chance to really change your life for the better. Think about how bad you would feel if Olivia got severely obese like you presently are. Let's make it a new goal to eat better and smarter; it can help us all to be healthier and happier. Let's do it as a family and see what happens. I'll help you all I can. Let's be a good example for her, you know that children learn three ways: example, example, and example.

With encouragement in her voice, she added, "I'm very excited to see you again at your normal weight. I want the strong, normal sized, nice looking man that I married, back in my bed, not a chug-butt."

He lowered his head in agreement.

CHAPTER EIGHT
SIXTEEN MONTHS LATER

Just over a year after Narvelle was shot, a small article appeared in The Los Angeles Times, it was hidden on the third page. A friend of Linda's noticed it and brought it to her attention.

It read: MAN SHOT ACCIDENTALLY in a drive by shooting sixteen months ago loses weight because of the surgical procedure that saved his life. The surgical procedure, stomach stapling, decreased the size of his stomach so that he feels full easier.

He is now on a new diet. He and his wife are changing the way they eat and both of them have lost weight and claim to have more energy. Being accidentally shot in the stomach has turned out to be a blessing for him. His name is Narvelle Phelps. He claims that he has lost around a hundred and twenty pounds since his accidental shooting over a year ago. His goal is to lose one hundred and eighty pounds.

He and his wife tell us that they went to an alternative health provider and were taught how to eat in more healthy ways. They eat more raw vegetables and fruits now and drink natural juice that they produce at home. Their diet now consists of less fatty foods and more natural or organic foods.

CHAPTER NINE
NEARLY TWO YEARS AFTER NARVELLE WAS SHOT

"Blap!" said the handball on the back wall. Narvelle dived for it, hitting it low and hard, it died in the lower left corner on the front wall of the court. "Game point coming!" he yelled.

His best buddy from the war, Fragile, was breathing hard from running his tail off. Narvelle served the ball again, hard, low and fast. Fragile returned it with a precisely hit ceiling shot, again, hoping it would bounce over Vel's head, and die on the back wall. Narvelle ran back to the back wall and scooped it precisely off the wall, and slap-shot it to the front wall in the right lower corner, about six inches off the floor. The ball died right there, again, hit perfectly. The game was over; Narvelle had won twenty one to sixteen.

He looked good and he felt great, since his accident, Narvelle had physically transformed. With tremendous energy, he felt like a Marine again, capable of moving about the court like he did when he was twenty years old.

In the shower, Harold "Fragile" Glasscock yelled across the room, "You have got your old self back my friend! You haven't beaten me in handball for many years. Way we go man!"

Narvelle smiled and said, "It's all that fru-fru stuff that my wife makes me eat. The shot to the gut probably helped some too."

"How much weight have you lost since you got shot?"

"Around one hundred and sixty pounds I think."

"Holy shit brother! I knew you were large. How much do you weigh now?"

"I weighed in at two hundred and fifteen pounds, this morning, before I took a shower. Hey, I gotta go, I'll see you and John tomorrow night at Vinnie's around nine, O.K.? We can drink some brew, shoot a little pool, and check out the babes!"

"See ya there my friend!" yelled Fragile.

Narvelle jumped out the door of the gym and skipped like a child, pretending that he was making "kill shots" with a handball.

He did, indeed, look and feel like he was normal again.

The next evening they were all sitting at their favorite bar, Vinnie's; Narvelle, Johnny, and Harold, the three old war buddies, good friends, brothers. Fellow sufferers of nightmares and visions. John ordered more beer and cracked a few jokes as they waited for their favorite pool table to become available.

"What do you call a cow that just had a baby?" Johnny asked dryly. No answer. "Decaffeinated." They all laughed, politely. The bartender grinned, just a little at the feeble joke.

Johnny was ahead of them with the booze. He knew it and purposely slurred, "I'm not as drunk as some of you thinkel peep I are. I've got all day sober to Sunday up on. I've only had tee martunies. Starkle starkle little twink, who the hell you am I think." Fragile and Vel laughed again at his clever mouthful of interesting bullshit. John was the intellectual of the group so anything that came from his lips was either funny, poetic, or dreadfully serious. They gave him respect.

Harold piped up, "Hey, I've got a good one."

"A lady was driving around town with a personalized license plate on her car that read DAM. A cop pulled her over, he thought it might be inappropriate for her to be driving around with DAM on her license. He asked her if the license plate stood for something. She said, "yes sir, Mothers Against Dyslexia."

Even the bartender laughed loudly at that one.

Vinnie's was less than half full of people that night, however all of the pool tables were full. The three amigos were up next for the best pool table in the house.

Narvelle looked around to scope out any pretty ladies, not to attack them, just to admire them. He had never fooled around on his wife and had no intention of doing so tonight.

To their left, just two bar stools away, sat an immense, rotund, young woman, bent over a large beer. The rolls of fat around her huge waist billowed and ballooned over each other in an explosion of waves, she was nearly round with rubbery, blubbery fat. Her shirt was pulled up in the back, exposing a naked white bulge of skin.

She looked lonesome and abandoned, she was. Her eyes were downcast, sadness permeated her very being.

Suddenly, all three of them were looking at her at the same time, she could feel their heat. She slowly looked up, turned her head in slow-motion, and then stopped, as her pretty blue shark eyes, peered lifelessly into Narvelle's curious gaze.

Long black eyelashes shot from her lids, her face was absolutely beautiful. A trail of long blue-black hair glistened in the red-yellow-green bar lights of the cascading waterfalls that advertise beer. Her porcelain white skin was without a blemish; full, luscious, ruby red lips and a small delicate nose completed her beauty. She stared at Narvelle with her suddenly seductive blue eyes for a few long seconds, saying nothing, then slowly turned her head straight forward and again bent over her lonesome beer, expressionless as a china doll.

Narvelle was in shock, amazed, eyes wide open. Time stood still as his heart missed a beat, and his breath quit him momentarily.

"What the hell?" he gasped quietly to his friends.

Narvelle was sitting the closest to her, so he hadn't noticed that his buddies were also staring at her with disbelief and wonder.

John's mouth was open and his eyes looked like pie plates as he whispered in slow motion with a real slur, "Well I'll be an armpit-smelling-son-of-a-bitch!" Then he added, "That chick has got one hell of a purty face!"

Harold and Narvelle nodded their agreement as their heads wagged up and down at the same time.

"It's a shame her body looks like shit!" unexpectedly came from their lips, in unison. All three of them said it at the same time. Their chorus response surprised them and the barkeeper, who smiled, "big time," at their comical retort.

The rotund lady heard them too, loud and clear. Insulted, her head went farther down over her beer, trying to hide, wanting to escape.

"Hey Johnny Cake, you guys are up now on table number four!"

The three wild boys returned to the real world of the bar as Fragile suddenly, from out of nowhere, cracked a joke.

"Hey, I've got a good one. How do you screw a fat woman?" Harold quipped loudly. No answer came, as Narvelle and Johnny looked anxiously around the bar.

"You roll her in flour and screw the wet spot!"

They all laughed wildly at that. Then, the three of them, like a puppet chorus, all at the same time, as if mechanically chained, turned their heads and ventured a peek at the fat girl next to them. Angered and surprised, she patiently let the insult of the joke soak into her space. Then her face flushed purple-red as steam vented from her ears. She was stunned, angry and deeply hurt.

Disgusted, she quickly pushed her beer away, without a word, slowly stood up and exited the bar, devastated.

"Aw fuck her, if she can't take a joke, fuck her and the horse she rode in on," Johnny rudely added with a drunken slur. They all laughed again as they stood up and headed towards their pool table.

"It would have to be a damn big horse to haul that broad." Fragile smiled slyly, his beer talking.

"I thought fat folks were supposed to be all jolly, happy and gay," Johnny added as they arrived at their game table.

"Not that one!" said Narvelle, who hadn't said much up to that point. "Now she was truly a---a—a—a-- FAT FOX!" he said as they racked the balls on the table, the other fellows agreed.

After the pool games were over they stepped out into the street. John reached into his pocket and pulled out a wrapped package containing some "stuff" for Narvelle, gracefully slipping it into his hand as they shook hands. Narvelle was glad to get some more LSD. He had gone for many months without it; he was excited to get some more of what he called, his, "favorite trip ticket."

It was an extraordinary night for all of them, a night that none of them would ever forget. Narvelle thought about how devastated the large lady was by the bad joke that Fragile had put on her. He drove home quietly, wishing that he could undo that evening of insult and humiliation for her.

He clearly and painfully remembered what it was like to be so large, unbecoming, undesirable, and the brunt of fat jokes.

The hurt on her face made him cringe as he shook his head in disbelief.

"That was pretty damned rude to insult that woman, right in her face."

CHAPTER TEN
CHARLOTTE, THE FAT FOX

Charlotte Johanson was a librarian, she lived alone, her obesity demanded it.

Everyone that met her said that she was pleasant to be around. As a young child, she had been the center of attention among her girl friends because she was so quick witted and full of interesting information, however, her gregarious behavior changed when she became an obese teenager. No longer did she seek out the comfort or friendship of others, she became painfully aware of the little jokes and innuendos that were made in her presence. Statements such as fat girls stink, are stupid, and should be ashamed of themselves, continually diminished her, through her school years. "How can she let herself go like that," she heard a dozen times as a teenager.

One sad day, Charlotte cried for hours after a rude boy in high school recited a poem to his friends. Acting as if she was invisible, he spit out his poisonous venom, just six feet away from her. "Fatty, fatty, two by four, couldn't get through the bathroom door, so she did it on the floor, and licked it up and did some more."

Being obese slowly withdrew her from the normal fun things of high school, and later on, early adulthood.

As an obese adult, she only had a few friends, very few.

She and Vivian Black have been best friends since they met in college, many years ago. Vivian was an average looking young lady, twenty eight years old, high school math teacher.

Charlotte, at the age of thirty three, was still a virgin. Her tremendous weight problem had repelled men from being anything more than barely polite to her. At her last physical, she weighed, a whopping three hundred and eighty four pounds.

Because of her obesity she had suffered from an unending series of embarrassing events. One of the worst humiliations occurred when she was twenty four years old, she attended a "breathing class" with a girl friend who was pregnant. The class instructor was teaching the class of pregnant women how to breathe diaphragmatically. He went around the room from woman to woman, placing his hand on their stomach and asking them to breathe and push his hand upward as they inhaled. As the instructor went from woman to woman, he finally arrived to where she sat, without hesitation he placed his hand on Charlotte's large stomach and asked her to breathe. Poor Charlotte blushed, as she defended herself loudly, "I'm not pregnant!"

Six pregnant women laughed out loud, while the remaining others smiled and the instructor begged forgiveness, with a grin. She was devastated, again.

Charlotte loved to cook, play chess, eat, read, and was a kind and polite young woman, but she was, understandably, lonesome.

Then, there is that other problem that she carried around with her, a beautiful face. Her face, was as intimidating as is the face of any extraordinarily beautiful woman. Somehow, Charlotte waded her way through life carrying those two unique contradictions.

Charlotte's parents divorced when she was twelve years old, her excessive eating started after that, to comfort her. By the end of high school she was seriously obese.

Her brother Mork, had maintained his weight through high school by being physically active as a wrestler. She was proud of his wrestling accomplishments as well as the fact that he was an excellent student, academically. Straight A's in everything were easy for him.

As mentioned earlier, she loved to play chess. She and Vivian got together once a week, for four hours, on Sunday, to play and eat.

Sunday evening at Charlotte's apartment, she explained what had happened at the bar. "So, I was at Vinnie's last night, getting a beer after work, and this jerk-face next to me told a joke about how to screw a fat woman, it pissed me off and humiliated me terribly. The stupid ass said it nice and loud so everyone could hear it, of course it was directed at me. It was a really mean thing to do. I was so mad that I got up and left without saying a word. I couldn't even think straight. What I should have done was slap the hell out of him."

Vivian comforted her, "Don't worry girlfriend, God will punish him, what comes around goes around. Next time that happens to you, call me and I'll come over and help you kick the beans out of him."

Vivian cracked a smile that could dry anyone's tears.

A beautiful pink and black alabaster chess set, handmade, from Italy, separated them at the table. Charlotte's father had given the chess set to her when she was fourteen years old. He had purchased it from an importer who specialized in "one of a kind" items. It was strikingly beautiful, with it Charlotte won the high school chess tournament, when she was a senior.

It was time to play chess. "Your move," Charlotte said as she regained her composure and popped four olives into her mouth. The game began with a large plate of black olives, cheese and cracker snacks, a large jar of cashews, wonderful thick homemade lasagna, buttered garlic toast, and a two quart bottle of Coke.

CHAPTER ELEVEN
VEL TRIPS OUT

A few years after sighting the FAT FOX, Narvelle lay in bed one evening with the lights out, thinking of the beautiful, obese woman that he and his friends had insulted, years ago. He had never forgotten her, thoughts of her drifted in and out of his mind, almost daily, a slight obsession. Her pretty, sad face haunted him, hurt him, and made him wonder about her life, wonder how she felt to be so pretty in the face, yet, obese and unattractively large.

Earlier that evening he had been tripping. The flashbacks that he was experiencing kept coming and going. Some were good, most of them were bad. A million thoughts and visual images flashed and tumbled around in his head.

Linda was cuddled up close to him and from her gentle snoring, apparently asleep.

The LSD that Narvelle had put into his system six hours ago kept his mind flipping in a wild series of thoughts and vivid visions. Suddenly his "trip" changed from pleasant hallucinations to a recant of horror. Now, he saw ghastly sights of dead bodies and the horror of war, corpses with guts hanging out, and men trying to push their intestines back into their body cavity. He saw soldiers being decapitated as blood spewed from their headless bodies, and horrific faces, without eyes, that spun around in a bath of blood; he could smell the stench of death, mixed with the flavor of wet jungle muck and acrid gunpowder.

Narvelle needed a break, needed some fresh air to clear his mind.

Slowly, he got out of bed and headed for the bathroom, for a drink of water. After filling his glass with water, and gulping the water down, he placed the glass on the sink, and stared at the water drops dripping from the faucet. Drip, drip, drip, drip, drip, drip, drip, they continued vividly, for forty five minutes, as Narvelle stood there, entranced, fascinated by the fact that the drops kept coming, and the extraordinary way that they splattered. Then, forcing himself to move, he ambled cautiously out to the deck, under the starlit night, to escape the flashbacks.

Narvelle uttered, "I am going to be a dead man one of these days, just like all my dead buddies. It seems like half of the people I knew in Nam are already gone. I have done very few things in my life that have helped anyone. My life has been a waste."

He paused and closed his eyes hoping that his mind would reset to normal, but it didn't.

"I go to work and do my thing, then come home, watch TV, get high, play a little pool once a week, and sleep. That's about it. What kind of life is this? My wife is gone most of the time with her friends. My daughter is over at her girlfriends house all the time, so I don't get to talk to her much either. Playing pool is about my only entertainment. What I really need to do, is get my hands on an old car, to putter around with. I need a hobby, something to keep me busy. I wish I had a cool old car to restore. That would be "the ticket" for keeping me from being bored."

His mind briefly switched tracks to a religious vein, again, as he peered into the endless sky and begged wisdom. "Where did I come from, why am I here, where will I go when I die?"

Then, his drugged mind jumped tracks one more time.

"That mercy killing doctor who was on the news when I was in the hospital, a couple of years ago, is the most interesting character that I've heard about in a damned long time. That sucker has been helping people die who are going to die anyway, now that's original as hell. What a cool son-of-a-bitch he is, to go against the grain of society. I'll bet my ass-to-a-tea- kettle that he finds that every day is exciting. He probably doesn't say "same shit, different day," when he gets out of bed, like some folks do. History will remember him as a pioneer, someone who made a difference.

I need to find something that would make my life exciting and interesting; maybe I need to get into some program where I help people, or maybe it would be fun to do something that is just plain controversial. If I hadn't got shot in the stomach, I would probably be dead now from a heart attack, or have some other damned disease on its way."

Then, as his mind flipped from one subject to another, he stopped abruptly. The most radical thought that he had ever come up with, jumped like a lightning bolt from his walnut shaped tissues and escaped through his lips. It came as a complete surprise. Narvelle was startled, amused, fascinated!

Looking up at the endless sky, he said, "I ought to find some lard-ass, like I was, and help him by shooting him in the gut."

His mind stopped transmitting electrical sparks as he listened to what he had just said, out loud. Then an unusual wave of enthusiasm and excitement warmed him from head to foot.

"Now that's an original thought if there ever was one. That is truly a unique, wild, original thought!"

Repeating himself loud and clear, he said it again, "That is a totally fucked-up, unique, wild, original thought!"

For a few seconds he was quiet, then he began again, "It would be really far out and totally cool if I shot some dude and he had the same result that I had, it would be like spreading the luck around. I could help someone to help them self!"

Then, from the dark side of his mind, Narvelle suddenly remembered the sad "fat-lady" at the bar. The FAT FOX. Her beautiful face, and the insulting situation where he met her dead-pan, blue eyes, became an enhanced vision. He winced and shook his head.

"What a beautiful face."

"If I popped her just right, she could get her stomach stapled exactly like mine was. I'll bet that she would benefit from it just like I did. It would be a sort of an apology for that joke that Fragile nailed her with. I have done really well since I got shot, why wouldn't she do just as well? Why wouldn't anyone do well, just like I did?"

In through the bedroom door he tiptoed to where Linda was sleeping peacefully. He stared at her for a minute from her side of the bed, then he walked around to his side of the bed, got in and turned off the light. With his pillow tucked under his neck he closed his eyes, hoping to drift off towards sleep, but it didn't work, his eyes were wide open with unusual excitement.

"My mind is scrambled badly," Narvelle thought as he lay there waiting for sleep to overtake him.

As he retraced his thoughts, another tingle of excitement made the hair on his neck and arms stand up as he thought of her, the beautiful fat lady, the new target of his desire.

"What a cool thing to do, shoot her, to help her. It would be a really gutty thing to do,------------ I could do it if I wanted to," he convinced himself. "It would be easy, just find out where her stomach is, and pop it with a piece of lead."

Narvelle grinned as he remembered back to some of the wild and crazy things that he had done as a teenager in high school. A smile slowly raised the corners of his mouth.

CHAPTER TWELVE
DEADLY PRACTICE

The long, straw colored hair shook suddenly in the constant desert breeze, as the checkered red shirt exploded with holes from front to back. The plump wide-eyed body wiggled a little with each explosion, then jerked and rotated with slight spasms. Wisps of straw flew out from the holes in the back of the shirt.

Pop, bang, bang, bang, POW, POW, the air exploded with the sound of Vel's rifle going off, the scarecrow target that they had constructed, twisted a little each time a bullet passed through it. The crucified dummy was nailed on a wooden cross, stuck in the dirt on an isolated hill, in the desert sand, east of Los Angeles, it was as big as a normal sized man.

Narvelle and Fragile had built the dummy in Fragile's backyard, a week before. "Mister dummy" had big, black, button eyes, but no mouth or nose, he was anybody and everybody.

Vel again started shooting his rifle from fifty yards away. Pop, pow, bang, bang, pow, in rapid succession. This time the first three shots missed the entire target, the fourth through sixth shots hit the target in the head and shoulder.

"Damn it, it's been a long time since I shot a weapon!"

"Squeeze it slow and gentle my man, breathe out and relax," urged Fragile. "Remember how we were taught to do it, in boot camp. Try it again, but this time slow down and fire a few deliberate single shots, make it a surprise when it goes off, gently squeeze the trigger."

"Maybe we should get a little closer for a few rounds," Vel suggested, casually.

They moved up to thirty yards from the target. Pop, pow, pop, again went his rifle, but in a slower more careful fashion, this time two of the three shots went straight to the heart, the third one hit the shoulder area.

Narvelle and Fragile shot their rifles that afternoon for nearly an hour, one hundred rounds each.

Narvelle counted up his number of hits on the target, to the heart. Of one hundred shots, he hit the heart sixty six times. He missed it, thirty four times. As he predicted, Sgt. Fragile Glasscock had done a much better job, after all, he was rated as a sharpshooter in the Marines.

Finally, with their bullets gone, it was time to return to the city.

A random thought whizzed through Vel's mind.

"Maybe I could get Fragile to hit the FAT FOX, I don't want to kill the chick."

He was still convincing himself that what had happened to him could be easily done to someone else.

"Can't do that, he would think I'm completely crazy if I asked him to do such a strange thing."

Fragile and Narvelle packed up their rifles, targets, and gear, in Fragile's jeep. "I need to practice some more if I'm ever going to get a deer again with you guys," Narvelle said as they bounced along in the jeep, down the hillside to the road.

The luscious dry desert air cooled them both as they headed for home.

Suddenly Vel felt his lips move before his brain got in gear. "Hey Fragile, I've got a strange question for you," he blurted out.

Narvelle was seriously toying with asking Fragile to shoot the FAT FOX.

"It could be a hell of a problem to miss and hit her somewhere else," he thought.

"Sure, my man, whass up?" Fragile replied.

Vel paused for a few seconds, looked in the distant desert, then, "Aw,--hell—uh—oh-- never mind, I was just thinking of some weird stuff. Skip it O.K."

"Sure, man," Fragile said without any questions asked, a true friend.

Narvelle's mind spun around in a whirlpool of thoughts as he tried to force himself to erase the idea of such an unusual deed. He began convincing himself that he was no longer going to think about the FAT FOX, that it was over, all over.

As he lit a cigarette, he turned the music up on the radio to distract him, and his best friend.

The recent rains had caused the desert to blossom with small gardens of wild flowers and had created a collage of beautiful colors that exuded puffs of delicate perfume.

"It's beautiful out here in the desert, isn't it?" came from Fragile.

"Yeah buddy, I love it. Peaceful!"

CHAPTER THIRTEEN
EVENING AT NARVELLE'S HOUSE

The lights were low; the TV was on at the Phelps household, stars danced in the evening sky. Walter Cronkite had just delivered his evening salute and told everyone watching, "the way it is." Linda sat on the couch with a large medical research book in her lap, Narvelle was nearly asleep in his big, brown, leather, easy chair. Legs up, and half numbed from the usual, boring, redundant, regurgitation of world news.

"Honey, before you go to bed, listen to this!" Linda requested. "There is now medical research substantiating the fact that obese people are at a much greater risk of having some of these serious diseases. Cardiovascular disease, type 2 diabetes, sleep apnea, some cancers, and osteoarthritis now are all definitely associated with obesity, according to this recent medical journal. It talks here about the success of stomach stapling and by-pass surgeries. Listen to this. After your stomach is stapled, you feel like you are full with only one cup of food. Researchers theorize that you will live longer and be healthier from a stapling procedure. Over ninety four percent of the people who have had a stapling procedure, and/or, by-pass surgeries, have had major success. Isn't that neat?"

He listened carefully as he thought of the FAT FOX and her predicament, then said, "yes," to Linda's question.

"You are so lucky! I told a few people at work about you, and they all giggle and make little remarks about how it was a heck of a way to go on a diet."

Narvelle smiled, got up, kissed her and headed up stairs to bed. On the way to the bedroom, the significance of what she said finally registered with him, deeply. "Serious ailments can follow obesity!"

"What a strange blessing is was for me to get shot in the gut," he mumbled as he entered the bathroom.

While he brushed his teeth, his mind drifted again towards mischief.

"If I don't shoot the FAT FOX, what will become of her in the future? She has a hell of a good chance that she will eventually end up with some serious diseases and be miserable the rest of her life. What the hell, she is already miserable. She really needs to lose weight. She deserves to lose weight. Her problem is that she just can't make herself do it, or she would have done so by now.

That girl had such a pretty face. I wonder if she has a boy friend, I'll bet that she doesn't have one. She looked so miserable that night, what a raw thing of us to laugh at her, and for Fragile to hit her with that stupid joke. Maybe I should check her out and see what is really going on in her life. It would be interesting to see how her life would change if she lost a bunch of weight."

Narvelle smoked his final cigarette, then crawled into bed; a few minutes later he began to dream. He dreamed a wildly luscious dream of the FAT FOX as a beauty pageant winner, walking down the walkway to accept her prize. She was smiling, with tears in her eyes and a sparkling crown on her head, her arms full of roses. The crowd exploded loudly, yelling her name over and over. Her body was normal, her face was extraordinarily beautiful. She looked happy, radiantly happy, beaming.

Suddenly Narvelle sat up in bed, wide awake; he knew that he had to do it for her, that she couldn't and wouldn't do it on her own. He knew that it would turn out O.K. for her just like it did for him. The mold had been cast, the die was set, his mind was made up. The dream had convinced him. "Dreams are significant messages from the great unknown."

CHAPTER FOURTEEN
WHERE IS YOUR STOMACH?

Eggs sizzled in the pan the next morning as Linda put the bread in the toaster, meanwhile Narvelle grabbed the orange juice from the refrigerator. Then he put the plates on the table. Olivia sat down at the kitchen table and quietly began to eat her cereal.

As Narvelle and Linda started to eat, he had a question.

"Sweetheart, Linda girl, could you tell me where exactly my stomach is, and where my intestines are?" he asked. She looked at him as if to question, why. "Why do you want to know?"

"I was just wondering exactly where all that stuff is inside. I don't know anatomy like you do."

Then he spoke casually, "I'm just curious as to where all that stuff really is located. I always thought that my stomach was here." Narvelle rubbed his lower abdomen, on purpose, pretending not to know.

Nurse Linda, patiently showed him where the stomach was and explained how the intestines wind around in the body cavity. Then she clearly explained where the heart, lungs, liver, and spine are.

"By the way, sugar, you look great now that you have lost all that weight. Thank you so much, I am very proud of you," she thankfully added. "I told you this might all turn in to a blessing in disguise."

She kissed him sweetly on the cheek. "Sometimes bad things turn out for the good, we are both very lucky."

Then his wife, Linda, added, "Hey honey, a nurse at work told me that obese people generally live an average of 24 years less than people who are of average build and weight. So you are going to be around for us to love on, for a long-long time.

Also, I just read a study that says that people who live to be 100 years old, only have two things in common. None of them eat anything in excess and none of them are overweight, they are all thin. Isn't that something?"

Narvelle smiled and agreed as he slowly lifted his fork to his mouth, analyzing what was on the fork, and how much of it there was.

After finishing his eggs and toast, with a sudden gulp of coffee, Narvelle looked up at the clock on the wall, jumped up and said, "Gotta go, I'm late." He thanked Linda for breakfast with a kiss on her lips, ran his fingers slowly and lovingly through Olivia's hair, then he hugged her. Quickly, he grabbed his keys and left for work. He was excited.

All day long, he looked at people differently as he delivered his packages, imagining where the stomach is and where the intestines are. He remembered what Linda said about where the heart and spinal chord were located. By the end of the day, Narvelle was comfortable with the fact that the stomach is pretty much located in the same area of the body, in everyone, almost.

"The only thing that could vary is that the stomach has got to be bigger in the really fat folks," he explained to himself as he analyzed a large man walking down the street.

"I guess that it would be easier to hit his stomach with a bullet, than to hit a really skinny guy."

CHAPTER FIFTEEN
VEL GOES FOX HUNTING

The bartender at Vinnie's told Narvelle the name of the FAT FOX. Her name was Charlotte Johanson. He explained to Vel that he had never seen her with a male companion, or a female one. She had been coming to the bar, off and on, for the last six years. Always came in alone, maybe one or two times a month. Always left alone. Never got drunk, had three or four drinks, that's it. Seldom spoke to anyone, is a librarian, that's all he knew.

Narvelle looked up Charlotte's address in the phone book, and on his bonus day off, he drove by her apartment and scoped it out for an hour. He waited patiently until a neighbor finally appeared, then asked the man who exited the apartment next to Charlotte's, where she works. Vel lied to him and told the man that he was an old friend of hers. The helpful neighbor pointed in the direction of the nearby library, without hesitation.

As Narvelle entered his car, his mind drifted back to a story that he had heard many years ago. It was about the carving of the famous sculpture, "David," by Michelangelo. Narvelle remembered the story of how a huge chunk of stone was selected by the artist, who would then imagine a body inside the stone. Michelangelo would then carve away what was not needed and leave only what was needed, allowing the form of a body to emerge.

"In each fat person hides a normal sized body waiting to come forth," he explained to himself, continually justifying his thoughts, talking himself into doing "the daring deed."

Narvelle then drove over to the library where Charlotte Johanson worked, it was 8 pm. There she was, her beautiful face behind the desk, quietly reading a book and looking painfully alone. The library was scheduled to close at 9 pm, so Vel left, ran his errand and returned to the library thirty minutes later. He waited patiently in his old station wagon about 200 feet from the front door of the library. At precisely 9:02 pm. Charlotte stepped outside and walked to her car, in the parking lot.

The street where the library was located was very quiet, not a soul other than him and her could be seen.

She drove straight home, about five miles from the library. He followed her car, like a sniper, it ignited the Marine killer instinct in him. His heart pounded as he thought about actually shooting her. What a crazy thing to do, and at the same time, what a cool thing to do, he reminded himself.

"No one in the history of mankind has ever done such a bold thing," he thought. "I am a true pioneer!"

Vel practiced intently three times, the next week. He made sure that the bullets he was going to use, were the kind that would enter and leave the body without making a large exit wound. His objective was to precisely puncture her, not blow a hole in her.

He practiced again the day before he finally decided to do his famous deed. His accuracy was vastly improved. Everything was ready. His rifle was sighted correctly, lubricated, and shooting true.

A small voice inside kept urging him on, saying, "You survived being shot, so can she."

The excitement of successfully doing it, really turned him on. Adrenalin squirted in his veins, each time that he thought about the actual process. Narvelle had always liked doing daring deeds, in the past they had helped him get past his nervous nature.

Once it was done, he would no longer be, just as ex-GI, wasting his life on a boring job, pool games, and dope.

Vel knew that a strange blessing was on its way for the FAT FOX, like what had happened to him. The only difference was that he would be the one to deliver it to her, with good intent, and on purpose. He was truly excited.

Narvelle Phelps, ex "fat-bastard," was about to do something extraordinarily good for mankind.

CHAPTER SIXTEEN
THE STRANGEST CHRISTMAS GIFT

The evening was cool, typical for December in Southern California. The daytime high was seventy degrees, the nighttime temperature was forty six. It had been one of those rare clear days when you can see the mountains that surround Los Angeles.

Vel had drilled a three and a half inch hole in the tailgate of his old station wagon, with a large hole saw. No one noticed it very much because his wagon was dented, had paint falling off, and looked dingy. He parked the wagon with the back of it facing the front door of the library, he was hidden away on the floor, waiting, no more than thirty yards from the front door. All of the streetlights were on, beautifully illuminating the quiet street, not a soul in sight. He lay on his stomach, methodically biting his finger nails off, patiently peering out through the hole in the tail-gate. The large street light next to the library, lit the area perfectly, everything looked good. It was exactly 9 pm. when his heart began to pump stronger, sweat beaded up on his forehead, and his breath quickly became heavy. Vel was about to shoot his first innocent person. Then, as if by magic, Charlotte was standing at the bottom of the library steps, a spot light glare of light from the overhead street light profiled her rotund shape, like crimson on a storm cloud.

She stopped walking to remove a stone from her sandal, and then slowly turned sideways, again, in a profile position. It was a picture perfect shot, he had to do it now. Vel carefully aimed the weapon at her, as he blinked the sweat out of his eyes.

"Now is the time," Narvelle told himself, trying to convince himself that it was time to act, time to get it done.

But he couldn't do it. He was shaking with small tremors and his hands were so wet that he let the rifle slip out of them on to the blanket on the floor. His head was suddenly pounding as his heart raced a mile a minute.

"Damn it!"

Charlotte slowly ambled up the street to her car, totally unaware of the impending danger lurking in the back of that old gray station wagon. After a few minutes Vel crawled into the driver's seat and collected his wits, slowly. This same nervous reaction had happened to him in Viet Nam a few times. The sound of his buddies taunting him with the childhood echoes of "don't go Narvelle Phelps on me," bounced in his cranium. After waiting for five more minutes, he calmed down, started his car and slowly headed for home, he was relieved and irritated, at the same time.

Suddenly Vel pounded the steering wheel with his fist.

"Damn, damn, double damn! I stressed out!" He yelled to no one.

"Next time I'll smoke a joint before I get into the position!"

Two weeks later, it was one week before Christmas. There was a haze of smog that enveloped the entire city, sort of like a ground fog, but it smelled moldy. Vel, the new perversion of Santa Claus, again prepared to deliver his unusual gift to the FAT FOX. He positioned his wagon as before, then looked both ways to make sure that the street was empty. Everything looked good. He waited until just before 9 pm, then smoked a joint and carefully got into position to deliver the gift of lead. Like clockwork, out the door she came, right on time. This time she hesitated as she buttoned up her coat, another perfect profile position. Vel took a breath, let it out slowly, aimed for her stomach, squeezed the trigger gently, and sent the hot lead flying. It hit her exactly where it should have, a perfect shot.

Charlotte stopped in her tracks as her belly jiggled abruptly from the impact, but she didn't say a word. She thought she heard the muffled pop of a firecracker as she looked around, but no one was in sight, the old station wagon didn't register with her. A burning, full sensation, was spreading throughout her gut like the pains before bad diarrhea, her broken ribs hadn't sent their information to her brain yet. She bravely stepped towards her car not believing that she truly had been shot. The sting in her side was unusual, she said, "Oh my goodness, my stomach hurts, maybe it's something I ate."

"I can't be shot," she explained quickly. "Why would anyone want to shoot me?"

Then she put her hand on her stomach where the pain was slowly becoming stronger. Warm, wet, sticky, goop told her that she had been shot, but she still didn't believe it, couldn't believe it.

Charlotte made it a few feet before she slowly collapsed to the sidewalk, unconscious. Vel calmly started his car and drove to the nearest phone booth, near a gas station. He called 911, in a matter-of-fact-tone gave them the address, told them that a woman was down, then he drove home. Mentally prepared to be relaxed, Narvelle walked through the front door of his house, only to find that Linda was not there. She and Olivia left a note on the kitchen table saying that they were out shopping for Christmas presents. He got out his stash of dope, smoked another joint, and went to bed with the lights down low. Stereo music gently filled his room with a song from his favorite Johnny Cash record. He could hardly wait to hear how Charlotte responded to "the sting."

Meanwhile, back at the scene of the shooting, the silence of the night suddenly screamed, as the ambulance slid to a stop near the front of the library, a blinking cop car was right behind it. No one else was on the street near the library except Charlotte, collapsed quietly in a puddle of blood and urine. A brief minute later the fire truck arrived with three strong-armed firemen. With serious effort, the rescuers lifted Charlotte into the emergency vehicle that took her to Belvedere Hospital.

She was unconscious when she was taken out of the ambulance. Luckily all of her vital signs were still good. The surgeons on duty took her to the surgery suite immediately. Their decision was to staple her stomach after cutting out the destroyed part. The surgeon also removed half of her liver and a portion of her small intestine. Later, the doctor who performed the surgery smiled cautiously as he exited the surgery suite.

He turned to the attending nurse and said, "When she makes it through this trauma, this may be a major blessing for this large woman."

The nurse solemnly nodded her head in agreement.

The next day, the local newspaper had a small article in it about what had happened. It was in small print on the second page. It merely read: WOMAN SURVIVES SNIPER ATTACK. Last night Charlotte Johanson was apparently shot by a sniper, no known motive. She was not robbed or sexually harassed. She is expected to make a full recovery according to her doctor at Belvedere Hospital. The shooter is still at large. Any information leading to the arrest and conviction of the shooter will be appreciated greatly. Please call the police department and refer to case no. 436573-JD.

Narvelle read the paper as he drank his morning coffee, and was totally relieved and elated. A small smile crept upon his face as he looked up at Linda who was cooking pancakes, she didn't see his grin. Narvelle had a secret.

It was in the cards; everything was going to turn out all right, he knew it, could feel it. He smiled all day long at work as he ached to tell someone about his glorious deed.

CHAPTER SEVENTEEN
A CHURCH FULL OF HAPPINESS

The small, slate roofed, elegant stone church was nearly full of people. The stained glass work in the arched windows was spectacular. Quiet prevailed as the packed congregation waited patiently for something to happen, their looks of expectation seemed to fill the air as people peered curiously in all directions, anxious. Large bouquets of flowers were neatly placed up front near the pulpit. The preacher arrived and conversed in low tones with the folks near the flowers. He was a serious looking young man, dressed in "the cloth," and super shiny, slick, black shoes.

Suddenly, the music started with a bang as someone fired up the organ and the building vibrated joyously.

"Here comes the bride!" welcomed Charlotte as she entered the church through the front door. Immediately everyone stood and looked around to see the newly transformed butterfly. As the congregation stood, waiting her arrival at the pulpit, the groom and the preacher got together up front. As the music continued, Charlotte slowly walked past the stares and polite gasps of the crowd. She was as beautiful as everyone had said she would be. Next, the bride's maids entered, it was time for a marriage.

The service was short and sweet, a few songs, a brief protestant sermon, then everyone listened carefully and quietly for the wonderful magic words.

"I now pronounce you husband and wife," the garbed one finally proclaimed. As Glen and Charlotte exchanged rings, the preacher finished, "You may now kiss the bride."

Glen raised the veil covering the face of his stunningly beautiful wife. Her "Snow White" countenance glowed with happiness and glistened with tears of joy. He kissed her, gently, and said "I love you, Miss Charlotte." She returned his kiss, gently, then answered back, "I love you, Mister Glen." They hugged each other as the congregation burst into yelling, clapping, and jubilant shouts of joy; the flower girls tossed their flowers as happy tears flowed everywhere.

Charlotte was dressed in a flowing, long white dress with beautiful, white, handmade flowers and pearls interspersed along the train. Her diamond ring was a three carat beauty that lit up when light from any direction hit it. It was top quality. Glen was dressed in the traditional penguin tuxedo and looked like old money as he stood next to her, in awe, smiling like a Cheshire cat.

She walked in beauty.

Two hundred or more people showed up for their wedding. Glen Jones, an established architect, had taken for his wife, the lucky librarian, Charlotte Johanson. She looked marvelous and beamed with confident happiness. Everyone in the crowd knew of her transition from a blimp into a butterfly. Charlotte's parents bawled with joy, they were both sitting in the front row, separately, with their respective new spouses.

Hidden in the crowd was Mork Johanson, Charlotte's sad, obese brother, crying loudly. His emotional upheaval was noticed by everyone around him for twenty feet, some people smiled, others grinned, everyone else was annoyed. None of them knew that his tears were for him, more than for her. Mork shed tears for her because of her profound transformation, tears for him because of his obesity shame. He was an emotional mess before he got there, it didn't take much to set him off. Dixie, his wife, had been yelling at him, earlier, about his serious obesity problem.

Charlotte didn't know all of the people at her wedding. Later at the reception, she greeted everyone like a Queen would, trying to remember each of their names as she repeated them, after they were introduced to her. Her gracious smile and warm hugs were shared with everyone, except her brother Mork, who went home early, and an uninvited guest-spy, Narvelle Phelps.

Narvelle had tucked himself into the crowd at the back of the church just before the wedding ceremony began. No one knew him; he looked and felt quite normal. He quietly slipped out the side door as Charlotte and Glen joined hands, just before the preacher officially married them. After the wedding was over, an unusual feeling of accomplishment filled his mind. He was ecstatic.

"I think I'm going to find someone else and do it for them too," he surprised himself with a crazy-quick thought.

The next day, the wedding announcement in the local newspaper included a special attachment. An article about Charlotte was written by the famous, Sum Ting Wong, a famous Chinese herbalist. Two pictures, side-by-side, of Charlotte, were followed with the story of her life. Mr. Wong wrote of the unusual experience that Charlotte had endured two years earlier, and about her transition from unhealthy food to healthy food. He described the physical activities that she was now able to participate in, such as tennis, swimming, and ball room dancing.

Mr. Wong also wrote about how her strange experience of being randomly shot in the stomach had turned out to be a wonderful blessing. He addressed the psychological difficulties that most obese people have, and the rejection they suffer at the hands of modern society. He spoke about the difficulties facing obese folks who travel on airplanes, the problems they have going to a movie, going to the rest room, their lack of sexual involvement, and their loss of social interaction because of social rejection. Finally he explained that many obese people feel like second class individuals because they often suffer job discrimination.

Two days after his article appeared in the Los Angeles papers, it was snatched up by the major national news media and became national news, ending up in over 170 newspapers throughout the United States. Weight loss programs everywhere suddenly wanted to get involved in the selling of healthy products to seriously obese people. Within a month, pictures of Charlotte, before and after, showed up on one hundred and eighty bill-boards all over America. The agent who represented her, explained to the media that the money generated from her photographs in the advertisements was going to be donated to UCLA, to help create an obesity research grant at the university.

The only down-side to Mr. Wong's interesting article and Charlotte's national recognition, was the jokes made on late night shows by the TV hosts.

"What is the best way to go on a diet? Hire a good shot," Johnny answered.

"What are the two best things that you can put in your stomach to lose weight? A staple and a bullet!"

"What did the fat guy say when he was asked what he wanted to eat? Aw shoot, I don't know."

CHAPTER EIGHTEEEN
VEL BOASTS

Narvelle couldn't contain himself any longer, he had to tell someone about his wonderful deed. Two years is a long time to keep a secret, especially one like he had.

One evening as they were playing pool, he grabbed Fragile and pulled him over to a quiet area of the bar and sat him down, a very serious look on his face.

"I've got to tell you something, but I want you to promise to keep it to yourself. O.K.?" Vel's eyes pleaded earnestly.

Fragile looked deeply into Narvelle's eyes, and then took a few seconds before he said, "Sure, I'll keep it secret, what the hell did you do, kill someone?"

"Not quite," he answered slowly. "You know how I was shot in the gut and how it helped me to get back to my normal weight. Well, do you remember that story in the newspaper a couple years ago about a fat lady who had the same thing happen to her? Here's the scoop, I'm the one who shot her! She was the grossly fat chick, here at the bar, back a few years ago, with the super beautiful face. You remember her, I called her the "FAT FOX?" Well, I just went to her wedding a couple of weeks ago, and now she is trim and as pretty as a speckled pup!"

"Holy shit bro!" Fragile's eyes stared, wide open, worried. "You shot her in the gut, so she would have to lose weight like you did!?"

"Thass right my man. I know it sounds sort of fucked up, but I dreamed about it for a long time, and I finally decided to do it, so I did it, and it has all worked out, just right.

It worked for me, so I figured it would work for her too."

Fragile spit it out, "Now that is the strangest shit I've ever heard! Holy cow brother, that's some super serious stuff! Wait a minute, hold on;----------- this is a fuckin' joke, right?"

"No man, I really did shoot her!" Vel was serious.

"I know that it's weird. It is kind of like being in Nam, scary and exciting, all at the same time. The really cool part is that it all worked out, just right. You should see her now; she's a gorgeous knockout, absolutely beautiful, sexy, and totally changed. The best part, she is getting a new lease on life, I made her do something that she wouldn't do herself. I'm going to keep track of her and see how her life continues to change for the better. This is a pretty cool thing that I've done!

Look at it like this, if you will please, it's sort of like the boy scout taking an old lady across the road before she asks for help."

"I'll be damned!" Fragile announced. "That is un-fuckin-believable!"

"You are a strange unit, my friend!" Narvelle's friend declared.

Then Vel started babbling again. "So here is the rest of the story, I want to pop another one, or maybe do a series of them, like a serial murderer, except in my case, it would be cool to go down in history as a serial helper. I'm really excited about this.

You have heard of Dr. Savornin, right? Personally, I think that what the Doc is doing is right on. His name will live on forever no matter who thinks he's right or wrong. So will my name be famous, if I do a series of extraordinarily good deeds, I'm going to shoot some folks and document how their lives change for the better. If I get caught, which I won't, I don't care. What is a jury going to do to me if they find out, arrest me for helping people get healthy? You see it's a win/win situation no matter what happens. Can you imagine them putting me in jail for helping people lose weight? Hell, the folks that I've shot will come and bail me out.

If this all goes as planned, a hell of a lot of fat-asses around our country will reconsider all the junk they eat, and many of them might just lose some weight out of fear. It just might start a true weight-loss craze. You know that there's an epidemic of obesity in our country and that over ninety five percent of all those diet programs don't really work in the long run, all they do is make some greedy businessmen rich."

Fragile stared at him as he tried to see the logic of what Vel had just said. His face was still twisted with disbelief.

"Fear is a great motivator," Vel reiterated as he smiled slyly at Fragile.

With serious emphasis, Narvelle continued. "If, for some strange reason, I die too soon, and I ain't famous yet, would you let the newspaper folks know it was me who did it? I know it sounds a bit conceited, but I've thought about it a lot. What I am doing is not only original but it's a pretty gutsy thing to do, so I feel that I should get the all the credit."

Total silence engulfed that area of the bar. Fragile couldn't say a word. Narvelle shut his mouth waiting for his buddy to digest it all. They sat there, looking at each other as the seconds ticked away. Then, gradually, Fragile started to laugh quietly. His laughter kept building up until he laughed so hard that he started to cry, tears eventually ran down his face. Vel joined in, he couldn't help himself, the laughter was contagious. They both laughed so loud and long that people in the rest of the bar stopped talking to see where all the ruckus was coming from. When it was finally over, they were gasping for air, tears were running down their cheeks as they forced themselves to regain composure.

Then another long silence, and Fragile spoke again, trying to be serious. "Are you telling me that there is no guilt involved in what you are did?'

"None at all my friend. How can I have guilt when all that I have done is push someone to change their life, for the better? Can't you see that I have helped her to have a better life?"

"It seems pretty risky to be shooting someone with a damned rifle, I hope like hell that you have done your homework about where to shoot them. You could kill someone if you screw up!"

"I have, son, I've got it all figured out: you do remember that my wife's a nurse!?"

"Well, I'm your blood brother, we have been through hell together, but this is absolutely the goofiest crap that I have ever heard of, in my entire life. It beats the shit out of anything that anyone could make up. I love you man, even though you are one crazy son-of-a-bitch." He stopped. "So, I promise on my life, not to tell anyone, no matter what. Not a word will be spoken until you're dead, right?"

"That's all that I'm asking of you." Narvelle was through.

"Fragile" Glasscock, shook his head and grimaced, bewildered, his chin hung on his chest, as they headed for the pool tables.

PART TWO

CHAPTER NINETEEN
CHARLOTTE'S BROTHER MORK, A FEW YEARS BEFORE SHE WAS SHOT

Mork Johanson came from fine Swedish stock, so did his sister Charlotte, she was three years older. He was a state champion high school wrestler in the heavy weight division and a straight "A" student. When Mork graduated from high school he was a powerful and fit two hundred and forty pounds. He was intelligent, nice looking, and undefeated in the last year of his wrestling career. He never lifted weights like the other wrestlers in his school, he was a genetic gift from God.

The University of Utah, UCLA, The University of Iowa, and The University of Oklahoma all offered him a full scholarship to wrestle for them. He turned them all down to work with his father, Ovard, who was a bricklayer. Mork Johanson had other more important things to tend to after high school, his girl friend Dixie was pregnant.

Two weeks before graduation from high school, he suddenly married his high school sweetheart, Dixie Morrell. She was 18 years old and declared pregnant, three months before they graduated. Because of this good or bad luck, depending upon how you see it, Mork missed out on the opportunity to go on with a wrestling career in college, or professionally. Their son Kaine was born six months after they were married, a beautiful normal baby boy with laughing blue eyes and true blond hair. Kaine Olaf Johanson was the next true Norseman, in the making. Because Mork felt that he should be a responsible parent, he immediately went to work after high school to support his family.

After six years of extremely hard physical work, Mork noticed that he was experiencing low back pain at certain times. His job was a real back breaker. He told people that his job was to carry "hod." This means that he carried brick and wet concrete to professional brick layers as they worked. At least he was paid generously for his back-breaking job that no one else wanted. He sought relief by going to get adjustments, three times a week, for the next nine months, however they didn't seem to give him long lasting relief. Then things worsened, the final four adjustments didn't help at all, but made his pain worse, so he quit. Two months after that, he started having pain all the way down his left leg, so he sought medical help.

An orthopedic surgeon, examined him and ordered some tests, the MRI test confirmed that he had a significant bulge in one of his discs in his low back. His leg pain was apparently coming from a pinched nerve in his low back. Mork was put on anti-inflammatory medication and told to go home and go on strict bed rest for two weeks. He followed the doctor's orders exactly.

The big man was on his back with his knees bent, and a pillow under his knees, for the entire two weeks, getting up just to walk around, eat, shower, and go to the bathroom. Mork ate and slept and ate and slept and ate, continuously. Dixie waited on him hand and foot, frustrated because he kept eating and gaining weight. She blatantly reminded him that Sumo wrestlers plump up by eating and then immediately go to bed. Mork didn't seem to care, he gained another fifteen pounds during his two weeks of bed rest. Mork was a hundred pounds heavier, six years after graduating from high school

After the prolonged bed rest, the back and leg pain finally went away, so Mork returned to work.

Dixie, his slender wife, continued to complain about him getting heavier. Verbal fights became a common occurrence, as she tried to pressure him to quit pigging out and gaining weight.

A few months after he returned to work, their marriage slowly went to hell.

CHAPTER TWENTY
THE DANCERS

Bright colored lights of every imaginable hue lit up the stage, flashing on and off, some twirled and others reflected off of angled mirrors. The pulsing music was loud, very loud, pounding the air from the six massive speakers that surrounded the stage. It was impossible to hear yourself think. Heavy-duty rock and roll had the crowd in an arm waving, big eyed smiling, shouting frenzy. The crowd was all women, women of all ages had come for their ladies night out.

There were purple haired grandmothers clutching their purses, giggling and laughing loudly, like school children. Dozens of middle aged, well to do party chicks, were dressed to the tees in their bright blouses, large hair, monstrous jewelry, and spandex pants. Carefully exposed breasts bulged boldly throughout the crowd, showing cleavages of all sizes and shapes, as their owners proudly showed off. Shy slim secretary types were clustered in small groups around the room sipping on their frozen daiquiris and cosmopolitans, trying not to show their delight with being there.

Everywhere, cigarettes burned as if lit from both ends, while the air increasingly became difficult to breath. Booze was on the tables or on the way. Up front, next to the stage, thirty or more women were jumping and shouting as they waved their hands full of paper dollars.

Excitement filled the air.

On stage were the famous, 'Stud-Muffin' dancers, bumping and grinding. The show consisted of twelve of the most beautiful men that a woman or man had ever seen, doing their versions of dirty dancing. Their skimpy little g-string suits barely covered their bulging packages, hundreds of dollars, stuck inside.

Each of them was different. Damon was exceptionally tall and beautifully built, still had on his red fireman hat which made him seem even taller. Steve, the only black man, was powerfully built and shined like a body builder in the Mr. World competition. Carlos, the handsome Latin looking guy, looked like the actor, Omar Shariff, except he was much shorter, a beautiful oversized sombrero adorned his head. Waylon, the cowboy in the middle of the group, had on a black ten gallon Stetson cowboy hat, gorgeous hand stitched Llama boots, and a g-string with tassels on it. Each man's body was impeccable, without an ounce of fat between the dozen of them.

Sometimes only one man performed to the beat of a song, at other times two or three of them performed together. They always started in full dress as a fireman, baker, preacher, teacher, policeman, doctor, lawyer, or welder, and then slowly disrobed to the hoots and screams of the wide eyed anxious women.

The show had been going on for nearly two hours when suddenly, the overhead lights flashed on and off repeatedly for thirty seconds. Slow music began. As it announced the finale a minute later, twenty four beautiful naked buttocks lined up, cheek to cheek, side by side across the stage. The slowed down music became a sexy grind as the dancers tightened and relaxed their butt muscles in succession like a wave, in front of the frantic women. Then a strobe light fired up and entranced the crowd as a reverse wave of butt tightening seemed to happen without premonition. It started on the right side of the stage and pulsed to the left side. Wilder screams and shrieks of acceptance exploded around the room. Hundreds of dollar bills flew onto the stage from the screaming women.

Suddenly, abruptly, the show was over as the overhead lights blinked on and stayed on, and the music stopped. The dozen "hunks" lined up together in front of the women for their final bows and a few kisses. There were women throwing keys to their hotels and homes, up on the stage, six pairs of wet panties lay anxiously on the floor under the dancer's feet.

Dozens of women wanted to put more money into the g-strings, and some pushed the money down the forbidden front area that was already packed. Then the women began to scream and shriek louder, as pandemonium broke loose, they didn't want it to end.

Magically, ten smiling police officers appeared from nowhere, to calm the mini-riot. Amidst the screams of the women, the cops joined arms and formed a line separating the stage and the performers from the crowd.

On stage, a really good looking man, the best looking one of the bunch, Robby Rich, the dancer on the far left, stood smiling quietly and soaking up the experience, he was trying to Zen the moment, in spite of his adrenalin rush.

He had been doing this job for the last five years and had traveled all over the country, making good money, enjoying himself and meeting all sorts of women.

It was a fun job, Robby liked being a 'stud muffin dancer.'

CHAPTER TWENTY ONE
MORK'S WIFE DIXIE

Dixie Johanson, Mork's wife, had been a cheerleader in high school, her genetics molded her into a beautiful young woman. After she delivered Kaine, she worked on regaining her slender figure that was hers in high school. A strong commitment to remain, "normal" dictated what she ate and that she exercised. Her disgust with Mork and his obvious weight gains, also helped motivate her to do the opposite thing.

A year after her child was born, her body looked perfectly normal.

Dixie was blessed with unusual, green tinted hazel eyes with slight golden specks, almost white skin, a perfect oval face, and radiant auburn hair that hung past her shoulders in natural ringlets. Her sweet smile would melt the 'Grinch.'

After her son turned six and began going to school, she worked at a local gymnasium as an assistant office manager. She loved to workout with weights, to swim, and to play tennis. While working at the gym she met a lot of really interesting and fun people. From time to time she would flirt, a little, just to make sure that men still thought that she was desirable.

Her flirting didn't go unnoticed. One quiet afternoon as she sat at her desk, Dixie met a young man named Robby Rich, and her life changed dramatically after that. Robby, let everyone at the gym know that he was a, 'Stud-Muffin' dancer. Curly black hair that bounced on his wide shoulders, framed his twinkling blue eyes.

He didn't care very much about the fact that Dixie was married, he saw the ring on her finger. To him it only meant that she was experienced. A powerful physical attraction to her was immediate and immense, so he had to check her out.

One afternoon, following his work out, they met. Casually he strolled up to her office window. Robby had decided to see how far he could get with her, because she was a real 'looker.' At her office window, he looked her squarely in the eyes for five seconds without saying a word. She couldn't help but stare back at him.

Then his bull-crap began.

"Hi sugar lump," he started with a mischievous smile. "When do you get off?"

It took her by surprise, she blushed as she continued to gaze at him, then, a few seconds later, she coughed up, "Five-o-clock, wh,---why?"

"I was wondering if you would like to come up to my apartment and see all my diving medals," he brazenly boasted.

"And,---why would I want to do that?" she asked. "I'm a married woman!" Her face went red as she awkwardly tried to defend herself.

Robby continued smiling as he sensed the need to back off, "I know that." He hesitated, then quietly added, "I was just checking you out."

Dixie was obviously embarrassed, her face and neck were still red. She looked nervously at the clock on the wall, wanting it to rescue her.

"I've seen you flirting with some of the guys from time to time and I didn't know just how married you are."

Robby laughed gracefully and stuck out his hand. She looked at his hand, then looked at his face again, with questioning in her eyes, then refused to shake hands.

"I'm Robby Rich, what's your name?" He asked politely as he lowered his hand to his side.

"Mrs. Dixie Rich, uh--uh---oh!--- I mean Mrs. Dixie Johanson," she stammered awkwardly.

His smile lingered. Dixie was finally flustered to the point of action. She stood up, looked him directly in the eyes, briefly, then excused herself, escaping to the restroom.

What happened there, whatever it was, happened in slow motion to each of them at that moment in time. The electricity between them zinged hot, she knew it, and so did he.

Frame by frame, Robby watched her go, as he wooed her with his wicked eyes. A moment later, regaining his full senses, he casually reached across her desk, grabbed her pen and an empty piece of paper.

Dozens of pickup lines quickly crossed his mind as he thought about all the women that had approached him, as well as the dozens of women that he had tried to approach. He knew the game very well. He was good at it.

"This pretty girl needs something very special," he thought. He decided that it had to be clear and to the point, where no mistake about his message was possible. Nothing silly or funny would do.

As Robby looked around the workout area of the gym, at the men and women working out on the machines, it finally hit him. The lines came from nowhere, like a gift.

"I want to billow in your thighs. I want to burst beautiful, a moment within you." He printed the words perfectly on the paper.

Then he put a time and date on the paper, as well as his address, but no phone number, and no name. He folded the paper in half carefully and placed it on her desk, with the pen placed precisely, on top.

Hoping that his magic words would do the trick, he turned to leave.

Smiling confidently, he shrugged his shoulders and strutted away from her desk, like the conqueror of a battle. Thoughts of Helen of Troy and how a woman moved a man and an army, followed him.

"A beautiful woman can slay many men," he told himself.

Outside, he jumped into his shiny, new, red Corvette, that waited patiently with its top down. Off he sped, still smiling, wondering if Dixie would respond to his invitation.

"I hope those magic words work. I could stare at her all night long."

CHAPTER TWENTY TWO
ROBBY AT HOME

Robby opened the door to his apartment, and entered, carrying a bottle of wine, a bag full of long cream colored candles and a beautiful bouquet of fresh flowers. He whistled as he carefully set the candles in their candle holders over the elegant stone fireplace. Then he put the wine in the refrigerator, as he headed for the stereo, to sort through his music selection; something special was needed for this exciting evening. Next, he pulled the sheets and bedspread off from his bed and put on new sheets, freshly washed and lightly perfumed, his "crib" was nearly ready for action.

Over Robby's bed was a beautifully framed poem written in old English penmanship.

WHENAS IN SILKS MY JULIA GOES

Whenas in silks my Julia goes, then, then, methinks, how sweetly flows, the liquefaction of her clothes. Next, when I cast mine eyes and see, that brave vibration each way free; O how that glittering taketh me!

By Robert Herrick 1674

Robby was an intelligent young man that graduated from college with a Masters Degree in English Literature at the age of 23. He worked as an entertainer because of the ample amount of easy money that it generated for him, it was a fun job and he liked it. His grandfather told him one of the most important things that he ever heard, "never work at a job that you don't like." He took that to heart.

His goal in life was to enjoy it all. He was a scuba diver, sky diver, motorcycle racer, oil painter, author, and a struggling poet.

An excellent condominium in the Splendid Shores section of the beach, that overlooked the Pacific Ocean, was his abode.

The porch on his second floor was spacious and inviting. The low plastered walls around the area, were covered partially by red bougainvillea, making it private enough to make love there, the only witness to such an occasion would be the sky. The inlaid wood floor on his porch had an expensive hand woven American Indian rug, a hand carved apple-wood Italian easy chair, and a beautifully carved glass table. The area was elegant and nicely done. Down below, lamp lights danced up and down the street in front of his porch, and wound along the edge of the road, down to the beach not far from his house.

As he straightened up, the door bell rang with its five chimes chiming. Robby opened the door to the big-eyed face of Mrs. Dixie Johanson, pretty as a picture, smiling cautiously, right on time. "Well I'm here," she spoke softly.

Robby led her inside his lair and then he turned to grasp her gently by the arm. "I knew you would come, by the way, I lied about the diving medals." He put on his sexy smile.

She smiled back and said, "I figured that out the moment I saw you." As Dixie slowly looked around his apartment, she coyly smiled some more. It was then that Robby knew that he had her hooked for the evening.

"What did you say your name was?" Dixie couldn't help asking.

"Robby Rich," he whispered secretly. "It's nice to meet you, Dixie girl."

The music in the background was soft and low. The sweet sea breeze from the porch bathed them in warm, sweet smelling wisps, the candles later created a cathedral of light. The night was perfect for love.

Later that night, the candles burned down to just nubs and the music finally gave up the ghost.

Silence.

As Dixie rolled over and crawled carefully out of his king-sized bed, his beautiful blue glass bong hit the floor and broke into a dozen pieces. Dixie was exhausted, sweating and out of breath. She slowly walked naked across the room to the bathroom and closed the door. The shortened, dozen candles, elegantly shivered and quaked on the hearth of the fireplace, bouncing reflections on her tight curves.

Robby pretended to be asleep, but he wasn't, he squinted at her in the dancing candle-light as she crossed the floor. She was as pretty naked as she was clothed.

The overhead fan ticked a tune as he pulled the sheet over his head and whispered to himself, "Life is good. I'm a very lucky man."

CHAPTER TWENTY THREE
MORK GETS TOLD

The radio on the kitchen counter at Mork and Dixie's house, sang softly in the background. All of the lights in the house were off except in the kitchen. Dixie silently put the dishes away in the cupboard, as 'Love Hurts' began to play on the radio. The Everly Brothers sang it sweet and smooth. Dixie peeked into the living room at Mork and muttered something about how much pain she had months ago. She remembered the last time that they had sex; his fat belly had literally squashed the breath out of her, and it did hurt, like the song just said.

Mork sat in his easy chair watching the evening news and eating his traditional late night snack. Dixie glared disgustedly at Mork for thirty seconds, as he sat there with a large bowl of ice cream and a full box of Oreo cookies. He was like a machine, gorging himself before going to bed, it was his nightly thing. His big belly bursting with food from dinner, he still needed more. Food was his only friend in times of mental stress and he was terribly stressed about his love life, or the lack, thereof. For many months Dixie had not made love to him. Some of her excuses were obviously fake and unreal, he knew something was bothering her seriously. He had finally made up his mind to find out why she wouldn't be with him anymore, like she had, when things were good between them.

"Hey Dixie! I got a question." Mork started politely with a question, as he downed another spoon-full of ice cream.

"Sure, what do you want to know?" she answered in a nonchalant, non-involved way. She put the last glass into the cupboard and turned around so she could hear him clearly, her full cup of scalding hot coffee was carefully placed on the table to cool.

"Can I ask you a question, and for once not get any illusive answers from you?" he said firmly, his tone of voice changed.

A look of defiance cautiously crept across her face, her eyes narrowed and her lips tightened, as she readied herself for battle.

"You can bet your butt on it!" she replied quickly.

"Don't get pissed off at this question, O.K.?" He paused a few seconds. "How come you don't want to make love to me?"

There it was, the message was angry, as it arrived. Dixie had heard that tone from him prior to the verbal fights that they had had, many times before. The message was loud and clear. Because she knew there was a serious storm brewing, she slowly counted to ten, then cautiously began to speak.

"Do you want to know the honest to God truth Mork, no holds barred?" she flatly asked as she tried to remain emotionless and cool. "You are not going to like hearing what is really on my mind. If you think you're man enough to handle what I really think, I'll be more than glad to share it with you."

"Yeah, put it on me. I'm a big boy, I can stand it. We ain't got it on for damned near a year, I'm starting to think that you don't like me. You always have a splitting headache or some goofy stomach pain, or something else going on when I want to get a little "diddle." I'm starting to think that maybe you got a boyfriend or something, you sure as hell ain't been putting out in this household."

Dixie began to lose her cool, she could feel the pulse in her forehead pound and her neck began to ache.

Then she began to spout, like 'Old Faithful.' "We have been married for over seven years now. Before we got married, my girlfriend told me some weird crap about marriage that I didn't want to believe, but now I do. She told me that a lot of people get fat, dumb, and happy after they are married for awhile. I always thought it was just an expression, a figure of speech. Now I know it's true for some people. As far as I'm concerned, you, are now guilty of all three of those things!"

Dixie continued, "Fat, dumb, and happy. Happy to be fat. And dumb because you don't apparently know that you look gross! The problem is that I'm not happy at all with how much weight you have put on since we got married, and you look like hell. You should be ashamed of yourself!"

Mork remained quiet, she caught him off guard.

"Who in their right mind would want to screw a whale?" she suddenly exploded. Then she paused, knowing she was on a roll. Her eyes were on fire, her body began to tingle as she felt the sudden urge to hit him.

"I hate to be seen with you or even walk next to you. It's like Jack Spratt could eat no fat and his wife could eat no lean, in reverse! Apparently you don't give a damn about how gross you look!"

Dixie continued burning his soul. "Look at me for God's sake! Take a good look! I look as good as when I was a cheerleader in high school, a hundred freaking years ago, and I've had a baby!

So tell me the truth, fat ass! What is the real reason you have let yourself go?"

Mork said nothing, he had never heard her talk exactly like that before. A look of surprise still registered on his face.

"Why have you let yourself become a damned porker?" she growled. "I have pleaded with you over and over to lose weight, for years now, and you don't do a damned thing but get fatter and fatter. What the hell is up with you?"

He looked like a deer caught in the headlights. Too shocked to speak for the moment, he remained silent for a few more seconds. The truth hurt deeply as it sunk in. Then, as he slowly regained his wits about him, he could feel his blood begin to boil.

Explosively, the shit-hit-the-fan, as Dixie finally yelled, "I don't find you physically attractive anymore, you fat-ass! I hate how you look! Fat jerks like you smell funny, and look stupid!"

Then, it was Mork's turn. "You conceited bitch!" he finally snapped back at her. "I work like a slave, doing hard labor, to provide food and a place for us to live, and I deserve to eat like a King. If this is such a big deal with you, why haven't you said anything about this before now?"

"I have, you stupid ass! you just don't listen when I complain about your gluttonous ways!"

Silence and hatred filled the room. He glared at her, mad as hell. Daggers of hurt shot from his angry eyes, as Dixie stared back at him, with a look of deadly defiance.

"You really piss me off!" he yelled back at her. "I ought to smash your pretty face for being such a goody two shoes, self-righteous, prom queen bitch!"

Dixie suddenly reached over and grabbed her coffee cup, which was full to the brim with hot coffee, and threw it directly at him. The blistering coffee drenched his shirt, but burned less than her words already had. She whirled around and stomped out of the room, halted at the front door, turned around again and defiantly yelled back at him,

"You know what? You have turned into a fat, ugly mass of crap, just like your blubber-bellied sister, Charlotte, did years ago. Not giving a damn about how you look, must run in your fat-assed family!"

Mork stood there, like a totem pole, silent again.

"I hate you!" Dixie screamed as she slammed the door. "I'm leaving, and I'm never coming back!"

Their son in his bedroom, woke up and began to cry.

As she headed for Robby's apartment for the last time, Mork wiped the tears from his eyes as he went in to comfort their son. He sat on the bed, holding Kaine's hand as he nervously tried to relax his mind. He felt terribly alone again, in the wounded silence he suddenly remembered one of his favorite sayings. The sobering words came to him clearly.

"Life is some kind of loathsome hag, who is forever threatening to become beautiful."

Sadness escaped from Mork's lips as the big man began to cry, softly, "Such it is with my marriage, Damn it, I always hoped that it would have been better than this."

CHAPTER TWENTY FOUR
AFTER DIXIE LEFT HIM

A year after Dixie walked out on him, Mork was no longer the man he once was, strong, powerful, contented, resourceful. He was spiritually broken, and he was still way overweight.

They never communicated on an even keel after the big fight, their marriage was over and they both knew it. She shortly packed up and moved out of his house to live with Robby. She and Robby raised Kaine.

Mork started drinking more and more. His weight was approaching three hundred and fifty pounds when he lost his job with the bricklayers, a few months after she left him. His back and leg pain returned with a vengeance. He ate powerful pain pills like they were candy. Then he ate pills to keep his stomach from burning, then he ate pills to keep from aching all over, then he ate pills to keep from being depressed, then he ate pills to go to the bathroom, then his pills ate more pills to keep the other pills down. Two handfuls of pills stared at him daily, waiting to be eaten.

He eventually had back surgery to remove the ruptured disc, and remained pain free for a few months. Then some pain returned, but it returned to his back, only. It was constant and varied in intensity. The surgeon told him that it was caused by scar formation as a result of his surgery, and that nothing could be done to remove it.

He lost the will to thrive and said that he wanted to kill himself, but he didn't have the courage to do so. A new bumper sticker showed up on the back of his car, it said it all for him. "Life is a bitch and then you die."

Mork was continually tormented by his sister Charlotte's, good luck, her fame, her loss of weight. Life seemed so good for her now that she was married, and was no longer obese. He saw Charlotte many times during the next few years and each time he would return home more depressed than before he went to see her. She was trim, and beautiful, famous, on television and billboards all over America. The last time that he saw her, a few months ago, she beamed with happiness; she told him that she was going to have a baby.

Mork tried to diet again and again, without success. He purchased new packages of diet food and forced himself to eat them, much of it tasted like flavored sawdust. It left a funny taste in his mouth and never really satiated him. He tried to exercise, but had to stop when he pulled some muscles in his shoulder. Walking wasn't any fun either, his feet hurt like hell from walking just two blocks.

After he lost his job with the brick layers, he got a new job at the super-market as a cashier. Standing killed his feet so they let him sit or stand, as needed. He couldn't keep up with the other cashiers, his movements were slowed by his weight.

Unable to afford his house payments, Mork had to sell his house and move into an apartment, with another man who was also down on his luck. His apartment mate was once the owner of a used car company, but he lost it all. He drank so much booze that his wife and family left him, shortly before his company collapsed. He now worked at a car wash, washing cars. They had many things in common because life was a bitch for both of them.

A couple of years after his divorce, Mork decided to do what everyone else in California does, he went to a shrink; he got his own therapist. He found a psychologist in the phone book and called her. The sexual fascination of talking to a woman shrink enticed him to spend his money. He told her of his wishes to die, and how bummed out he was about his life. He told her that he was going to kill Robby and Dixie someday, then commit suicide. She always appeared unmoved as she listened carefully at each meeting and asked him how he felt about this and how he felt about that, as if his feelings were important to him. Mork didn't grasp the significance of his feelings, all he wanted was someone to talk to and someone to listen to him with compassion. He continued to feel sorry for himself, so, after a year of unproductive therapy, he decided to stop seeing his therapist.

Mork overdosed on sleeping pills one evening, but he didn't die from them. His apartment mate called for help, which arrived promptly, so he haplessly returned to the life of pain and misery that he was trying to escape.

As he kept a watchful eye on Charlotte's wonderful new life, he frequently mentioned to his apartment mate, about how his pretty sister had lost a ton of weight, and that now, after being shot, her life was perfect. A few times he said that it would be great if someone would shoot him and help him too.

"Shoot me in the head or the stomach, your choice. In a way, they would both be therapeutic. I don't really give a damn about anything anymore."

PART THREE

CHAPTER TWENTY FIVE
VEL'S NEXT TARGETS

Many months after Charlotte's wedding, as Narvelle delivered a package to someone's house, he noticed a very obese man next door slowly getting into his truck. His belly was so large that he had to push his seat back as far as it would go. The adjustment on the steering column raised the steering wheel, allowing him to squeeze under it.

"I'm going to follow this guy and see what's up with him. He looks like he might need some help."

The big man drove to an office building about three miles away. He took his time as he painfully exited his truck, with cautious steps in slow motion, he walked the fifty feet to the office. The sign on the office door read: Weight Loss Clinic. Vel waited patiently until the big man came out from the office to get back into his truck, he had been inside the building for half an hour. Vel couldn't help himself, he jumped out of his delivery truck and ran over to him as he was slowly getting into his truck.

"Excuse me sir, please don't be insulted, I have a friend who is really overweight and is looking for some help. Has the clinic, in there, helped you any?"

An expression of pain and agony presented itself on the big man's face, he didn't say a word at first. After he got himself situated in his truck he took a couple of slow big breaths, then after he burped a big belly burp, the grin of a five year old child covered his face. He thought about the question for a few seconds more before he replied, then he spit it out.

"This, so called specialist, has got me on a diet that would kill a damned canary, and I'm still fat. I have to take fiber every day just to take a crap. My blood pressure is sky high and my cholesterol sucks, I have reflux and everything hurts, I take a handful of pills every day. Now I have to take more pills to help me take the original pills. Heartburn is the result of everything that I eat that tastes good. After going to this quacko-doctor for three years, I feel like I'm barely alive. Is he helping me? Since I don't know what the hell else to do, I guess so."

"How old are you?" Vel asked politely.

"I'm fifty four years old, but I feel like I'm a hundred years old," he answered with a painful laugh. Physically his body and face looked like he was in his late sixties. His hair was mostly white and getting scarce, and he had a dozen liver marks on his wrinkled face and neck. His belly was immense. As he tried to smile, the pain in his eyes told the true story.

"Thanks for talking with me," Vel said as he turned around and slowly walked towards his delivery truck.

"He is in definite need of some help. Number two is coming up! He is in for a big surprise because his life is going to change dramatically. I'll see to that."

Vel did a little research.

The big man was named Andy Killborn. He was six foot tall and weighed four hundred and sixteen pounds. Andy had been slowly getting more and more overweight from the time he quit playing professional football twenty years ago. When he was playing ball, his fellow football players called him 'Wild Man' because of his fun, enthusiastic, and unpredictable behavior. He had been an excellent athlete, his professional football weight was around two hundred and forty pounds, which he had handled nicely.

Now he had gout, osteoarthritis, high blood pressure, high cholesterol, and bouts of severe indigestion. He presently lived alone. Andy's wife of twenty two years, died from colon cancer a year earlier. She was only fifty two years old. Andy used to be a great bowler, and he loved to ride motorcycles but had not done so for many years. Vel decided to help Andy because he apparently wasn't doing very well with the program he was on, and mostly because he looked so pathetic and miserable.

Narvelle stalked Andy for three months and tried to observe his ritual behaviors, this was a difficult thing to do because Andy did not come out of his house on a regular predictable basis. Vel had to work, so he could only observe Andy when time was available for him. Finally his three months of sporadic observation, paid off. Vel discovered that when the weekend came, Andy would leave his home in a more predictable manner, he would regularly go to church. Andy was a Catholic, he would usually leave on Sunday evenings at about six pm and end up at a church fellowship meeting for men. He usually returned home at around eight thirty pm. Vel finally had it figured out as to where he could hit him.

The easiest place that Vel could sting him would be at the church. He observed that when Andy went to church he would always drive around to the back of the church fifteen minutes before the meeting actually started, he would honk his horn and in about two or three minutes a couple of men would come outside with a large wheelchair. Andy could not walk more than a hundred feet without becoming seriously fatigued. The church fellows would push him inside the building, where he would remain for an hour and a half or so, and then they would return him to his car, after the meeting was over.

Andy would stand outside of his car for about two or three minutes, prior to them coming to transport him into the church. That would be when Vel would shoot him.

The day arrived. It was time to strike his new target. Vel drove his old vehicle around behind the church an hour and a half before the Sunday meeting was to begin. As he slowly came around the corner of the church, he nearly hit a police car head on, they both jerk-skidded to a stop. The cop was patrolling the parking lot and the neighborhood. Vel's couldn't believe it, his loaded rifle was uncovered in the back of his station wagon. Worse than that, he had just recently put a home-made silencer on it. He looked at his rifle and then he looked back at the cop and forced a smile and a wave. The cop smiled and waved as Vel regained some air into his lungs. The cop car slowly proceeded and exited the lot.

An hour later Vel cautiously returned and parked his wagon near a wall of trees, far from the back door entrance to the church. Even though it was approaching evening, it was still light out.

There was no traffic around the back of the church so everything looked good. Three cars were parked at the other end of the building. The shot would be just less than 50 yards. Narvelle was ready and excited to do it again. He had practiced faithfully on his private desert dummy and was hitting it regularly, on the dime.

He positioned himself on the floor in the back of the wagon. Through the hole in the door he could see his target area clearly, one hundred and thirty feet away, he needed to make this a perfect shot.

The time had come to strike. Andy pulled up and parked his car. He got out and lit a cigarette as he stood by his car, waiting for the wheelchair crew. Then, Andy's time for a life change came with a bang, he felt the hot bee sting and like most gut shot victims, didn't cry out in alarm. He looked surprised. He placed his hand on the wound and observed blood spilling out, but he just stood there, in shock, as if it wasn't real. He remained standing for a minute until the ushers appeared with the wheel chair, they sat him down and one of them ran to the phone for help. A few minutes later an ambulance arrived. Andy was still alert but totally in shock, his eyes were wide open and he looked bewildered, frustrated. The ushers loaded him on board the "cracker box," and away he went to the county hospital.

No one suspected the old abandoned station wagon parked so far away in the parking lot. No sound of a gunshot had been heard. Vel casually drove off around the other end of the building a minute or so after the ambulance left and the ushers went back inside.

The shot was perfect, it destroyed half of Andy's stomach and a section of his liver and broke a couple of his ribs. The surgeons were in agreement to staple his stomach and that's exactly what they did. Andy left the hospital two days later and his life began to change for the better.

Vel called the hospital the next morning after the shooting, just to check up on Andy and to make sure that he was O.K.

Because the procedure went so well with Andy, Narvelle came to the final decision that he was going to shoot a total of seven people, and then stop. Seven seemed like a lucky number. He would document each case and eventually write a book about how he chose his target, then document how well each target responded. The end goal would be to record how each of them responded, and how their life improved.

When Narvelle arrived at the fine old age of fifty five, he would write each of his targets a letter explaining how and why they were chosen, then he would publish his book and wait for fame to strike him.

That was Narvelle's plan for the future.

CHAPTER TWENTY SIX
ANDY IN STURGIS, TWO YEARS LATER

Sturgis in the summer is capable of having both hot and cold weather on the same day, or within the same hour. Thousands upon thousands of motorcycle riders converge there every year to raise hell, eat, and drink till they either puke, get high, laid, or sick. It is the largest motorcycle Mecca in the world. Many of them regress to acting like a five year old child, showing off, and acting a fool, as they ride their motorized toys up and down the streets of Sturgis and through the mountains of South Dakota.

A pack of six motorcycle riders from California cruised along, headed for Sturgis. They had their dew rags on their heads, sunglasses, leather jackets with patches and emblems on them, and three weeks of purposely grown beards and mustaches. The wonderful blue sky was cloudless as they roared into the Black Hills of South Dakota, and pulled over to rest at the next beer stop, Lefty's tavern. Their burnt cheeks fanned out from their dark sunglasses.

They dismounted their Hogs, as they parked them backwards on the sloping pavement in front of the bar. The rear end of their bikes stopped near the concrete curb, so they could drive up and away without having to push their heavy bikes back up the incline. Into the establishment they sauntered like gunslingers from the Old West, cigarettes and cigars were hanging from their lips while black gloves still wrapped their hands.

The group consisted of a tough crew, a Dentist, an Accountant, a Truck Driver, a Plumber, a Gynecologist, and

Andy, the retired football player. Professionals on their hogs, trying to look like "bad boys." They bought their beer and then went upstairs to the landing, to watch the unending parade of motorcycles going past on their way to Sturgis.

Their conversation with each other was gentlemanly, and of no significance until they saw a tall biker-dude pull up and park in front of the bar. He parked his white Honda Goldwing with the front end downward towards the bar entrance door, front tire next to the curb.

The tall biker was inside the bar for a brief minute, then he went back outside. With his information in mind, he straddled his bike and slowly, but easily, backed it up the incline, and rode away, on the road to Sturgis.

"Did you see that?" the dentist asked curiously.

They all said yes.

"That was the strongest son-of-a-bitch I've ever seen. I have never seen anyone back a big motorcycle like that, up an incline, without huffing and puffing!"

The others laughed at him and shook their heads.

"That Honda, ol' buddy, has a reverse on it, like a car," Andy explained. "It's the only motorcycle that I know of that has a reverse gear."

Andy fake punched the dentist in the ribs and they all laughed out loud again.

The bar lights of night were going on everywhere when they pulled into Deadwood. The bar where Wild Bill Hickok was shot in the head, and killed, loomed up ahead, it was packed with people and had a line of bikers waiting outside. The group of six, rode on by, and pulled over at a Motel 8 for the night, they got the last three rooms that were available.

After a great steak dinner at the Belligerent Bull Restaurant, the "six pack" assembled in the parking lot near their motorcycles. Puffs of smoke shot from their nostrils as they talked about the weather, motorcycles, women, and the excitement of coming to Sturgis for their first time. Next to them, not twenty feet away, three gnarly looking bikers were sitting on their bikes, shooting the breeze and drinking beer, drunk as skunks.

"Gents!" Andy spoke up. "Here's a good joke. This guy was on an airplane bound for Orlando. He sat next to a nice look young lady. He asked her why she was going to Orlando. She told him that she was going to a nymphomaniac convention. He looked surprised, and then asked her if she had ever been to a convention like that before. She said yes, that she went last year and learned a lot. She told him that she learned that Jewish men have all the money, American Indian men are the kindest, and that the guys that are the most fun are Rednecks. Then she paused and said, I'm sorry, I didn't introduce myself. My name is Dawn, what's your name? He hesitated for a couple seconds and then said, my name is Tonto Rosenbloom, but my friends call me Bubba!" They all laughed out loud.

One of the nasty looking bikers, next to them, drunkenly blurted out, "Hey ass-breath! Did you call me a redneck?"

Andy calmly turned and looked at him, then roughly growled, "Mind your own business big shot!"

The bleary eyed drunk, dismounted his parked bike and staggered boldly up to Andy and awkwardly body bumped him. "I'll whip your ass, Grandpa!" the drunk slobbered his words.

Without hesitation, Andy's right fist hit the drunk, three times in rapid succession. First he hit him in the neck, the second punch was to the solar plexus, and the finishing blow was nicely aimed at his crotch. One, two, three, the drunk was on the street, writhing in pain, barely breathing, gurgling like a broken water pump. The other two nasty looking, "self appointed tough guys," slowly came over and dragged him off towards their room. As they hauled him away, they were cussing and yelling, threatening revenge.

The dentist timidly piped up, "Gentlemen, perhaps we should go find a nicer place to stay for the night."

The six bikers fired up their Harley's and headed off towards Sturgis, in the light of the three quarters Moon. Later, the doormen at the Hilton Hotel hauled their bags inside, with a grin.

The next morning was glorious, the "six pack" walked down the mile long row of motorcycles parked in the middle of the street, in downtown Sturgis. Swarms of motorcycles drove by, slowly cruising and showing off. Then a motorcycle with a Corvette engine came by, burbling and snorting, and shocking everyone; immediate approval from all of the bystanders was evident.

"That's a Boss Hoss!" Andy yelled. "It's a bad sumbitch. Only has one speed, fast!"

Then, to everyone's surprise, a delightful parade of scantily dressed young ladies on the back of bikes, and some riding their own bikes, came by. A tee-shirt on one of them said it all, "bitches on bikes." Every man on the street hooted, whistled, and yelled as they putted by, long hair floating in the dry wind.

Downtown Sturgis was a sight to behold: bikes, bellies, bikers, babes, beauty, boobs, butts, bodies, bedlam, bad boys, bald heads, bare breasts, and beer.

Awe, continually gripped the six riders as they enjoyed the public spectacle of the people and their outfits.

After the girl parade was over, the dentist asked, curiously, "You damn near killed that jerk last night?" Andy explained, "I told him to mind his own business didn't I? I'm not used to taking crap from anyone. I hope you guys are all right with that.

Besides, I have been wantin' to punch some son-of-a-bitch for a long time, but I couldn't until recently. A few years ago, I was way overweight." He grinned and they looked confused.

"I don't know if you guys know this or not but I use to play professional football. I retired and I got really overweight, ----blimpy, actually. A couple of years ago I had a freak thing happen to me, I have lost around one hundred and fifty pounds since then. I'm not down to my football weight, but I'm getting pretty close. I feel really good and since that jerk was, a little nasty, I felt like someone needed to punch his lights out, so I did. I have always liked hitting people who need to be hit, it's good for them, they learn stuff." He grinned with his naughty-boy grin.

"What kind of freaky thing happened to you?" the chubby, out of shape, dentist asked.

"Well, this is going to sound unbelievable, but I was gut-shot one night as I was going to church. A bullet came out of nowhere, I didn't hear a gunshot or nothing. Someone shot me, or maybe he was shooting at someone else and missed and hit me, I don't really know how or why I was shot. I wasn't robbed or nothing. As far as I know they never caught the guy who did it. I had part of my liver, and part of my stomach taken out. It's been a crazy thing in a way, since then, because I can't eat a lot like I used to. I haven't been on a diet or nothing; I have just steadily lost weight since then.

I feel like a young man again. My doctor says that I will continue to slowly lose weight for about one more year, and then finally reach a point of stabilization."

"You look pretty damned normal to me," spoke the dentist as he rubbed his belly that hung over his belt. He was around 60 pounds overweight, himself.

"It's also very interesting that I don't have all the aches and pains that I used to have. I have stopped taking all the medicines that I once took, except two baby aspirin a day and my blood pressure medicine."

"You know what?" the dentist replied. "I read in the newspaper or saw it on television a few years ago about a woman who had the same thing happen to her. She was hit by a stray bullet, or by a sniper, and she ended up losing a bunch of weight, too. I think the article was written right after she got married to some famous architect. There was a picture or her in the paper. My wife said that she was real pretty in the face, if I remember right. I never saw her picture. I don't think that anyone was ever arrested for it, or if it was just ruled, a freak accident."

"Speaking of 'purty,' what say we drop in that bar over there and watch some young chicks dance, and have us some beer?" Andy enthusiastically asked, as he pointed towards the Zinger Club. Everyone instantly agreed to that. In, they went, cigars in hand, eyes wide open, grinning like possums, ready for a few beers and "some fine entertainment."

The stage had four good looking young women, sort-of dancing, with nothing on but a G string, a garter belt to collect cash, and a smile. An anatomy class at an art school would have been jealous. Dozens of men were whistling, yelling, and talking loud. The country music boomed as body parts bounced, and the beer flowed.

Andy and his group sat in the back and waited for the beer lady to arrive. After she took their orders, Andy got up and sauntered up to the bar, where he started talking to a pretty woman, sitting unaccompanied. He came back in a few minutes with an excited smile on his face. "I tell you fellers what, I just met a really cool woman! She is an artist and likes to ride motorcycles, I got her phone number, and sure as hell, I'll be talking to her later on tonight!"

Carefully, Andy shook some salt into his beer, then added thoughtfully, "Her name is Lucretia McEvel, funny name huh?" He wagged his head, looking puzzled.

CHAPTER TWENTY SEVEN
HO, HO, HO, A GIANT

Just over a year, after Andy Killborn was shot, Narvelle and Linda went to the state fair with Olivia and two of her girlfriends. They enjoyed the fair and tried all the weird stuff to eat. They ate fried cheese, fried Twinkies, fried Snickers, fried pretzels, and fried tomatoes. They all felt like they were sick to their stomach, and laughed quietly when Olivia threw up after riding the children's roller coaster. It wasn't much of a roller coaster.

Later, as they walked around the fair, Vel was secretly on the lookout for his next target. Suddenly out of nowhere, there he was. The next one to be shot was one of the biggest men Vel had ever seen, he was a giant of a man. He stood 6 ft. 6 inches tall and looked like he weighed around five hundred pounds. He was immense in girth with his belly hanging way down over his belt. His thighs were so large that he couldn't walk normally, they rubbed together, like sandpaper. He tipped from side to side as he moved forward, like some goof-ball from a horror movie. His movement up the street was deliberate, slow and painful. Denim overalls wrapped his massive body and he truly looked like a monster as he lumbered down the road. Folks stopped and stared at him as he approached them.

Growling at people, the giant pushed through the crowd, sometimes bumping into folks on purpose, just to watch them fall off balance. As he disappeared into the crowd, Vel knew that he would be hard to identify if he stayed put, there, with his family. Somehow, he would have to find out quickly who this man was, he needed to go find out, now.

But he couldn't just ditch Linda and the kids and run off. Narvelle was perplexed for just a minute, then it quickly came to him.

"I have really got to go to the bathroom," he blurted out. "I can meet you guys at the ice cream stand over there in a few minutes. I'll be right back." Off he scampered after the giant.

Down past the concession stands are the row of barns and stalls where the pigs, chickens, cows, and horses are kept. Because the giant wore overalls, Vel guessed that he might be a farmer or a rancher. No one else in the crowd was dressed like him. Vel darted into the first barn. It was full of cows and a few young boys and girls washing and grooming their cows.

Then Vel jumped into the next building. It was full of chickens and dozens of people. He methodically looked up and down the aisles for the giant, but he was not there either. The next building was the pig pen. Standing up against the wall was the giant. The huge man was standing near the largest pig that Narvelle had ever seen. It was white and appeared to weigh a thousand pounds. Vel watched the giant from a distance. As he wondered what to do, the giant was approached by a cute teenage girl in a blue band outfit. She had a clarinet in her hand. The big man bent over and she whispered something into his ear, then he pulled out his wallet and placed a few paper dollars in her hand. Then she ran off, towards the far end of the building. Vel stepped outside and hustled his feet in her direction.

The band was getting ready for their daily march around the fairgrounds. The clarinet player was talking to three other young ladies who where holding their musical instruments in their hands. The director of the band was putting on his marching hat, some fifty feet away. Vel calmly walked up to the young lady that he had followed.

Politely, Vel spoke to her, "Excuse me, I'm John Dunne, and I want to buy that big white show pig from your father. I have been to the pig pen twice and your father was not there. Is there some way you could give me his phone number so I can contact him?" He smiled his kindest smile as she looked curiously at him. The young girl acknowledged his question as she ceased her conversation with her friends.

With a little giggle, she answered his question, "He's not my father, he's my uncle. His name is Richard Head. He lives out past Riverside. I don't know his number but I'm sure you can find it in the phone book. By the way, don't call him Dick Head. If you do, he won't talk to you." She winked, then added, "Good luck."

Vel hustled back to the ice cream stand and joined his wife and the girls. They had their loaded ice cream cones in hand, and Linda was holding a double scoop of chocolate ice cream for him.

"Lets all ride the roller coaster, together, after we eat our ice cream," he suggested.

After they rode the roller coaster they walked around slowly on the fairgrounds, heading towards the exit. Suddenly, they all stopped at the same time in front of a shooting gallery. The barker invited them in with a promise of winning a prize. The girls wanted to win something. Even Linda was in the mood to win a big stuffed animal, as a memento of the state fair. Narvelle went along with their desires. They paid the young man the money and took their rifles in hand and begin to fire at the moving targets. There were dancing pigs, roosters and chickens, regular round red and white targets, and Martian space craft, all mixed together, moving from left to right, with some of them popping up suddenly for a few seconds, and then quickly disappearing. Narvelle aimed his gun at the row of dancing pigs, pulled the trigger, and then his vision skewed.

He was suddenly dizzy as his blurred eyes envisioned grossly obese men and women, all naked pink and blubbery-round, moving from left to right, next to the pigs. There were three or four fat people, then a pig, then two obese people, then two pigs, then a single person, then three pigs, then five fat people, then four pigs, then two obese people "doggy style"............ He blinked his eyes as on and on it went for a few more seconds, until he closed his eyes tightly to stop it. Anxiously, Narvelle opened his eyes to realize that he had, again, not been in touch with reality. It happened to him from time to time.

"What the hell!" he said out loud with innocent alarm. Everyone heard him. Linda gave him an understanding look of forgiveness.

Conversely, the girls all looked at him strangely and paused from their shooting fun.

Linda asked quietly, "What's the matter honey?" as she peered into his far away gaze.

"Just bad memories. Damned flashbacks! War stuff, you know, all that crap. The movement of the targets triggered it, I think." He blinked his eyes a few times, then kept them shut for a few seconds.

They all understood, and said no more as they slowly returned to their shooting game. He put his rifle down, turned around, and walked humbly towards a nearby bench.

Narvelle slowly sat down, lit a cigarette, and waited patiently for the girls to finish their fun. Then, suddenly a headache washed over him like a tsunami, instinctively, both of his hands cupped his temples, as he squeezed his eyes shut, once more.

Dressed up soldiers were standing, next to the walls of the dance floor. Large, colorful, paper constructed, Chinese lamps, swung to and fro from the ceiling. The music in the background was the Guy Lombardo orchestra, with saxophones and violins, mixed with trumpets and trombones, playing sweet and low.

Charlotte, the large pretty faced woman in the corner was staring at the lamps and crying. Three or four dozen men and women were dancing, cheek to cheek, gracefully across the dance floor. Then the music slowly drifted off key, like a record player slowly loosing power, until it stopped. Looks of confusion painted the faces of the soldiers.

"Ladies and gentlemen, boys and girls, it's now time for a ladies choice dance. Ladies, now's your chance, find the man that you would like to hold in your arms!" boomed clearly from the ceiling speakers.

Narvelle was talking to Harold and Johnny when he felt a light tap on his shoulder. He turned around, and there, smiling beautifully in front of him, was Charlotte, the fox, all four hundred pounds of her. Narvelle graciously accepted her invitation to dance, as the orchestra began a waltz. Gliding across the floor, seemed too easy, Charlotte seemed unreal as she moved lightly, floating next to him. Their bodies didn't touch at first, then Narvelle felt the desire to pull her closer to him. Like a kite string, he pulled, she resisted, he pulled, she slowly came closer. He felt her breasts and belly, bump into his body. The more he pulled, the slower the music went. The roomed faded into colored pools of light, as he kept bringing her closer and closer. Then, her soft cheek gently touched his face. Narvelle was shocked as he stared at Charlotte, her body was changing, melting away, while he hugged her. The fat was disappearing, she was getting smaller and smaller as they continued to dance.

Finally his arms wrapped completely around her, and he felt her entire body up next to him. Like a skin covered skeleton. She was warm, and smelled like gardenias, roses, lilacs, and honeysuckle. The rest of the people on the dance floor, had stopped dancing. They were in a big circle around Narvelle and Charlotte, applauding, whistling, and making cat calls.

"Narvelle! Honey! Are you all right?" anxiously came from Linda as she placed her hand on his shoulder and shook him strongly, bringing him back to reality. He looked like glazed cake. A far distant look in his eyes.

Another damned flashback.

CHAPTER TWENTY EIGHT
HOT RODS

Every year after Narvelle and Harold came home from the war, they would go to the annual hot rod show. This year, a week after the state fair where Narvelle spotted the "giant," his best friend Harold, finally bought his long deserved, dream car. It was 1957 Chevrolet Bel Air, two door hard-top, red. It was very nice, in excellent shape.

Narvelle felt the pressure to act. He and Linda, also had been saving money to buy a dream car, so this year, because his friend had done so, he asked Linda if he could buy a special piece. She agreed. They bought an amazing, rare vehicle, a 1955 Chevrolet convertible with a continental kit. It cost them an arm and a leg, took all of their savings. It was a real beauty.

The car was lowered front and back and stood barely four inches off the ground. Tall speed bumps were a definite "no-no." The hood was leaded in, and it boasted two dozen louvers. There was the original manual three-speed shifter on the column. It had chrome reverse rims with baby moon hub caps and white-wall tires. The unusual, six chrome scavenger exhaust pipes, underneath, stuck out under the rear bumper like tuned trumpets. Three, special, one barrel carburetors, hung sideways on the special intake manifold that fed the motor. It's custom exhaust pipes ran straight from the rebuilt original six cylinder motor, without mufflers.

The car made a hell of a racket when he would down shift and let the pipes rumble. Foot stomping acceleration sounded like a top fuel dragster. The car's sound was totally illegal, but cops didn't say a word when he passed by. The car was way too cool.

The extraordinary, hard to find, Chevy convertible, was painted mirror black, with black, diamond tucked leather seats, and a black soft top.

Fragile and Narvelle would get together every so often, to wash and wax their cars at Fairmont Park, under the huge trees, in the shaded afternoon. They would bring some beer and turn the "oldies" on the radio.

Sometimes, Narvelle parked his '55 Chevy in the driveway at his home, for the neighbors to admire. It was pure art. People would stop and offer to buy his car, at least once a month. Narvelle was "world famous" in his neighborhood, because of the black beauty. He called it the "Black Marauder."

The car became Narvelle's major link with reality.

Special Saturday nights gleamed with classic style when Narvelle and Linda would pack their pride and joy, full of Olivia's friends, and haul them to the movies. Later, they would pick the kids up, and take them to the Oldies But Goodies Diner, for banana splits, or root beer floats. Once a month he took Linda to the local church square dance, in the Chevy. Everyone there, loved their car, some lady dubbed it, "the cat's meow!"

After work, Narvelle and Linda loved to ride around, in the countryside. Driving with the top down, seemed to purge his soul, for a while, from the torments that frequented his mind.

Linda loved to sing songs to Narvelle from the radio, as the wind whipped her hair into knotted ringlets.

Their black Chevrolet ran perfectly on a dozen trips up Highway 1, to the wine country, as well as to San Francisco, Carmel, Santa Barbara, and Yosemite.

CHAPTER TWENTY NINE
RICHARD HEAD, NINE WEEKS AFTER THE STATE FAIR

Rain poured down on Southern California. It never rains lightly in California, it usually pours. Vel had his windshield wipers on, full tilt, because he could barely see thirty feet ahead of him.

He was hunting for the giant, it was time to puncture another obese belly. Little did he know that his next target was not going to be so be so easy.

Vel's old grey station wagon was creeping along at ten miles per hour on the road towards the giant's home. Blankets of rain had suddenly slowed him down, making driving treacherous. He had done his research and knew where the giant lived and his phone number. According to his map, the giant lived within two miles of where Vel presently was. What he still didn't know, was exactly what Mr. Head did for a living, and how to get to the man, to inflict his "good deed."

Narvelle stopped at the next gas station, filled his tank with gas, finally making his way into the gas station to go to the rest room. Inside, he approached a man who was buying cigarettes, and asked him if he knew anyone around that area who had a big white pig. The man said no, that he did not live around there; he said he was on his way to San Francisco and had taken the wrong road in the blinding rainstorm.

Casually Vel then approached the unusual looking woman at the cash register. "Do you know anyone around here that raises or owns prize hogs, pigs, or whatever you call them?"

She looked annoyed. "Why do you want to know?" she snapped.

Nasty looking woman, nasty response.

She had a two inch long hair growing out of a dark mole on her chin, and a face that would scare a scare crow. Her hair was cut short, chopped up, and looked greasy. Dark, piercing, rat eyes, that were too close together, sent their message of distrust. No makeup attempted to grace her face. Her lips were cracked, and when they separated with speech, yellowed, rotted teeth appeared inside her foul-smelling mouth. A wad of chewing tobacco bulged from where it was squirreled in her left cheek.

"I was at the state fair a while back and I found a hundred dollar bill near a pig barn. It was on the floor next to a great big white pig. I think the pig was a prize pig or something special. No one was around, so I asked some lady in the next stall who the owner of the big pig was. She wasn't sure. She said that the owner was probably a man named Richard Head. She said he lives out here in Flander, somewhere near Riverside. That's why I'm here, I came here to give him his dues. Do you know anyone named Richard Head?"

"You're shitting me, right?" she snarled. "Who the hell are you, the good Sam Martin?"

Vel looked perplexed, didn't know how to take her.

"You know, Samaritan, like in the Bible! What the hell, it's a joke, sir!"

" Na, No, ah,... not really. I-I-I guess I'm just trying to da-da-do the right thing," Vel stuttered as he lied with the same breath.

"Well, if you don't know, Mr. Dick Head, is a real piece of crap. It just happens that he owns the house that I rent. He owns this shit-hole of a gas station, and a couple other homes around here. He is a stingy old ding bat, and no one likes him! That sucker is a mean man; he will throw you out of his rental properties if you miss just one payment. He did that to my sister about three years ago. Then, the jerk took her to court and sued her for damages to that piece of crap house that she rented from him. I don't know why anyone would want to be nice to him, someone ought to shoot that fat prick!"

Narvelle smiled, rolled his eyes, and calmly said, "The lady at the fair said that Mr. Head is a real big sucker, I mean that he's as big as his prize pig. Is that true?"

"That's about it, he's a pig raising a pig. His wife probably slops him and the other pigs at the same time," the nasty clerk answered back. "He's actually a small time farmer that raises a few head of cattle, and some pigs, for show. He ain't poor. I think he also owns about forty acres of land that he raises hay on."

"What does he do for entertainment? I mean does he get out much?"

"The only thing I've ever seen him do was ride around his farm on his big-assed John Deere tractor. I have never seen him here, in a grocery store, or anywhere else. I have only seen his face two times in my whole life, and that was from a distance. He's sort of a recluse, if you know what that word means.

I heard that he ran over his four year old kid, with his big tractor, years ago. The kid was playing in the yard and he apparently didn't see him. Smashed his head flat as a pancake, they say. Everyone says that he's been mean as hell, and grumpy, since then."

"Well, I'm heading on over to his house to give him what he deserves. Wish me luck."

"You ought to give the dough to me for even talking to you about that pig of a man," she angrily mumbled under her breath as he headed for the door.

Vel stopped, looked at her pathetic face, slowly reached into his wallet, then methodically pulled out five, twenty dollar bills, and placed them into her chubby hand.

"Well I'll be damned!" she blurted out.

In his car, Vel sat and pondered the situation. He had learned that his target is a recluse. That he is not well liked, and that he is fat as hell. Mr. giant sounded like he was a mean man. Vel's conclusion, he was next to be shot.

Now the game was on as to where and how to shoot him.

Vel knew that he could be patient if he had to. He told himself that part of the intrigue of this hobby was finding a situation where he could pop the weasel. Vel needed a plan, in order to find a place to hit him, a way to entice his target out of his secure space. He put his thinking cap on as he listened to the radio on his way home. A few miles up the road he suddenly stopped at the next gas station.

An idea that might work, popped up.

He went to the phone booth, called the number to the giant's house. It rang a few times, then suddenly he was voice to voice with his next target.

"It's your dime!" the giant growled as he answered the phone.

"Sa,--Sir,-- I know this might sound a little bit unusual, but I would like to rent your prize hog, the one I saw at the fair. My name is John Dunne."

"It ain't a hog, wise acre, it's a pig!" Richard Head snapped. "Why on God's green earth would you want to rent my pig?"

"I,I,I, I'm making a movie," Vel stuttered awkwardly. He was suddenly nervous. He went just a little "Narvelle Phelps" for a few seconds.

"What about?"

"It's, it's, ah,-- about a young boy who buys a hog, I mean pig, and, and, and, it grows up to be a national champion."

"What you going to call the movie?" Richard asked coarsely.

"Well, I haven't fully decided yet," came Vel's reply, trying to buy some time to think of a good name. "Maybe------- SUPER SIZED PIGZILLA, or ROTUNDA, or something catchy like that."

"I'll think about it, it's going to cost you," the giant said. "Call me tomorrow morning about 10 am."

Click. He slammed the phone dead.

What happened the next day put the fear of God in Vel.

The next morning at precisely 10 am, Vel called Richard Head. The big man decided that he wanted a thousand dollars, cash, for renting his pig. He agreed to rent the pig, for four hours, and said that he would deliver the animal to where Vel wanted it, on Saturday of the next week. Vel told him to meet at an abandoned farm house that he had noticed about 10 miles East of Mr. Head's farm. The prize pig would be kept in a fenced in corral over at the farm. Vel told him that all of the filming was to take place at the abandoned farm. Richard Head knew the abandoned farm well; he had known the previous owner, who passed away a year or so ago. So it was all set.

The time for the meeting was set at 9am, next Saturday.

The weekend came quickly. Vel left the house with errands to do. His rifle was stowed in the old station wagon as he headed for the abandoned farmhouse out on Gholson Road. He arrived early and scoped out the farm and barn. The nearest neighbor was over a half a mile away, perfect. His old wagon ended up being parked near the barn, out of the way, almost hidden. Vel found a good hiding place in a small, old shack, about thirty feet from his station wagon, he waited patiently inside for his target to arrive.

9 am came and went, but no one showed up. Then it was 9:20. Vel was about to leave and go home, when suddenly a big red Peterbilt, with the short trailer, slowed down on the main road, and then slowly pulled into the yard. The tractor slowly continued down to the barn.

The giant, inside the tractor, peered curiously around. He suddenly stopped for a moment, then the front wheels turned as the big rig lurched forward again, heading in a reverse circle, as if to leave. Vel knew he had to do something quickly, to get the man out of the tractor. Without further thought, he put his rifle down, and promptly ran outside, waving his hand in a friendly gesture.

The truck jerked to a stop. Vel yelled up to the open window and introduced himself to Mr. Head. He told him that the rest of the film crew would be there in an hour. Mr. Head responded dryly, "Let me see the money!" then, he opened the door of the tractor and very slowly lowered himself down to the ground. Around to the rear of the trailer, he waddled. There, he released the two lock chains to the cage with the pig in it. When he was done, he returned to the front of the truck and stood silently, waiting for his money.

"I'll be right back with the dough!" Vel yelled as he headed for the shack.

Vel entered the shack and quickly picked up his weapon. Without further ado, he methodically aimed the gun through a crack in the door, and promptly fired a round into the profiled belly of the giant. Vel closed his eyes for a second, then gently laid his rifle next to him as he turned and sat on a bale of hay, waiting for the giant to collapse. The shot didn't seem to bother Richard, all that much. The giant appeared to just be angered, by the hot sting. He looked toward the shack and yelled loudly, "You dirty little bastard, I'm going to kick your ass!"

Richard lumbered quickly towards the shack with a surprising cadence, covering 50 feet in a few quick seconds. Vel heard him coming and slowly looked up, he was shocked at the big man's speed. Then it hit Vel, the giant, Richard, was attacking him! All the hair stood up on Vel's neck and arms as his blood suddenly ran cold.

Yelling like a wild man, 'Big Bad Richard' angrily kicked the door to Vel's hideout, completely off of it's hinges, with one stroke. He was ready to fight!

Vel's military prowess pushed him to the other side of the shack, where he whirled around and fired point blank at the giant-enemy. It was just like when he was in Viet Nam; he aimed without aiming, and bang, bang, went his weapon.

His killer instinct was still intact.

The big man stopped suddenly, in ultra-slow motion he wobbled sideways, briefly, for a second or so. He tried to move forward, but couldn't. Then, he awkwardly dangled from side to side, teetering like a drunken puppet. Suddenly his legs buckled. Without uttering a word, he crashed onto the dirt floor, like a massive tree being felled.

Vel swore later that the earth, damn near shook.

"Dead as a doornail!" raced through Vel's mind. "Shit!"

The dust settled and it became evident that Vel had put the two chunks of lead into the big man's right knee. Richard lay on the ground moaning and cussing, very much alive, mad as hell, still ready to fight.

Vel quickly ran for his station wagon, started it up and left in a hail of gravel, scared witless.

Five miles from the abandoned farm house, Vel pulled over, inhaled a cigarette and called 911 from the nearby phone booth. Off, again, he sped to the drug store, picked up a prescription for Linda, and headed home. He was very upset that the situation had turned chaotic. The target had seen his face, what a mess this could be.

He could be identified.

"It's good that I don't have an unusual face that could be drawn up easily by a police artist," he thought, still seriously worried.

Vel figured that the newspaper or the television would surely run the story, and help him know what to do about it.

The next day, Narvelle carefully read every page of the morning and evening editions of the newspaper and intently watched two hours of local news at 7 and 9pm. There was no mention of a shooting, not a word. Big-Time-Worry set in deep as he turned the television off, after the late news. His hands started to sweat, as they gradually began to tremble and shake like palsy. Linda, on the couch next to him, noticed his behavior and asked if he was all right.

"Sh---sh---Sure," he stuttered a little. "I haven't been sleeping well, because of those damned nightmares and flashbacks about Nam. All that bad stuff on the news get's to me too. Honey, I'm going upstairs to bed now. Good night."

Panic pinched his ass, as up the stairs he climbed quickly. Looking for help, he grabbed the phone and called Harold. When things were serious, Vel called Fragile by his first name.

"Harold, my man, I have a big favor to ask of you!" Vel anxiously and quickly spewed over the phone. Fragile could tell that this call was important.

"Would you go to City Hospital tomorrow and see how a guy named Richard Head is doing?"

"Sure," Fragile's answer came without question or comment. Then a long pause as Fragile coerced an explanation as to why he should do this favor for Vel. Finally, Vel coughed it up as he sensed the need to explain.

"Uh, well, uh, ah----shit,---- I shot this guy with my pop gun, and the son-of-a-bitch saw me, saw my face. He's in City Hospital, I'm pretty sure. I just want to know two things. Number one, is he alive? And number two, can he identify me? Listen carefully, his name is Richard Head!"

"O.K. I'll scope him out for you. Richard, Dick Head huh? Cool name!" Trying to be funny, Harold added, "why didn't you shoot someone named Fat-Assed-Billy?"

"Listen damn it! don't screw around! this could be some serious shit! It might mean real trouble!" He sounded worried, he looked worried, he was.

The next day after work, Fragile drove to City Hospital in Los Angeles. The information lady told him, "second floor."

Fragile suavely approached the nurse at the desk. "Hi, I'm a neighbor of Richard Head. I heard that he got shot or something. How is that big buzzard doing?"

"He is doing pretty well now," the nurse replied with a serious demeanor, she didn't look up from her paperwork. Mr. Head is a tough man. He's been through a lot, he's lucky to still be alive!

Mr. Head is in room nine down the hall to your left. Visiting hours are over in half an hour."

"Who shot him? Do they know?" Harold casually asked.

"Well, you may or may not know, Mr. Head wears glasses, but he said that he didn't have them on when he was shot. The police were here earlier and I overheard them say that he was unable to describe the man who shot him, other than to say he was a white man, with a green baseball cap." The nurse supplied the answer.

"I won't be long," said Harold as he casually sauntered down the hall, he stopped at room eight, looked back, then past room nine. He peered back at the nurse's station again, saw that it was clear, and out the door at the end of the hall he went.

Fragile drove to Narvelle's home to comfort his friend, who looked like a "plucked chicken in a steam bath."

"Fragile" Glasscock returned to the hospital the next morning and found out that Mr. Head was still doing well and that he was to be released the next day. The news was still all good news. It put Narvelle's, no sleep, nervous as hell mind, at rest.

Another person had been helped!

CHAPTER THIRTY
PHYSICAL THERAPY

Two weeks after he was shot, Richard Head sat in an oversized wheelchair, waiting for a physical therapist to see him. His wife sat patiently in the waiting room. He had an unusually pleasant, calm look, on his face. People who knew him before he got shot, now said that he looked like a different person. A major kindness had crept in.

The therapist greeted him. "Hello Mr. Head, my name is Roger Sebastian. I'm your physical therapist. We're going to get you up and get you moving better."

"It's good to be here, if you know what I mean," Richard said with a wide smile. The therapist nodded, he had read his medical records.

The big man's right knee was hit by the bullets above the knee joint and below the knee joint. The bullet that went below the joint caused the most damage. It severed the nerve that raises your toes up when you walk. The upper bullet only caused muscle damage. Richard was fitted with a device that would keep his foot in a normal position, so that it wouldn't drag as he walked, like a stroke patient uses. His lower leg nerve injury was permanent. The physical therapist put the device on him and they moved over to the parallel bars.

"How are you doing with your new diet?" the therapist asked.

"I have lost eight pounds so far. The doctor says that I need to lose around two hundred pounds before he will be happy with my weight. I can't eat like I used to, I eat six times a day now, just a little each time. Strange blessing huh?"

Richard added, "That is pretty normal for someone who has had a stomach stapling procedure, I am told."

The therapist nodded "yes" as he examined the range of motion of Richard's right knee.

With a slow but mighty pull, up he went on the parallel bars. Richard stood there for a minute to make sure that he was not dizzy. Then step by step down the pathway of the bars he ambled, slowly, methodically.

Richard recovered slowly as he began twelve weeks of intensive physical therapy treatments. His three months of physical therapy ended successfully. He walked with a slight hesitation, without crutches, and appeared to be quite stable. He had lost another forty pounds during his therapy treatments.

Richard was very pleased and he enthusiastically told everyone that he met about how well he was doing.

Clinically, the gunshot to his abdomen had hit his lower ribs, punctured a hole in his liver, ruptured some major blood vessels, and hit the stomach as targeted. The internal bleeding that occurred was considered excessive by the surgeons who saved his life.

The physicians had agreed with each other that he was quite lucky to be alive.

His medical record said so.

CHAPTER THIRTY ONE
LAPD

The day after Mr. Richard Head was shot, cops discussed his case.

At the police department, like in a movie, the door was shut, the brown caged circulating fan on the desk purred quietly, as two plain-clothes police officers, smoking cigarettes and drinking coffee, faced each other in serious conversation. Through the glass windows that sequestered them, they could see a dozen police officers in their department, scurrying about like ants. Each of them had serious intent written on their faces.

"Let's continue to keep this particular shooting incident, relatively low key," the taller police detective said to his partner. Then he added, "A while back, I read about a man and a woman who were both shot in the stomach, just like Mr. Head was, for no apparent reason. We need to dig up the records on these two previous hits, and see if they are similar to this deal with the pig farmer. I swear to God, there is a similarity about the other two people with this one.

Who gets shot, only in the gut, for no reason? You know what I mean, no robbery or other stuff going on. This guy, Mr. Richard Head, was shot with no apparent intention to kill him or rob him. Very strange. Somehow, I think that the shooter, shot him at close range, on purpose, and wanted him to live.

The news guys were careful not to release any information on this pig farmer, like I asked of them. I called them yesterday, right after he was shot, and I asked them to downplay it. It's got a weird "serial shooter' smell to it.

I don't want to be blamed for creating some damned public panic, just yet."

CHAPTER THIRTY TWO
THE PRETTY MOON-EYED REPORTER
AND RICHARD HEAD. A YEAR LATER

The television was on in the bedroom at Narvelle's house. Linda had just returned from the neighbor's house where she had been making cookies with her friend. A plate of fresh chocolate chip cookies was placed on the nightstand next to the bed, a tall glass of milk accompanied it. She crawled into bed, gave Narvelle a kiss and positioned her body so that she could watch television for a few minutes. Olivia was doing her homework in her room. The house was quiet except for the television, and the crunch of cookies.

"We are at the California state fair today with one of the luckiest men alive," the beautiful moon-eyed reporter said to the Channel 9 camera.

"Next to me is Mr. Richard Head. He is the owner of this year's grand champion pig here at the fair. Just over a year ago, Mr. Head was brutally shot by a stranger for no apparent reason. He survived the gunshot wound to the abdomen and has continued to slowly lose weight.

Mr. Head is going to present a special gift to the Children's Hospital of Los Angeles. Did they ever capture the man who shot you?" she asked.

"No they haven't," Richard responded quickly, he didn't look the same as before he was shot; he looked vibrant, kind, relaxed, like a thinner friendly Santa Claus.

He had physically, mentally, socially, and emotionally changed.

"I know this sounds bizarre, but in a strange way, I would like to meet the guy who shot me, and tell him thanks. I really am doing great. I have lost one hundred and fifty pounds, and everything is good in my life,"

Richard Head's whole countenance had changed.

He was still overweight, but he looked amazingly healthy. A kind smile continued to cross his face. The mean, angry looking, sad man, no longer existed.

"I have a picture of you about five years ago, a few years before you were shot. Our viewers can see that you have changed quite a lot," she said as she held up an old photograph of Richard, years before the shooting.

"Is it true that you are going to auction off your champion pig and give the proceeds to the Children's Hospital of Los Angeles?"

"Yes I am. I am thankful, and lucky, to be alive and well. I should be able to get around eighteen thousand dollars for my pig. His name is King Tut. I'm glad to donate the money to a worthy cause.

I chose the Children's Hospital because they do so many wonderful things that help disabled and crippled children. I lost my only child many years ago in a tragic accident and have never really got over that, so I want to give the money to help children that need financial assistance."

Richard's face continued to glow with light. His eyes glistened with tears, a sincere ring of thankfulness in his voice.

The moon-eyed reporter was touched, she placed her hand on Richards arm, smiled and said, "Many people will be helped by your generous gift, thank you sir, you are a very nice man."

The reporter then paused and carefully read from the notes in front of her. She wanted the viewers to know a little history about Mr. Head.

"Mr. Richard Head has given me permission to share a little history about his life. Richard was born, and raised, in Billings, Montana. He graduated from high school and immediately was drafted into the Army at age eighteen. He was stationed in England for two months prior to the invasion of Normandy. As he landed on the beaches of France, four of his good friends were killed by machine-gun fire, in front of him. They were his shield from the onslaught of bullets. Richard was then engaged in combat with the German Army for a few weeks. A call came for volunteers, for what looked like a suicide mission. He joined up, immediately.

The assignment was to parachute with one hundred other brave young men, into German occupied territory. Their job was to destroy an electricity generator, at a dam site. Most of his buddies were killed in their parachutes, on the way down to the ground, by the Luftwaffe. Twenty two men survived the ordeal, and were finally led to safety, to the French underground, by a ten year old German boy scout. They did accomplish their goal.

Richard returned home and vowed to be a boy scout master. He did so for ten years, then quit, the day after he accidently ran over his only child, with his truck, on his son's fourth birthday. He admits to having become a recluse, until he was shot in the stomach and luckily, survived. His tells me that now his life is full again, that he has a new lease on life.

Mr. Head raises cattle, and has raised prize winning pigs for the last eight years, he was recently elected president, of the Porkbelly Club of Greater Los Angeles, a non-profit club. He and his fellow members donate money that they generate to worth causes, such as The Children's Hospital."

She glanced at the clock, it was time to end the interview.

"And now let's take a look at the weather," she continued as the T.V. flashed to a picture of the storm coming in from Hawaii.

Narvelle smiled slyly and turned the television off, his secret life didn't seem real. His patience and planning had paid off again. But he wanted more. More recognition!

Down deep he wished that everyone knew that it was his skill and determination to help, that had prompted the shooting procedure, that had helped Mr. Head morph into a happy, productive, kind, and generous man.

Someday, he would be famous, but he wanted accolades, now!

Linda pulled the pillows from under her head and rolled over on her side. "Good night sweetheart," she said as she drifted off to sleep. "Good night my love," Narvelle whispered as his mind toyed with a few questions.

"What shall I have them put on my tomb-stone?" he asked himself. "How about, here lies Narvelle Phelps. With his accurate shooting, he popularized stomach stapling and weight reduction programs that really work."

Or, "Here lies Narvelle Phelps, the father of the biggest weight loss craze that ever hit America."

Or, "Narvelle Phelps, unsung hero, perhaps the bravest man that ever lived. He helped people improve their lives, with his accurate shooting."

He smiled again, as he closed his conceited eyes.

PART FOUR

CHAPTER THIRTY THREE
VEL SEEKS FAME

"It's time to strike again," Narvelle thought. It had been many months since he shot Richard Head. "I think I will find a rich fat woman who is very famous, this time. I want some big time publicity that will make the national news. Not a damned word was in the newspapers after I helped that last guy, that ain't right. What I'm doing is so unique that it should become a nationally known phenomenon. I want fat folks everywhere to look around and wonder if they could be next." A smile slowly thinned his lips as he realized that he really liked what he was doing. His life now had a purpose.

The conversations that he had with himself continued to convince him that it was his fate to do what he was doing. Life, had brought him to this point. It was his destiny. Somehow, he felt quite normal with the whole process of finding large people and shooting them. His step across the line of sanity, was no longer challenged.

Time to go shopping for a new target, the mall was a perfect place. Saturday at 5 pm, Vel sat quietly on a bench in the newly opened mall in Long Beach. He was people shopping. Folks of all sizes and shapes were there for him to gawk at. A lady came waddling by with a body that looked like two people, from different body builds, had been glued together at the waist. The top half didn't belong to the bottom half. Her head was small, as were her shoulders, chest, and waist.

The contrast started with her hips, that were much wider than her shoulders, and literally stuck out sideways, three inches, on each side. Her butt was a true, honest to God, bulging "muffin ass." She was narrow at the shoulders and broad at the beam.

Her body was pear shaped.

Another grossly obese lady pranced by slowly, white shorts wedged up her butt crack. Her face was plump, her ankles were plump, even her hands were plump. Her dimpled butt had rolls and divots that looked like an elephant's butt. Rolls of fat stuck out from below, under her "too small," tee shirt. At the same time, around front, her obvious "camel toe" bulged, begging attention. The undersized red tee shirt, read SEXY, with its large glittery sequins. Her appearance was so disgusting that Narvelle laughed a little, then looked away, as she strutted down the main aisle of the mall.

Her right hand was clasped by a beautiful, normal sized, six year old girl that skipped along holding her doll in the other hand. As Vel returned his gaze towards the obese lady, the little girl turned unexpectedly and locked her eyes on him, smiling warmly. Their eyes met. Narvelle wondered what the future would bring her. Suddenly, she cheerfully waved at him with her doll in her hand, he gulped and bowed his head in silence as a dry lump choked his throat.

"What will the future bring her?"

Ten minutes later, he became intrigued with a very large young girl near the ice cream store, a teenager, that appeared to be around sixteen or seventeen years old. Her profile begged to be shot. Her belly looked like buttocks as it drooped towards her knees, enormous breasts lay like watermelon flaps over her stomach. Three other obese girls were with her, eating their triple dips of sugar, creamy fat and ice. "They all need to be shot," he thought. "Especially her."

Narvelle walked up close to them, and studied them carefully, listening for clues about them, looking for a reason to help.

"Should I pop a kid?" he asked himself. "Naw, it might not be a good thing to do, their stomach and the stuff inside probably isn't mature enough to tolerate the trauma. I guess I best stick to grown ups."

Vel looked at his watch, it was late. He got up and headed for home, enough shopping for a while, enough "side-show" for one evening.

He returned to the mall again two weeks later, later in the evening, just before sunset. The mall was full of people this time. "Obesity" was walking everywhere, as usual. Just for the hell-of-it, he started a count, to figure out how many people out of 100 were overweight. As he counted 100 people who walked past him, he was shocked to realize that 46 of them were obviously overweight and 16 others were grossly obese, like blimps, like he used to be. The total was 62 that appeared to be abnormally heavy, out of the 100 that he counted. 62%!

Real blimps have good spinal posture, Vel noted, perhaps because they had to keep their spines erect in order to hold up their enormous bellies. As he continued looking around, trolling for a fat catch, through the crowded mall, he suddenly spotted an obese lady looking in the window of a store. She was about 150 feet from him, really big, her belly way out in front, thin husband by her side.

"Jack Spratt and his wife! Honest to God!" he announced happily.

They both were dressed elegantly, he was in a dark suit, she had a long, expensive looking, red coat, that nearly touched the ground. They were the kind of people he was looking for. After they looked in the window of the store for a few minutes, they walked away from him, heading outside of the mall. He didn't see her face, but he memorized her long red coat in case he lost view of her.

He jumped up and took off after them, it was dark outside. As Vel exited the building, he saw them get into a long black Rolls Royce that pulled up close to the curb. The car was a big give away, they were obviously very "well heeled."

She, automatically, was the next one to be helped. This wealthy obese lady would be his claim to fame, he thought.

Under the parking lot lights it was obvious that that their car was black, new, shiny, and very elegant.

The car almost whispered as it passed, "these folks are THE super-rich people."

He couldn't see the obese woman's face through the darkened windows as they passed, but he tried. Loudly he voiced and memorized their personalized license plate, "PARTEEE," as the car whisked off into the night.

Later that week, he asked a police officer friend of his to find out who owned the car. Vel told the cop that a package had fallen off the trunk of a black Rolls Royce at the mall and that he wouldn't mind returning it to them as he drives his delivery route. The package was full of underwear and a nice watch, he claimed.

His friend complied, and called him the next day with the phone number and the name of the owner. The cop confirmed that the car was indeed a new black Rolls Royce, owned by a big time socialite with a lot of money, a Mr. Stephen Manson of Beverly Hills, a multi-millionaire.

CHAPTER THIRTY FOUR
VEL AND FRAGILE DISCUSS HIS NEW TARGET

Narvelle dropped by to visit his buddy Fragile. "Hey man, how are you doing?"

"I'm as happy as a pig in warm poo," Fragile smiled cheerfully, he always seemed to be happy.

"I've got to tell you about my next find. Since you are the only one who knows about my little hobby, let me lay some seriously heavy 'poop' on you."

"Sure, my friend, whass up?" came Fragile's reply.

"I'm going to hit a really rich broad, here's my thinking on this. She or her husband is very rich and they might even be famous. I know her husband's name. I'm checking them out now, before I hit her. After I hit her and she gets all skinny and all that good stuff, the newspapers will make it known nationally. They ride around town in a new Rolls Royce and live in Beverly Hills with all the other rich pricks. It will be national news because what happens to us poor folks ain't nearly as interesting as what happens to the rich folks, you know what I'm talking about. I ain't been getting a lot of national recognition about this shooting business, so, this one will do the trick.

Here's what I want, I want people all over the country to know about it and to be curious, and a bit nervous. I want the grossly fat people to start wondering if they will be next. This one will definitely start a public awareness program like there has never been before. I've got a feeling that this one is going to be spectacular."

Fragile winced at that, he knew that the aberrant sounds from a nut bag, had just hit his ears.

"Am I right?" Narvelle pleaded, waiting for his acceptance.

"Well it sounds like a fucked up plan to me, you crazy cotton picker!"

"There was no mention of my last target in the newspaper. That really irritated me. Nothing made the news until a year later when that giant of a pig farmer was on television, telling everyone how much weight he lost, and selling his pig for charity. By then it wasn't big news anymore. I wanted more recognition than that. This time I'm sure that I will get some real serious national recognition."

Then Vel returned to the subject of his next target. "Now that I've done three of them, it's become a piece of cake. It's actually a very easy thing to do. Think about it, your stomach can only be located in a reasonably consistent place, it's not attached to your knee or your elbow, you know what I mean? This next hit will scare rolls of blubber off of fat folks all over the country, there will be people losing weight just to keep from getting shot." He laughed sarcastically.

"Then again, it has worked so well, some fat folks will be lining up, begging to be shot. Hell, I might have to start a clinic!"

Fragile interrupted his madness, "Some copycat ass-hole will probably start shooting fat fucks too. You know there's a lot of weirdo's around!"

"Hell, I don't care! Like I said my friend, it might start a new craze, like the hula hoop. Lot's of cool shit starts here in California. Maybe even a doctor or two will "fire up" a cannon to get more patients to work on." Vel laughed. "Greed is a powerful thing, I heard about a dentist that would fill teeth when there was nothing wrong with them. He would tell people that they had a cavity when they didn't."

Narvelle waited for it to sink in, then he added, "Haven't you ever wondered about how many surgeries are done, that weren't really necessary?"

"No," eked from Fragile's lips.

Vel continued his rant, "I'm going to write a book about this wild experience that I'm having. I pretty much have complete records on the first three, and how well they have done.

You really should have been there to see how beautiful the FAT FOX was at her wedding. Congratulations were in order. What a doll she is now, and happy as a lark!

What I'm doing ain't all that bad compared to some of the shit that happens in society. It ain't nearly as bad as all the gang murders that are going on, or how the bankers, politicians, and preachers are dishonest and greedy, continually screwing the public. What I'm doing is helping people to help themselves.

It's exciting, being determined and confident enough to actually pull the trigger, and it's a lot of fun figuring out how to get to them, to shoot them." He was winding down.

There was a long, cold, silent pause as Fragile studied his eyes, wondering what to say. He wanted to say something that would stop the madness, but he knew that once Vel had made his mind up, it was too late to convince him otherwise.

"I guess its cool, my friend," Harold finally said. "I still think it's a bit messed up myself. I sure as hell would never do what you're doing, it seems like it's too damned risky."

"Naw! it's a piece of cake."

"I hope you don't fuck up and cripple or kill somebody!"

CHAPTER THIRTY FIVE
NOT ENOUGH INFORMATION

Narvelle asked a few people where he worked about the Manson's of Beverly Hills, gleaning a few interesting things about them. They were indeed famous, at least in Los Angeles. They were also serious party animals and very wealthy.

Mary Lynn Manson and her husband Stephen Manson, apparently lived a life of luxury, fun, and excess. Stephen came from an extremely rich family that owned a significant amount of oil stocks. His father was a stock broker and died at the age of forty seven, from a heart attack. Stephen inherited a large fortune at the age of twenty eight.

The Manson's lived in Beverly Hills amidst all the other extremely rich people. Mary and Stephen loved to throw huge garden parties. Guests at their mansion got to listen to live bands, drink the free booze, smoke a little pot, or snort free cocaine. The parties often got written up in the newspaper. Wild, costumed, Roman toga parties were given twice a year and everyone who attended, apparently loved them.

Behind their beautiful outdoor swimming pool, the Manson's had a vomitorium similar to those used by the ancient Romans. It was a separate and distinct building with a dozen beautiful, naked, Italian marble statures surrounding it. It was publically known that many of their friends would gorge themselves and then throw up and eat some more, like the ancient Romans did. True gluttony. The Manson's was "the place to go," for excessive eating, partying, and throwing up.

During their Toga parties, the vomitorium was equipped with open showers, two private rooms with beds to rest or recreate in, or do whatever you want. There was also a separate room with a pro wrestler looking lady, Swedish massage therapist, some fresh clothes or togas, and a full time medical doctor. A certified colonic nurse was also on duty during the excitement that lasted for two days running.

The joke at the parties was that you could get any kind of relief that your want, from either end, anyway you want it.

Their strikingly beautiful house was a sprawling 15000 square foot mansion styled like an Italian Villa, with 24 foot ceilings in many areas of the house, and beautiful arched windows. The building was shaped like the letter U, with a swimming pool, waterfalls and a reflecting pool easily seen from the column of pillars that surrounded the inner porches. The estate was nicely nestled in Beverly Hills. The yard was meticulous and beautifully landscaped.

Vel began his surveillance and data gathering mode, he drove up and down the street in front of their mansion numerous times over the next three weeks. However, again, he was forced to be patient. As he parked respectfully on the street for hours, he never saw anyone enter or leave the house, it was like studying a closed museum. The lack of people coming in or going out perplexed him.

The Manson's cars were hidden purposely behind a beautiful five foot tall, brick wall that had been swallowed elegantly by English ivy. An old, beautifully restored, rare, red and black Bugatti, and the newer cars: Mercedes Benz, Aston Martin, and Bentley, hid in the five car garage that encased them. The guard parked his new Volvo, outside the garage, near his private little stone cottage.

Narvelle's creative phone calls to the house were intercepted by the voice of the resident guard. He changed his voice and called again later and asked to speak to Mrs. Manson about her insurance policy, but was told to call her agent. Vel pretended that he was from the newspaper and was told to call her publicity agent. He claimed to be an old friend and was told to call the entertainment coordinator. He tried to deliver a package with his truck and was stopped by the guard as he approached the gate. It was frustrating him severely that he couldn't break into this rich ladies life patterns. Vel kept reminding himself that part of the fun of his new hobby, was the chase involved in finding out who the target was, what they did, and finally how to get to them.

What he didn't know, was that Mary Lynn and Stephen left the country on an extended stay, right after he saw them that evening in the mall. They had flown to Italy and were staying with guests in their multi-million dollar vacation home on the isle of Capri.

Narvelle learned of their trip overseas, when he accidentally read about their impending return home to Beverly Hills. The newspaper read: BEVERLY HILLS FAVORITE PARTY COUPLE to return home on Thursday, from their vacation on the isle of Capri. The paper said that the Manson's were coming home to host a large dinner party in order to raise money for Harry Lungrease, the state Senator, a true scumbag politician that they had befriended.

The fun part of the chase was on again for Vel, he could feel himself become alive. The process of the hunt got his adrenaline stirred up and all of his hunting instincts reactivated. Being forced to think and then react, instantly, really turned him on. He called Air Italia and found out which planes came in directly from Italy on Thursday. There were two flights, one came in at noon and the other at 8:15 pm.

He loaded his station wagon, and then drove to the airport; it was 9 am when he arrived. He went inside and approached the information and ticket desk at Air Italia.

entry to the area, three on each side. No dogs were on the premise or nearby. No other cameras guarded the house or the yard. Vel scoped it all out in military fashion.

The evening was perfect for an approach to the yard, the sky was dark and cloudy. It had been threatening to rain, off and on, all day long, the evening blanket of dark was descending upon the neighborhood. Vel arrived at the mansion around 8 pm. He told Linda that he was going out to play pool with his buddies, as usual, no problem.

In the cloak of darkness, he got out of his wagon three long city blocks from their mansion, wrapped his rifle in a blanket and put it in a guitar case. The end of the barrel stuck out of a hole in the case, a golf club bag was slipped over the end of the barrel. In the darkness it was barely noticeable. He walked slowly to their house without seeing a soul, luck was on his side, again.

Vel found a perfect place to hide along the fence where he could clearly see into the back yard. The next door neighbor's house was over four hundred feet away. Everything was set. He waited and relaxed, then suddenly, a long black limousine pulled up the winding driveway from the street. The guard walked out and opened the gate and the car slowly pulled into the backyard. Vel was ready. Stephen came out first, he walked over and shook hands with the guard. The guard went to the trunk and picked up two large suit cases and headed for the house. Stephen then walked around to the side door and opened it, Mary Lynn slowly and carefully stepped out, Stephen then turned and immediately headed for the house. Mary Lynn wore her large long red coat, carried a purse, and clutched a special bottle of wine. Excited to be home, she let out a war hoop that bounced around the back yard walls. Stephen smiled, and quickly answered with a war hoop of his own, to add to her good vibrations.

"I'm from the newspaper and I am supposed to write a little tidbit about the Manson's when they return from Italy. There are two flights coming in today. Your first one lands at noon. Could you confirm for me that the Manson's are on that flight?" he asked politely.

"I'm sorry sir, do you know their first names?" the ticket agent asked coldly, with a nasal twang to her voice. She obviously didn't know who Vel was talking about.

"Yes, Mary Lynn Manson and Stephen Manson are their names," he said. "You don't know who they are?"

"No, sir, I don't. A moment please," a brief pause, then again, she coldly replied, "They are on the 8:15 flight, number 786. They will land on concourse D this evening. Next in line!"

"Thank you for your help," Vel said quietly as he left with the answer.

"Cold bitch!"

Now he had to work fast to find a place to hit her. He quickly walked the airport and decided that it was not a good place to do his business, too many people, no place to hide, too many cops, a real security risk. He would have to hit her at her home. Later that evening, Vel headed for their house, hoping that they would go there and not somewhere else in Los Angeles.

Surrounding the Manson's estate were huge bushes, large well established trees, large parcels of grass and flowers. The long fence that surrounded the garage and their cars continued winding and wrapped the pool, the flower garden and the vomitorium. The guard resided in a splendid small stone home approximately two hundred feet from the ornate metal gate, inside the walled area. The entire yard was immense, covering two acres. The guard had a remote camera to watch the driveway. There were six beautiful five-bulb lamp posts, mounted near the metal gate that allowed

As she slowly turned to head for the house, the night suddenly exploded with another sound. This one was a loud boom sound bouncing around the back yard walls. POW! WOW-wow-wow it ricocheted. It sounded like rolling thunder that accompanies a close lightning strike. The echo bounced from wall to wall and then around again, coming from nowhere and echoed everywhere at the same time. Stephen stopped in his tracks and slowly looked up at the sky. Then he turned around, not knowing where to look, he didn't realize that his wife had been shot.

"What the hell was that!" he asked as he finally turned back to look at his wife. "Thunder?" Then Stephen saw her.

Mary Lynn had collapsed on the cobblestones of their beautiful driveway, blood slowly was pooling around her on the elegant hand lain stones. She hadn't uttered a sound as she wilted like a flower in a blast furnace.

Stephen began to scream, "Oh my God, oh my God, oh my God!" as he rushed to her aid. "What the hell is going on, oh my God!"

"What has happened here?" He looked at his wife curiously.

"Has she been shot?" he shrieked. "That sounded like a gun shot, oh my God! I need to get an ambulance here immediately!"

He scanned the backyard walls for a few seconds, eyes darting uselessly, he saw nothing unusual.

Quickly, Stephen bent over and looked closely at her bloody, messy clothes and her lifeless face. The driver jumped out of the limousine and ran for the house; the guard came out of the house, ready to fight, as the sky opened up with rain, then a real burst of thunder shook the yard. The rich lady bled while Stephen screamed, "Oh no! Oh my God, oh my God, this can't be real!"

The slow motion nightmare soon became very real.

As Stephen screamed, Vel quietly slipped out the back side of the yard, down the street, and into his waiting car. No one saw him, and he saw no one, it was as smooth as smooth could be. He smoked a cigarette casually as he headed for home, radio booming the voice of Johnny Cash, "And it burns, burns, burns, the ring of fire, the ring of fire." He smiled and nodded his affirmation, again he had done his job well, it was all good.

"That was as easy as it gets," he said to himself, as he calmly drove along. "Now let's see how much the national news recognizes the significance of this proverbial, shot in the dark."

The hospital emergency room was packed when the medics wheeled Mary Lynn in through the door. Her eyes slowly opened and she went wild, as she looked around and realized where she was. Suddenly, she screamed an agonizing, blood curdling, cry of horror. Immediately the doctor injected her, and whisked her off to surgery.

A few long hours later, after the surgery, the doctor entered the waiting room to address Mr. Stephen Manson, whose face was deranged with anticipation and concern.

Stephen knew for sure that she was dead. He looked pathetic.

He remained silent as all of the color left his face, then the doctor finally spoke, telling him the bad and good news.

The baby had been pronounced dead, as he performed the emergency cesarean section. The bullet had hit a major blood vessel supplying life to their unborn son. The child bled to death. The good news was that the quick arrival to the hospital had saved Mary's life. The surgeon informed Stephen that his wife was in fair condition. Tears of thanks spilled from Mr. Manson's eyes.

After the surgery, Mary Lynn was taken to a recovery room and Stephen was immediately given sedating medication by the attending physician, then instructed to go home to get some sleep.

Stephen didn't remember his ride home.

The next day there were two, beautiful, excessively large bouquets of flowers, in Mary's room. Around noon, the doctor and a nurse entered her room and approached her slowly, with grave expressions on their faces. The doctor's head hung down, sadly, his shoulders heavy.

Mary Lynn was groggy, but finally awake, her eyes begged information.

He quietly and reverently began, "I'm Doctor Mot Dooley. I worked on you last night, you were shot in the stomach. You're going to be O.K." Mary looked at him like he was from outer space.

Then he paused and put his head down closer to her. Lovingly, the doctor took her hand in both of his and whispered gently, "I'm, terribly sorry, but your baby, didn't make it," his words drifted away as they slowly escaped his lips, he could barely utter them.

She looked at him in disbelief. Then quickly, shock set in, protecting her, preventing her from dying. For a moment she looked detached from the gravity of the situation, she didn't gasp or cry as she let his words slowly sink into her brain. Gradually the reality of what he said crept upon her face.

While the doctor waited patiently, he said nothing for a moment, then he slowly nodded his head up and down slightly. His compassion for her was quite apparent as tears quickly filled his bloodshot eyes. Mary didn't know that the doctor's wife was six months pregnant with their second child. She looked him squarely in the eyes for a few seconds and then hoarsely whispered, "I was afraid of that."

She closed her eyes as the gravity of the situation continued to depress her soul. Dark gloom pressed down upon her senses. "God is punishing me for my terrible life style," escaped innocently from her mouth in a whisper, a confession to no one.

Then the dammed up river of tears began to flow, explosive tears welled up at first, then they rained freely. She sobbed and sobbed hysterically, gasping for air as tears streamed from her eyes, her nose ran and her eyes turned bright red. The nurse reached over with a handful of tissue paper. Mary Lynn's emotional release was total, as she pitifully wept, inconsolable.

Minutes later the doctor spoke again. "You can let her husband into the room now for a brief moment," he whispered to the nurse, as he pointed to the needle in the nurse's hand, then he carefully left the room.

Stephen walked respectfully into the sanctum where his injured wife lay.

His eyes were nearly swollen shut from crying intensely, before entering her room. He cradled his wife and hugged her gently, and then he put his hand on her head and gently stroked her hair. Neither of them said a word as they sobbed and cried together. All of the tears that could be made by a human body were pressed out, drenching their clothes and her bed. The nurse kindly injected her with medication as he lowered his face to hers and gently kissed her cheek.

She whispered in her drugged state as she dozed off, "My little Stephen is gone."

"I know," he whispered back. "I am so sorry."

CHAPTER THIRTY SIX
THE LONGEST DAY

The next day, Narvelle appeared to be happy as he cheerfully exited his house via the front door. He whistled casually as he picked up the newspaper from the front porch, took it to the kitchen, the dog wagging along behind him. Inside, he grabbed his waiting coffee, sat down and read the large print on the front page.

Blood quickly began to leave his face.

MARY LYNN MANSON'S BABY DIES. Mary Lynn who? He read it again, then, like a ton of bricks, it hit.

The article followed with this: Socialite, Mary Lynn Manson, was hit by a rifle bullet at her home in Beverly Hills last night. There is no apparent reason for the shooting. She was pregnant with their first child. The baby, a male, was pronounced dead at the hospital. The baby was due to be born in three weeks. An ambulance rushed her to Presbyterian Hospital where she is in stable condition.

Her husband, Stephen Manson, said that they had just returned home from a vacation to Italy. The police have been asked to find the shooter and investigate this case. There is a $100,000.00 reward for information leading to the arrest and conviction of the shooter.

Narvelle Phelps was now pale as he went into brain overload, his hands shook with super-palsy.

"This can't be true!" escaped in a light whisper from his lips. He read it again carefully, slowly, one more time. It started to sink in that he had killed an innocent unborn child. Panic hit him as his head began to pound and throb, and the muscles on the back of his upper neck tightened like a clamping vise.

"What a damned mess this has turned out to be," he thought, nearly saying it out loud.

"Damn, damn, damn!" he finally blurted out, loudly. Linda looked up from the stove where she was scrambling eggs. She easily detected the unusual alarm that wrapped itself around his face and exited from his mouth. Cautiously she asked, "What's happened honey?"

Narvelle paused before he spoke. He needed to think this through a little before he let out the wrong words, or the right words. Somehow he managed to say, "Some crazy shit happens around here. It says in the pa-pa-paper that a lady who was pregnant was shot in a drive by shooting and that her baby da-da-died, but she is all right. How's that for some crazy shit?"

"I would have to kill someone if they shot our daughter!" Linda firmly said, as she continued stirring the eggs, a serious look on her face.

"Me too," he added firmly.

"It's a crazy damned world we live in isn't it?"

Vel conjured up, "It seems like every day someone is shot in a drive by shooting somewhere in this messed up city. Just last week an innocent seven year old kid was shot and killed as he was riding his bicycle home from school, remember that? A few months ago a seventeen year old girl was shot in the head and killed accidentally at a swimming pool in Bakersfield. Some teenagers were target practicing a mile away from her, and one of them shot a bullet in the air, just horsing around, and it killed her."

Narvelle's mind continued to whirl as disbelief was trying to be replaced with belief. He excused himself as he got up and slowly walked towards the door, lost in thought, he blindly heading for work, without eating his breakfast.

His head was spinning, numb. The unreal trancelike feeling continued to accompany him as he drove to work, he didn't remember the ride at all.

All day long he tried to shake the information out of his head, but it wouldn't leave. He imagined over and over what it would be like to find his beautiful daughter, shot dead. His replay button had been pushed and he knew of no way to turn it off.

That night after dinner he sat quietly alone on his front steps with his head in his hands, as tears streamed down his cheeks. Olivia came out the front door and wrapped her arms around his neck and kissed him on the cheek, she whispered, "I love you daddy," then, off to the neighbor's house she ran, no questions asked. She never asked about his problems, or questioned his behavior.

"What have I done? Oh, my God! This can't be real," he quietly moaned, surprised by the fact that he truly cared.

Later that night, Vel drove cautiously as he took the long way to Harold's house. He was a nervous wreck, he had to talk to his only true confidant, in person. He knew that Fragile was the only one who would listen and not judge him.

Harold quickly read the deep concern in his face as he ushered him into a quiet area outside of his house and waited patiently.

Narvelle began, "Well here it is my friend, I have totally screwed the pooch, my life is all bitched up. I just shot and killed an innocent baby." His face strained with anguish as he stopped for a second, for Fragile to digest what he said.

"The lady that I just shot, was pregnant, she wasn't fat."

Harold's mouth slowly opened. He closed his eyes, bowed his head and wagged it from side to side, but didn't say a word as he put his hand up and massaged his chin thoughtfully.

Narvelle seriously explained, "That quiet, small voice in my brain that I had when I was a kid, and went to church, is not totally dead. It ain't like in the war, where you're fighting for your life. I never felt too bad about killing some bastard that was trying to kill me, but this is totally different. I just killed an innocent child and I don't know what to do about it. I feel really bad."

He rambled on. "I really fucked up this time, by not checking her out better, what the hell am I going to do?"

"That's some really bad karma my friend," Harold finally said. "That's a hell of a good question! What are you going to do?"

"I never figured on this happening. Damn it!"

Narvelle paused and looked up into the eternity of the dark, star studded sky, looking for an answer. Then, in a fleeting moment a glazed appearance came from nowhere and Vel's eyeballs began to shake as he "lost it" for a few seconds. His head began pounding like an African war drum. Flashes of light and ghastly grimaces of dead faces spun in a bloody pool in the back of his mind.

His head felt like it was about to explode as he lost his balance and nearly fell over. Somehow he stayed standing as he went completely crazy for a while. He felt himself lose contact with reality. His head was spinning, his mind twirling, tripping without drugs.

Vel's hands went wet as he visualized his daughter's head flying from her body, as a guillotine dropped its blade. Orange-blue flames engulfed his vision, as blood squirted from her neck and her head fell to the ground. She smiled crazily and looked up at him with gigantic baseball sized eyes, and screamed, "Why has this got to happen daddy?!"

Then the hallucination was over.

Arms by his side, overwhelmed, head bowed, Narvelle closed his eyes as tears slowly dripped to the ground. "God forgive me," he said softly, and then gasping sobs took over, shaking his body. His friend stood next to him and honored the moment.

After a few seconds, Fragile wrapped his arms around his best friend. He held him tight in a man to man hug and whispered like a Priest, "Son, you got to get hold of yourself. Don't turn into a bowl of nervous pudding again."

Harold held on to Narvelle, to keep him from falling over, kept on holding him tight for a few minutes, as Narvelle's tears flowed like melting ice, onto his shirt.

CHAPTER THIRTY SEVEN
THE POLICE DEPARTMENT AGAIN

Lieutenant Fred Franklin had the reputation of being smart, super-smart. He graduated with honors from his class at the police academy, went to college, had a college degree in Criminal Justice. He had been a detective for twelve years. His partner Dave, the shorter of the two, had been a detective for eight years. Dave was no slouch either, he had solved a dozen very difficult cases, by himself, during the last five years.

The case of the Manson's baby shooting was laid on Fred's desk the day after the shooting by the chief of police. Dave sat across the desk from him, super anxious, waiting, and ready to go.

Fred began, "There it is again my friend, someone shot in the gut with a single bullet, only this time, a baby was killed. This one sounds like it could be murder!" He added, "What did you find on those other folks who were gut-shot a while ago?"

Dave replied, "Not much, just their names and their end result, they all seem to have recovered well afterwards. They are all famous for losing a lot of weight after being shot. I couldn't find any other similarities in any of their cases, no other patterns and no clear motives."

Fred continued to explain, "Well this lady who just lost her baby is the wife of a personal friend of the chief of police, as you well know, she is some rich Beverly Hills socialite. The chief wants us to put some special effort into this case. There's a lot of PR that will be bad if we don't come up with something soon. Let's pull up some hospital records from surrounding hospitals and see if there are clues that we haven't looked at?

Get the addresses of where the others were shot, lets go look around, we need to get a whole lot more serious about this case. Maybe some better evidence will show up. In the meantime let's go back to the Manson's place and scour the area again, the crime scene guys might have missed something.

Let's find out what the hell is going on here. We'll also see if we can dig up any motives from the Manson's friends, family, and work associates. These folks have a reputation for throwing some big, wild parties over the last few years. We need to check the entire list of people who have attended any of their parties for the last three years. Maybe Mrs. Manson was the target, not the baby."

Dave, the shorter partner, listened carefully then he added his two-cents-worth, "Why on God's green earth would anyone purposely shoot this lady? From what I know about her, Mrs. Manson is one of the best liked people in this whole damned city. She is somewhat famous for donating her time and gobs of money to folks who are less fortunate than she and her husband are. The thing that really bothers me is the way she was shot, it appears that it was not a guaranteed kill shot. Was someone just a lousy shot, from such close range? I ask myself, who was the target, her or the kid, or both of them? Maybe some sicko wanted her to bleed-out and kill the baby at the same time."

"The question is always why, isn't it? Next always is the question, who," Fred added, then ended with, "there is something very unusual about this case."

CHAPTER THIRTY EIGHT
MARY LYNN AND STEPHEN MANSON

Narvelle learned more about the Mansons, later, much too late.

He later gleaned that, Mary Lynn Young was born in St. George, Utah. She was a great-great-great granddaughter of the famous Mormon pioneer and church leader, Brigham Young. She was the fourth child of a Mormon family, of seven children.

Mary met Stephen Manson at Disneyland, married him after three years of dating. Her sense of humor, reputation for kindness, and generosity, was widely known.

Stephen Manson was a football player in high school, raised in the lap of luxury in Palos Verdes, California. He had two brothers, both younger than himself. He was a talented runner and was offered an athletic scholarship at three colleges, but he turned them down because of the financial situation with his parents. His father set up a fifty million dollar trust fund that would become his, a few years after graduating from college. The trust read that he had to go to college and graduate, and after that, he had to sustain himself for four years without any further financial help from his family. Stephen complied with the requests and graduated with an engineering degree from UCLA. Then he found a job capable of supporting himself, as he waited for the impending fortune to land on him.

Earlier, at the age of twenty three, he and Mary Lynn ran off and married in an out of the way wedding chapel in Las Vegas. Her parents were disappointed that she had not chosen a Mormon boy to wed, and that she got married in such an impulsive manner. His parents were shocked to say the least, they expected a heavenly wedding with heavenly bills.

Their early married life was fun, with many friends, lots of travel around the world, experiences that only the rich get to enjoy, and exposure to all sorts of drugs and wildness. Little by little, Mary Lynn allowed herself to experiment and experience things that she had been sheltered from at home.

After eight years of marriage they decided to slow down some, and start a family, she loved children. Mary immediately got pregnant, but lost the baby when she was three months along. They tried again a year later. The second time she lost the child when she was nearly four months along. At that point in her life she began her battle with alcohol and depression. Mary's psychologist sent her to a psychiatrist for some strong medication and intense psychological help, Alcoholics Anonymous welcomed her with open arms. She was clinically depressed to the point of suicide for over a year after her second miscarriage, it devastated her.

They considered adoption, but decided to try one more time. Mary attributed her horrendous losses to her acquired habits of drinking alcohol, smoking pot and snorting cocaine.

As preparation for her third pregnancy, she went for a whole year without using illegal drugs, before she conceived. Now this terrible thing happened to her that shook her faith in God and challenged her will to live, suicide again seemed like such an easy way out.

She spoke of it occasionally to Stephen.

CHAPTER THIRTY NINE
MARY LYNN GOES HOME

Mary Lynn arrived home four days after being shot, she looked weak, pitiful and forlorn. Stephen sat in the leather recliner chair in their massive bedroom, the fireplace danced with large flames and tried to welcome her home with a warm glow. Stephen had four large bouquets of beautiful flowers arranged artfully around the room. As she lay in bed, propped up by two large pillows, she thoughtfully said to Stephen.

"We have got to find out who did this terrible thing to us. The bible says an eye for an eye and a tooth for a tooth. I've never really thought that I could kill someone, but I am so devastated, I think I could. Why would someone want to shoot me?"

She added, "I know that the police are looking for who did it. If they do find him, he'll probably go to jail for seven years and be out for good behavior, I hate the judicial system in this state. In Utah, they believe in shooting or hanging a murderer. I think that we need to hire a private investigator to find the dirty bastard who did this to us."

Stephen spoke up, "I agree honey. I have already done so, I hired one while you were in the hospital, he is here in town working on the case all ready. He's from Chicago and has a hell of a good reputation. He is supposed to be one of the best in the country, kind of a Wyatt Earp type of guy, sort of expensive, but you get what you pay for. I'll tell you what, after we find the crazy bastard, I'll hire a hit man and we'll fix this situation ourselves." He looked unusually serious.

He added, "I wonder why someone targeted you. Do you think that someone wanted to kill you, or the baby, or both of you!"

She answered, "That's really been bothering me too sweetheart. I don't know why anyone would want to shoot me. Do you think someone really was trying to kill me? Who hates me enough to kill me? Why would anyone shoot me in the stomach, were they a poor shot? I don't understand why this happened!"

She covered her eyes with her hands and slowly started to cry. Then, it gradually built up to a hysterical moan with gushers of tears. "This all seems so unreal," she sobbed. "It's just not fair, it feels like I'm living in a horror movie!"

As she cried, it progressed until she was gasping for air, finally she had to stop. She painfully moaned, "God, I hate you wherever you are, how could you let this happen to me?"

Finally, amidst a few more tears, she surrendered, "I just want to die; I can't stand this any longer. All I ever wanted was a baby. What have I done that is so terrible that you would do this to me?"

Stephen couldn't help himself as he joined her with gentle tears of his own.

A sad, Eric Clapton song, came on the radio. "Would you know my name if I saw you in heaven? I must stay strong and carry on, because I know I don't belong there in heaven."

Bittersweet words wafted eerily in a dream state across the elegant bedroom, as Mary Lynn quietly started to cry quietly again. Stephen jumped up quickly and turned the radio off, so that silence could hold them, kindly, in their sorrow.

CHAPTER FORTY
HOT SHOT COWBOY

The hot Santa Ana wind blew dust and debris through the beautiful tall trees and around the perfect yards of Beverly Hills. Then God provided a lull in the wind and from it emerged a legend of a man, a breath of fresh air, strong at the shoulders, with a trim waist and narrow hips. Los Angeles welcomed Joshua Horlacher, hot shot detective.

Mr. Horlacher drove up to the Manson's estate two days after the shooting; Mary Lynn was still in the hospital. He gingerly stepped out of his large, rented, black, Cadillac, looking like someone had pulled him off the page of an advertisement for a Wild West movie.

Joshua was leathery, tough, meat. His wide shoulders and thin hips fit him perfectly. Ice blue eyes hid behind his black Maui Jim sunglasses, their piercing look could intimidate any man. He looked mean as hell, with deep lined dimples carved into his sun burnt cheeks.

As he emerged from the black Cadillac, he put on his black ten gallon cowboy hat, then he methodically twisted his long, bar handle mustache, on the ends, with both hands at the same time.

A .50 caliber Smith and Wesson pistol was legally concealed under his vest, except where he had purposely left, the hand carved white pearl handle, exposed, for the entire honest and dishonest world to see. His $4000.00 pair of Ostrich boots, Levi's, a hand embroidered turquoise shirt and a beautiful soft leather jacket, let you know that he was a tough, cool, son-of-a-bitch. He hummed quietly to himself, words from an old song, as he sauntered up the walkway to the mansion, "Get yourself an outfit and be a cowboy too."

The Viet Nam war had returned Joshua to society as a highly decorated Navy Seal, with seventeen confirmed kills, his four years were loved, every minute of it. After his military experience, he attended law school at Yale where he graduated number 1 in his class of 94 students. After practicing law for five years in Chicago, he became bored, that's when he decided to become a private investigator.

He owned and occasionally raced a 48 foot racing yacht, had a fine, kind, wife, and three small children to bless his life at home.

His mother promised him that he was born to succeed and never fail, so far, life had delivered that promise to him.

Joshua Horlacher cockily strolled up to the Manson's front door; the butler let him in and brought him to the parlor. After quietly introducing himself to Mr. Manson he asked for permission to snoop around.

The cowboy detective then went outside and walked completely around the fenced-in backyard, slowly, where he thoughtfully took a dozen photographs. He knew where the limo was parked and where Mary Lynn was standing when she was shot, from the police report and the stains on the cobble stones. He ended up standing exactly where Vel stood as he released the deadly chunk of hot lead. His imagination was wide open and capable of anything, reasonable or not, as he studied his suspected shooters spot thoughtfully. The surrounding area was next, then the grass and bushes, but nothing on the ground or in the grass was of any help. The cops had already been there he determined.

Joshua looked carefully around at the neighborhood and imagined where he would park a vehicle if he had done the shooting. Certainly back into the wealthy neighborhood would be the wrong direction. Thoughtfully, playing the roll of shooter, he left the wealthy area and slowly headed toward the area where Vel had parked his station wagon, it seemed like a logical spot. Somehow, he stopped just fifty feet from where Vel had actually parked. It was near a corner intersection where the wealthy people live on one side and the much less rich live across the street. Such is Los Angeles, walls separate lives all over town.

The doors of every house within two thousand feet of the intersection, were knocked on. Politely, the investigator asked if anyone had seen a vehicle that dreadful night, parked there, that didn't look like the kind of vehicle that belonged in the neighborhood. All of the neighbors had read about Mrs. Manson and wanted to help. An old lady, nearby, told him that an old Ford station wagon was parked there that night. Said she noticed it because she previously owned a wagon exactly like it, except hers was white. She told him that this one was maybe dark gray, or blue, or brown, finally let him know that she was a little color-blind, and she reiterated that it was dark out. He wrote it all down in his beautiful leather-bound book that appeared to be his note bible. Inside it he stored his work-plan and notes, all neatly written and organized.

The next thing he decided to do was to investigate the other people who had been gut shot for the last ten years in the Los Angeles area. It was simple to him, a lateral gut shot, not chest shot, seemed unusual.

Five days of intense research, hospital records, newspaper items, and police reports, dislodged some interesting facts and figures. Joshua wrote them down in his book. He looked up gut shot victims that were only shot in the gut. In the last 10 years, 64 people had been shot in the stomach in the greater Los Angeles area. He narrowed them down and categorized them. 39 of them had died from their wounds. 27 had multiple shots to the stomach. 5 were shot from the side by a single shot. 12 had been shot with shot guns only. 31 of them were gang type shootings witnessed by bystanders. 6 were drive-by shootings. 58 were shot directly from the front. 29 were shot at night. 5 were shot by the police in shoot outs. 2 were declared accidents. 1 was self inflicted. 60 victims were males. 40 were Mexicans. 12 were Blacks. 2 were Chinese. 10 were White. 18 shootings occurred during armed robberies. The oldest shooting victim was 68 years old and the youngest victim was 15 years old. 48 of these cases had been solved and arrests had been made.

After looking his statistics over, something inside told him to concentrate his focus on side-shot victims. 4 others also had been shot through the stomach from the side only, by a single shot, besides Mary Manson. These 4 were all obese when they were shot and some of their stories had been written up in the newspapers. Each of them had lost hundreds of pounds from having their stomach stapled or by having a gastric bypass procedure. One of them was a woman, the other three were men, all four were still alive. So, including Mrs. Manson, a total of 5 side-shot victims became the focus of his investigation.

First, he investigated Mary Lynn Manson's case, after all, she and her husband were the reason that he was in LA. He carefully read and re-read Mrs. Manson's medical records, noting the wounds, entry and exit, where they were located and how they appeared. He read about the internal blood loss, her physical reactions, and everything that could be noted about a human body being shot from the side. He wrote it all down slowly in a very organized way, looking for the logical and the illogical. She was the only one not shot directly in the stomach organ, probably because her stomach was pushed upwards from her pregnancy.

She was the only one who was pregnant!

A careful series of phone calls to the Manson's friends, neighbors, police and other confidants, pushed him away from his curiosity, for the time being, about someone wanting to kill her.

Next came the cases of Andy Killborn, Charlotte Johanson, Narvelle Phelps, and Richard Head.

Joshua went to the crime scene in each of their cases, but found nothing of major value. The only thing he found after five days of work was three bullet casings, in the small shack near the barn at the abandoned farm where Mr. Head was shot, heavy metal jacket type. He knew immediately that the bullet lead from these casings could enter a body and likewise, leave it, without blowing a massive hole as it exited. He theorized that these were probably the type used on Mrs. Manson because of the size of the exit wound on her body, medical notes described it clearly.

Further research disclosed that each of the five side-shot people had been shot with a bullet that enters and leaves with almost the same sized hole, except the first man, a Mr. Narvelle Phelps. From his medical records he had much more internal damage than the others and the exit wound was larger and expanded. Joshua supposed that a different type of bullet had hit him and broken apart.

Plan B. What to do next?

Joshua set about to interview each of the other gun shot victims and to see if he could glean any further information, he called them up and made appointments with each of them. He was curious as to why they each had been shot in such a similar way, perhaps they could help. It appeared that three of them were shot in an apparent attempt to hit the stomach only, except perhaps Mrs. Manson and Narvelle Phelps. It didn't make any sense. Why?

Before retiring to bed one night, the phone rang in Joshua's hotel room. "Hello, this is Joshua."

The policeman on the line spoke up, "Hi this is Fred Franklin, as you know we have been investigating the shooting of Mrs. Manson. We have heard of your reputation, glad to have you here in LA to help us work on this case."

"Thank you, sir," the cowboy investigator replied. "What have you learned?"

"Our first question is why anyone would shoot this popular lady. She's a socialite that apparently is well liked by everyone, thus far, we're without a motive or witnesses. Because she was gut shot, instead of head shot or shot in the heart, we wonder if it was done on purpose, to kill her child."

"There are four other folks who have been shot by single shots to the lateral aspect of their abdomen in the last few years. We are presently investigating three of them. We don't want to include the first one, because he was shot in a "drive-by" shooting, the other ones were apparently targeted. The rest, like Mrs. Manson were shot in a sniper type of scenario, so the first victim doesn't fit our profile.

Other than that we are up the proverbial creek without a paddle. Like I just said, there is no motive, and there are no witnesses, thus far."

"I understand sir," Joshua politely said. "I too have dug into the exact cases that you just spoke of, and also have found this to be quite a perplexing case, so far. The motivations or intentions behind the shooting of Mrs. Manson are still unclear to me, too."

"No jealous husband or wife has turned up, no robbery, and no patterns. We've asked around to see if anyone would want to kill her or her baby and nothing has been confirmed." Then the cop jokingly replied. "Perhaps some crazy cat just wants to practice shooting people in the stomach."

"Why would anyone want Mrs. Manson or her child dead? Maybe there is some other thing involved here that we don't know about yet, revenge or blackmail could still be out there waiting to pop its ugly head. At present, I am pursuing every avenue, I haven't ruled out someone wanting her dead," Joshua added.

"There is no dirt on this lady or man, only thing of note is that she has a long history of psychiatric treatment and she is an alcoholic, but who ain't? Her husband is very supportive and he's as clean as a whistle. The lady is pretty hysterical about it all, ya know she lost two pregnancies prior to this one. All of the people that we have talked so far say that she is a faithful and loving wife to Mr. Manson. We don't know why anyone would want to shoot her either." The cop paused, and then continued, "She's a Mormon for God's sake, they don't generally fool around, got the lowest divorce rate of any denomination."

"Thanks for the input," Joshua said. "I'll keep in touch with you fellows. I'll let you know if I find anything really hot."

"Hey I heard a good joke!" Fred piped up, anxious to be heard.

"Santa Claus, the Tooth Fairy, an honest lawyer, and an old drunk are all walking down the street together when they simultaneously spot a hundred dollar bill. Who gets to keep it?" He paused. "The old drunk, or course, the other three are mythological creatures."

Joshua quickly hung up the phone, "What a goofball-sumbitch! Some cops ain't right in the head!"

CHAPTER FORTY ONE
NUTTY NARVELLE

Narvelle felt like he was losing his mind, he had already been interviewed by the police and they didn't seem to believe him. He was worried witless about his up coming interview with the hot-shot detective named Joshua, that he read about in the newspaper. The cowboy detective was famous and apparently, very sharp, intimidating, and cunning.

Vel had quickly and quietly sold his old station wagon an hour after he read that the baby had died. When Linda asked him why he sold it, he responded that there were a lot of mechanical things that needed to be fixed and that it wasn't worth putting any more money into.

Since the shooting he had been nervously eating all kinds of unhealthy things, like the large pizza, the quart of ice cream and then a whole container of cashews, that he had last night after dinner. His stomach hurt like hell as he tried to find the solace that he once had found from food.

He was obviously a nervous wreck.

Yesterday, the family doctor put him on blood pressure medicine for the pounding headaches that he was now having, as well as the fact that his blood pressure numbers were elevated.

During his delivery job he found his mind tripping off into a daze, a dozen times a day. He would forget where he was supposed to be going and just drive around for awhile waiting for his head to clear. Sometimes he would stop his truck in a parking lot, in a trance, and just sit and stare at the moving traffic. Lost in space.

When Vel got home from work he was sullen and detached, drinking hard liquor a minute after he walked through the door.

Linda commented about his recent shift in behavior, suggesting that he see the 'shrink' again because of his obvious new wave of depression, she could see that he was obviously messed up.

Vel couldn't find an escape that would grant him peace of mind. His first thought of how to solve his problem was to apologize to Mary Lynn and her husband, but nothing that he came up with made any sense, he tried to think it out.

These lines just didn't work.

"I'm sorry I killed your baby, it was an accident."

"I thought you were fat and I was trying to help you," sounded like pure horseshit, for sure.

It was difficult to think of what to say that made sense, that might get him off the hook. "Hell, they might not believe me even if I did tell them the truth."

Today, Vel was scheduled to meet the fancy, scary detective. He closed his eyes as he slowly paced the floor in his kitchen; he was waiting for the super detective to knock on his door, nervous, jerky, on edge.

Suddenly the doorbell rang, and Narvelle jumped to attention, the joint he had just smoked wasn't working all that well for him. He cautiously opened the door to the cowboy gunslinger. A quiver of fear electrified his body as his eyes got a full view of Joshua's presentation.

Vel did his best to appear normal. It didn't work. "Ca-Ca-Can I help you?"

"Yes sir," answered Joshua politely. "My name is Joshua Horlacher, I'm the private detective that called you. I've been hired by Mrs. Manson to investigate her case. May I please come in and ask you a few questions?"

"Sh-sure" stammered Vel as he led him into the living room. Linda and Olivia had conveniently gone to a birthday party, Vel planned it that way.

"Would you like a da-da--drink or something?"

"No thanks, I'm fine, I would like to ask you a few questions about what happened to you, if you don't mind." He spoke softly and politely as he sat down. Vel sat across from him in his easy chair, chewing on his thumbnail, trying to relax.

"Could you tell me about when you were shot a few years ago?" Joshua asked nonchalantly, as if he really didn't want to know, very polite, laid-back, non-threatening in his verbal approach.

His outfit and demeanor did all of the talking.

The contradiction of his speech and his attire baffled nearly everyone, including Narvelle.

Narvelle had rehearsed his story a dozen times, out it came in memorized fashion, emotionless and objective. He went on and on about how it was a blessing in disguise and how much weight he had lost since then. He showed the detective the scar where the bullet went in and the scars where the bullet exited his body. Proudly he handed Joshua a previous picture of himself, when he was at his maximum weight, Joshua smiled politely.

"I'm lucky to be alive, I guess. My wife says that it's a blessing in disguise, it must be."

"Were you ever in the military?" The investigator casually asked. He had already checked this out and he knew the answer before Vel could say it, knew the entire history of his military time served, and that he was honorably discharged.

"Uh, yeah I was. Nam. How about you?" he tried to shift the questioning to the detective. Joshua read his redirection immediately and avoided any further discussion of military service.

"Me too," Joshua let it go at that.

"What kind of cars do you own, if you don't mind me asking?"

"I-I-I own a Jeep," Vel stuttered nervously. "And, and, my pride and joy, ma-ma-my '55 Chevy outside."

"Yes sir, I saw that black beauty in your driveway. Beautiful. I'll bet that baby is worth a lot of money."

Narvelle nodded nervously and wished that this interrogation would get over soon. "It's a rare one, only a few hundred were made. It cost me and my wife enough to buy two new Chevrolets."

"What do you do for a living sir?"

"I-uh-uh drive a delivery truck," Vel mumbled as if he had forgotten what it was that he did for a living.

Joshua appeared to be content as he politely thanked him; then he shook is sweating hand and left. He went to his car and wrote the whole experience in concise form in his note-bible.

"Mr. Phelps is a nervous mess. I don't know if that is his normal behavior. He owns a Jeep and a rare, '55 Chevrolet convertible, black, beautiful. He is an ex-Marine, honorable discharge, no police record. A drive-by shooting victim, Mexican gangs. He thinks it's a blessing to have been shot in the gut, lost a lot of weight since he was shot, a few years ago. He acts like he's not telling the truth about something. Appeared to be stoned or inebriated. Strangely nervous man.'

Joshua then headed for his next interview with Andy Killborn. He was told the story of how it all happened and how much weight he had lost. Again he heard that it was a blessing in disguise and that it had changed his life for the better. He wrote it all down in the little black book.

"Andy is a clown and likes to joke around; he seems honest and straight forward. Ex pro football player, etc."

The next day he interviewed Richard. The same story of getting hit by a single bullet to the stomach was told, but at this time he learned more, added to the story was that there were two gun shots, at close range to his knee, that he didn't know about. He add more information about an old station wagon being parked near the barn, that the wagon appeared to be gray with primer spots in a few places and looked like a piece of junk. He also gleaned the information about the shooter: white, male, six feet tall, wearing a baseball cap. Richard told him his story of how he got lured to go to the farm, rehashing the "cock and bull story" about the pig being hired to be in a movie. Richard ended with the statement that it was a true blessing in disguise.

"Another damned, blessed, sniper story," he explained.

He purposely refrained from telling Richard about the bullet casings that he had found.

Note in the black book: "It appears that a copycat shooter may have shot these last two men. Similar style of shooting. Both obese prior to shooting, both lost significant weight, gut shot from the side. Both think that it was a blessing to be shot like they were. A station wagon being involved may have been confirmed. Maybe I should put this information into the newspaper."

The next day he met the beautiful Charlotte. As she opened the door to him, Joshua immediately noticed that her finger tip was placed delicately between her front teeth. Sexily. He stared. (See the front cover of book)

Charlotte innocently spoke first, "I hit my finger with a hammer,------ oh, hello,-------- I'm Charlotte, please come in."

Eye-candy-surprise for Joshua! He had no idea that she was so pretty. Few women in his life had graced his presence, that had rendered him speechless, but she did, immediately. Like a lighthouse, she beamed with beauty, his attraction was obvious and instant. Innocent sexy smiles and glancing eye contact with her confused his thought patterns as he tried to interrogate her, he couldn't help himself. She apparently was attracted to him too, and his fancy outfit. He caught himself staring at her perfect facial features a dozen times, enjoying every pretty smile that she beamed back at him.

Charlotte told her story earnestly, with sincerity and gratitude, then ended the explanation with moist eyes, "What a strange blessing this experience has been for me, God works is mysterious. My life has changed so much since then, I am truly thankful for what has happened. I never expected to be so blessed, it must be a God thing."

Joshua thanked her as he left. His notes in the book were as follows: "Charlotte is strikingly beautiful. A real fox! Lateral gut shot, sniper fashion. She has lost a lot of weight since being shot. She now has a child, a kind and respected husband, dozens of new friends, a nice home, good health, and a new portion of self respect. In her case, it truly was a blessing to have been shot, the picture on the mantel of her before being shot is amazing and sobering, she was grossly obese, much worse than the others."

His final summary notes read like this. "None of these four victims stated that they owned an old station wagon. The first one to be shot, of the group, was a confirmed gang related incident. All four were gut shot from the side. All have lost weight. No other pattern except that they are all very thankful for what has happened to them. Found 3 metal jacket casings in Richard's case. Narvelle is excessively nervous, was hit in a drive by shooting. Question his behavior. The other four victims were apparently targeted by a sniper. Mary Lynn may be the fourth victim of a sniper. Don't rule out a copy cat. Don't rule out an unknown intention to kill her; the baby's death may have been accidental. Andy is a clown and appears to be blatantly honest. Charlotte is strikingly beautiful. Richard appears to be a very kind man, thankful for his new life, also was shot twice in the leg. Mary----alcoholic, depressed, hysterical and deeply hurt, may be suicidal. Can't blame her. None of this makes much sense. What is the motive? Where are the witnesses? Who profits from these shootings?"

Joshua was still stumped, so he decided that it was time to take a break and let it all settle. His plan was to return home and discuss his findings with his vastly intelligent friend in Chicago. Experience had taught him that sometimes it's good to detach yourself from a problem for a few days, if you are not making headway.

Before he left, the answering machine at the Manson's estate recorded, "Hello, this is Joshua Horlacher. I've decided to take a break for a few days to sort out the information that I have found thus far. I'll be flying home to Chicago to discuss the situation here with a good friend of mine, sometimes two heads are better than one. I'll be back soon, will call you and let you know when I have returned and give you a summary of my findings at that time."

A brief pause, then he added, "God be with you both."

CHAPTER FORTY TWO
CHICAGO AIR

Joshua slowly lowered his body in his first class seat on the airplane headed for Chicago. Four hours before his flight he had removed his mustache, his boots, and his entire cowboy outfit. He had his working outfit stored in his room at the hotel. His transformation into a serious looking businessman was complete, every hair on his head was perfectly cut to the right length. He had on a pair of brown penny loafers, khaki cotton twill pants, a subtle blue and gold sweater and a quiet refined Rolex watch.

Next to him on the airplane sat a small dark skinned man, they introduced themselves. The small man was a Baptist preacher. Joshua explained that he was a lawyer.

The preacher piped up and wanted to talk about his son who was not accomplishing much with his life. First he explained that he had a daughter who married early and now had two children, she only finished high school. Then the preacher went on about his son, said that his son was a wonderful person, smart and kind, but lacked motivation. He explained that his son was now 24 years old and still lived at home.

Then the preacher opened a book of wit and wisdom and read out loud from it.

"The young people of our time are a perplexity to our souls. They contradict their elders. They are lazy and non productive with their time. They want to argue and disrespect their parents and people of authority. They sleep late, stay up all night, and only want to party."

It was written by the great Socrates, five hundred years before Christ!

They both laughed.

"Nothing new under the sun," said the preacher.

"How did you gain respect and motivation for yourself as a young man?" the preacher asked cautiously.

Joshua pondered the question for awhile, no one had ever asked this question of him. He had thought about it but never had made an attempt to explain it to anyone.

"Long ago, as a teenager, I read about the ancient Inca civilization. Their standards were to my liking, don't steal, don't lie, and don't be lazy. So I started to practice them.

I would have to say that my work experience would be the basis of building respect and the motivation to go onward and accomplish other things. Success engenders success, and respect.

When I was a teenager, I also worked as a delivery boy for a pastry shop and did odd jobs for carpenters. Later after high school, it became quite apparent to me that I wasn't ready for college, so I joined the Navy. I believe that it is while I was in the military that I really grew up the most.

After my military experience, which was exciting and wonderful, I worked myself through college; no one helped me except the GI bill. As a summary, it appears that I figured it out years ago, respect is earned by doing something, anything that is a significant accomplishment."

It was all absorbed by the intense preacher man as he listened carefully. He hadn't spoken, but now it was his turn.

"Let me sort this out then," the preacher man said thoughtfully.

"I'm going to tell my son that in life, in order to gain respect, you must do something respectful, then you will have your deserved rewards. You will be what God has intended you to be. That is how a productive joyful person becomes motivated. This will also be the basis of my next sermon on Sunday, all of my flock needs to know this good stuff."

Thank you for your clarity, my new friend." He smiled warmly.

Joshua smiled and nodded politely, then he looked out the window at the world of the sky, for a minute.

Slowly, his head returned to straight ahead, gradually closing his eyes, he drifted off to sleep.

CHAPTER FORTY THREE
FRAGILE COUNCEL

A few days after the Joshua Horlacher interviewed Vel, Vel called Fragile, he asked him to meet him at their favorite pool hall. Vel needed desperately to talk about his problem. He asked Harold what would happen if he turned himself in, would be prosecuted for murder? Fragile was fairly well versed in a few parts of the law, his younger brother was an attorney. He told Narvelle that it wasn't first degree murder in any sense of the word because it wasn't premeditated. He explained that he would probably get a plea bargain for a manslaughter conviction because this act of repentance could sway a jury to be lenient. At worst, Harold thought that Vel might get from 1 to 4 years in jail.

Harold also carefully explained, that because Vel acted so jittery at times, he might get off totally, by being declared mentally incompetent. Vel's shrink might have to speak up for him.

"After all, shooting people in the stomach so that they can lose weight, is pretty damned crazy," he added with a serious look, a very serious look.

"What are you going to be like if you don't turn yourself in?" Harold plied.

"I ain't doing real well with this," Vel again bit at his thumbnail, nervously fidgeting, as he continued. "I've been having more frequent episodes of visions with babies blowing up, mixed with all that weird shit that comes from being in Nam, you know what I'm talking about, the guts and the gore. My head is so messed up that sometimes I think that I've gone completely nuts. Sometimes I forget what I doing, or where I'm going."

Vel told him that he had gained a bunch of weight during the last two weeks, also that his blood pressure was still 200 over 110 when he saw the family doctor recently. He told Fragile that Linda thought he was on the verge of a breakdown, because of his erratic behavior. She had called the shrink again and demanded another appointment for him. Then Narvelle let his friend know that his second written notice from work had been formally issued, explaining that he was not performing in a satisfactory manner. He had delivered packages to the wrong address, two times last week.

"You can see that I'm a mess, I'm so confused that I can't think straight. It is so helpful for you to talk to me. Thank you for not judging me. You are a true friend." Vel reverently spoke.

Thankfully, Narvelle ended with, "You're much better than any high powered shrink could ever be, most of the ones that I've talked to are crazier than I am."

CHAPTER FORTY FOUR
THE COWBOY IS BACK IN TOWN

The phone rang in Joshua's hotel room, he was fresh out of the shower, and was carefully putting on his bar handled mustache. The rest of his outfit was waiting neatly on the bed, no wrinkles. Mrs. Manson was on the line. She explained that her husband had gone back to Italy to take care of some important business, and that she would be available to receive any information about what his investigation had turned up. They agreed to meet at six pm, for dinner.

The butler let him in, Joshua had his outfit on in full array. Mrs. Manson looked like she hadn't had any sleep for a week, her hair was poorly combed, and her eyes were puffy and without makeup. The large dining table was set for two, three tall, lit candles separated them. The big house was darkly lit inside and empty of any happiness, except for the four elegant lamps, that bravely framed the opulent dining room.

Joshua sat down facing her. He explained that he had gone home and discussed his findings with his ex-partner, Joe Tanus, a brilliant lawyer with a creative imagination. They had been partners for a few years and had relied on each others opinions without reservation, before Joshua went on his own as a private detective. Fellow attorneys in Chicago, jokingly referred to them back then as the Bobbsey Twins.

He explained to Mrs. Manson about his findings and that the uniqueness of her case had never been written about in any of the books that lawyers refer to.

Joe, his ex partner, had a few theories about why someone would randomly shoot people in the stomach, most of them led nowhere. The exception was his theory about Mr. Phelps. He relied heavily on what Joshua had told him about how Mr. Phelps was unusually nervous. Joe agreed that Mr. Phelps may not be telling the truth about everything, Joe thought that Mr. Phelps was involved, somehow.

"We really don't have any good evidence or other leads to go on for now," Joshua explained apologetically.

"Here's a summary from my notebook. The bullet casings are common. The station wagon that was seen in two cases could be one in a million. The man who shot one victim was an average white man that we have no real workable description of.

The person who shot you might be a copy cat that is sick and wanted to repeat what he read about in the newspapers, or heard about on TV, or, I hate to say this, we can't rule it out that someone may have wanted to kill you. No motive has turned up yet, by me or the police. If you can think of anyone to investigate concerning that idea, please tell me as soon as possible. I have already done some looking around and I don't know of anyone who would want you dead, and that's an unusual compliment. The bottom line is this; I am stumped so far."

Mary Lynn kept her head down as she picked at her dinner, slowly, listening carefully to Joshua. When he finished, Mary said, "Please let me be the first to know if you find something important." He agreed.

"I don't think the police know anymore than you do, if I find out anything from them, I will call you and share it with you," she added with a sad look on her face. Her eyes were hollow, her voice flat, her demeanor demolished, she had taken a severe whipping from life.

Joshua was not a quitter, he left her house, with renewed determination to find the answer. He had the ability of letting information seep into the crevices of his mind, store it there, and not let it cloud fresh new thought processes. His approach from that point was simple and logical, go back to the very beginning and start all over, just like he didn't know anything.

The next morning he ran a large half page ad in the personal section of the largest newspaper, it read.

"A Reward of $100,000.00 will be paid for information leading to the arrest and conviction of the person/persons who shot Mrs. Mary Lynn Manson. The suspect is believed to be a white male, 30 to 40 years old, approximately six feet tall of average build. He may have been driving an old Ford station wagon. The vehicle is presumed to be gray and is apparently in need of repair. Call me at this number. Joshua Horlacher BR549."

When he returned to the hotel he called each of the other four victims and set up an appointment to interview them, again.

After the appointments were set, Joshua turned off his detective role. He called his wife and asked how she and the children were doing. Told her that he might be away from home for two to six weeks trying to solve this difficult case.

"I love you guys very much. We will all go for a fun boat ride on the big-sled when I get home. I'll call you again later tonight before I go to bed. Kiss the kids for me sweetheart."

CHAPTER FORTY FIVE
MAD MARY

Mary Lynn walked over to the window of her palatial kitchen and peered out Then, she walked around the dining area and peeped out through the cut-glass windows at the street. Three young girls were going home from school, laughing, skipping and singing happy songs; their happiness embittered her even more. No longer did tears fall from her sorrow, her sadness and anger only wanted revenge.

Later that afternoon, she was delivered to her psychiatrist, by her good neighbor from next door; the doctor greeted her somberly, their eyes never met. She greeted him in a belligerent manner as she ungracefully plopped down in the large brown easy-chair, anger twisted her face, mean lines accentuated the dark sculpture of her eyes.

"Mary Lynn, are you going to be able to talk to me today?" the doctor began.

"Yeah, sure."

"Is the medication helping you?"

"I'm sure it is. I don't feel like dying or killing myself all the time any more, that's good isn't it?" she spewed.

"That's good. How is Stephen holding up?"

"He's doing as well as can be expected. He's out of town, had to go to Italy to take care of some business and to solve all the problems of the world, he does that you know."

He stated flatly, "It sure has been nice weather lately. Have you taken the opportunity to get out and walk around your neighborhood?"

"Not really. I think it's going to take a long time for me to get over this shit!"

On and on the idle banter went for a half hour without resolution or benefit, nothing was solved, nothing could be solved, and nothing pretended to be solved. When it was over, as they headed home, Mary Lynn had her friend stop at the liquor store.

Once inside her door, she fixed a tall, triple shot, drink of vodka and orange juice, quickly sipping it down to ease her pain. Then she went to the closet where Stephen kept his hunting guns, took the key and opened the safe. She stared at all the beautiful rifles for a few minutes, and then she picked up the magnificent .357 Smith and Wesson long barreled pistol. It was a special model that had been given to Stephen by the Governor of California. Mary took her clothes off down to her underwear, put on a thin elegant pink bath robe, then slowly walked around the house pretending to shoot the lights out, the windows out, and to kill imaginary fish in the toilets; the vodka helped her aim.

Suddenly, the phone rang, it was her oldest sister calling to say hello and to check on her. It rang a dozen times until she grudging answered it. By then Mary had mixed another tall drink of vodka and orange juice, the first drink took a drink.

"Yup, what do you want?" she blurted out with just a hint of a slur.

"Hi Mary girl, how are you doing?" sis said, in a cheery voice.

"I'm getting drunk and shooting fish in the toilet," Mary Lynn answered sarcastically.

"What are you talking about?" She paused a few seconds. "Where is Stephen?"

"He's in Italy, trying to solve all of the problems of the world, he does that, he always does that, he's a fixer."

"Do I need to come down there and be with you? You don't sound like you're doing well!"

"No sis, I will be all right, my two good friends are here to comfort me. Thanks for calling, I love you," she said as she abruptly slammed the phone, hard.

Mary picked up the pistol and slowly began to examine it. Down the barrel she could see the rifling that makes the bullets spin as they exit the gun. The grip was beautifully carved in an intricate tight cross pattern. The booze was altering her judgment now as she aimed the gun at the overhead fan; then, slowly, like a robot, she aimed the gun at her forehead and held it there as tears began to stream down her face. Suicide crossed her mind. She imagined that there were bullets in the chambers and questioned whether she would hear the explosion of a loaded gun going off.

Russian roulette suddenly jumped into her thought processes, she sought a decision as to whether she should continue to live or die, right now. She looked around for a bullet, but realized that they were in the safe, too far away for her tired, wobbly legs to carry her. The excitement of surviving a try at Russian roulette teased her, enticed her. Let God be the judge, she decided, as she closed her eyes, took a big breath, and slowly tried to pull the trigger. It was an impossible task because it wasn't cocked. She lowered the pistol and carefully cocked it, then she pressed the business end of the barrel between her eyes and barely touched the trigger. This time the hair trigger went off with a magnificent bang, the loud metallic click sounded like a hammer smacking her brain. Her jaws clamped like a vise, making her teeth ache, breath escaped her for a long minute as her mouth hung open, fishlike.

She lowered the pistol to her lap and realized how fast and gracious that form of suicide would be.

"I guess God wants me to live. All I ever wanted from this life was a happy family with some children and a good time."

Her disturbed mind rambled onward. "This castle that I'm trapped in holds me wishing that I were dead most of the time, how bad is that, to have all the money in the world and still be unhappy? Why can't I have a baby like everyone else has? Is it my curse for leaving the damned church?"

She looked lovingly at the pistol. "What do you have to say about all that, Mr. Smith and Mr. Wesson?"

She cradled the pistol lovingly to her chest as she stared at the slow motion blades of the ceiling fan overhead. Round and around they went, silently, accomplishing nothing, just moving, mesmerizing, soothing.

The huge mansion was empty as the silence gripped her and wouldn't let go. Finally a flip of the remote control switch put a voice in the house for companionship, as the television blinked on.

While it warmed up, and the pictures changed from blurred to visible. Mary Lynn curled up in the big leather chair and pulled a large, beautiful, handmade Italian blanket over her legs, then up across her stomach. The pistol hugged her chest.

Life's problems faded further and further away, as she finished the second tall glass of anesthesia and stared again at the slow moving ceiling fan blades, escaping, drifting.

CHAPTER FORTY SIX
ANDY, LUCRETIA AND JOSHUA MEET

Meanwhile, Joshua started his second round of interviews, with Andy Killborn. Andy met a woman named Lucretia that night at the bar, in Sturgis, with the six-pack of riders. She was the lady working as a waitress, sitting alone at the bar, the one he had told his friends about. He immediately liked her smile and the way she carried on, cutting up, laughing, and cajoling with the bikers. Their attraction to each other was mutual and immediate, she liked his big-bodied look and the tough guy impression he gave as he recited the story of punching the drunken biker, ….. "one, two, three."

Lucretia McEvel was from a small town in New Mexico, called Wolverton. Her husband of twenty two years had been recently killed in a house fire, so she was on her own as far as making a living. Her three grown up children lived in Albuquerque, New Mexico. Lucretia had lived in Sturgis for two years prior to meeting Andy.

For her own entertainment she was an oil painter, but had never shown her paintings. Her art was excellent, but she refused to sell any of it because it was done in a spirit of love and for her own self-gratification, many of her paintings became gifts to her friends and family.

Andy got Lucretia's phone number when he was in Sturgis; a week later he called her. They met at his house in Los Angeles, ten days later, and immediately started living together. With a little encouragement from Andy, she finally allowed twenty of her best paintings to be viewed in an artist's street crawl, in San Francisco. She sold nine of her paintings the next week. That's how the artistic history of Lucretia McEvel started, thanks to her acquaintance with Andy Killborn, ex football player, comedian, tough guy.

Joshua Horlacher, cowboy investigator, rang the doorbell at Andy's house as he sought his second interview. Standing in the door way as the door opened to him, was a nice looking lady in her early fifties, a pleasant smile rested on her face. Her hair was dark, and her eyes were sparkling green. She was trim, with curves that resembled Marilyn Monroe. Turquoise with gold rings wrapped three fingers on each hand, her long colorful dress said that she was ready to go to a country square-dance at any time.

Grinning from ear to ear she invited the interesting looking, cowboy lawyer into her house. She introduced herself as Lucretia McEvel, got him a glass of water, then headed upstairs to fetch Andy. Joshua sat down on the couch and looked around the room at the eclectic collection of Southwest and Impressionistic art. A minute later he stood up and approached the paintings, they were all signed, Lucretia McEvel, interesting name he thought.

A minute later, Andy, the ex-football player, trotted down the stairs and sang out a happy, "howdy partner!" He entered the room and reached for Joshua's hand. After he purposely crushed Joshua's hand, he smiled real big and sat down. He still had a spare tire around his waist, but he looked healthy and happy as a lark, and moved like a young man in his forties. His hair was now dyed almost black and he had grown the three week beginnings of a mustache.

"Did ya get introduced to my girl friend?" he asked confidently.

"Yes I did. She's got her name on all those paintings." He looked at the walls. "She is one hell of a fine artist!"

"Well, thanks for that. What can I do for you today, sir?" Andy didn't like to beat around the bush.

"As of yet, I haven't hit the jackpot on this investigation. I thought that I would go over everything, from front to back, again, and see if I could pick up any new or better information."

They sat down as Andy slowly and carefully went over the entire story of how he got shot. While they talked, Joshua prompted him a little and asked him if he noticed an old Ford station wagon, gray in color, anywhere around the place where he was shot. He asked him to remember the backside of the building, and to try to remember anything unusual a few weeks prior to the being shot. Andy thought about it for a minute, and then it came to him.

"Now that you mention it, a couple of weeks before I got plugged, I was getting out of my car, behind the church, and an old station wagon drove by, behind me, I noticed it because I seldom see any other cars back there. It had a big hole where the key would have been in the tailgate, the hole was about the size of a baseball bat.

I'm sorry that I don't remember the color of the wagon, and, honestly, I didn't see who was driving it. For some reason I looked at the hole in the tail gate the most, it was really unusual."

Joshua stored the new information quickly in his minds computer.

"What kind of cars do you own?" Joshua asked Andy.

"I just have one car, just recently bought a new Cadillac Seville, and I have my motorcycle that my woman calls a Charley Harrison."

Andy acted like he was through talking. Suddenly he popped out, "That's it, that's all folks, ta da!" as he grinned his boyish grin.

Joshua persisted, "Did your insurance company pay for your medical bills?"

"Yep," up came Andy's answer quickly, he was calm and cool as a cucumber and very believable.

"I'll check it all out with the police department and the hospital," Joshua replied.

Joshua stood up and put his hand out, and said, "Thanks for your time, by the way, you look fit as a fiddle." Andy nodded thanks.

"I'm ready to kick-ass and take names!" Andy jested as he smiled widely and danced a little with his hands, shadow-boxing.

Before Joshua could get out the door, Andy thought quickly and casually added, "Speaking of, by the way, I might as well tell you a little, by the way, up front. Lucretius's real name is Susan Brown, she coined the name on her art because her real name is so common place. As you may well know, lots of people aren't who they look like or pretend to be."

Andy looked squarely into Joshua's eyes as he waited for a response from him. Andy the clown, didn't want any future hassle from the fancy cowboy investigator. He was trying to protect his girlfriend and to eliminate any future involvements with the law.

Little did he know about the cowboy and his facade.

Joshua grinned as he reached up with both hands and slowly twisted the ends of his bar-handle moustache, then with a twinkle in his eyes, said with a serious demeanor, "Yeah, I know that statement is the honest to God truth. You should never judge a book by its cover."

He headed for the door again, "Thanks for the information on Susan, you folks make a nice looking couple. The best of luck to the both of you. Happy trails."

CHAPTER FORTY SEVEN
REPEAT THAT PLEASE,
THE SECOND INTERVIEW CONTINUES

The interviews continued. Next came Joshua's second interview with Charlotte, the beautiful, he looked forward to gazing at her again. She beamed as she opened the door, the face of an angel. Again, Joshua noticed that her body was normal in size and shape. This time her beautiful young daughter stood by her side smiling sweetly. Her hair looked perfect, her eyes glistened like a doll's, and her skin was white and flawless as silk.

"What an absolute baby-doll!" he thought to himself. "Who on God's green earth would want to hurt her?"

Nothing new came from the second interrogation. Her medical treatments were covered by her insurance company, and she reported that she never saw an old gray station wagon.

When she was asked if she knew of any reason why someone would want to shoot her, she replied, "It was truly a God thing that happened to me, I told you that the last time we met. I repeat myself; I believe that what happened to me was definitely a God thing. It surely wasn't an accident, I believe that someone shot a gun into the air and that the bullet hit me exactly where it did, on purpose. God directed it to hit me so that my life would change for the better, he sent me a blessing in an unusual way. I believe in the Bible, and I believe in miracles.

I have a brother, his name is Mork, he is a very kind man, but he is obese, like I was. He needs a miracle like I received. My prayers every evening, are that God will somehow send him a blessing, where can lose his weight and get back to normal. He suffers so! His wife left him and he is in a lot of pain."

For a brief moment Charlotte was a perplexity for him. As she talked and explained her position and her desires, her countenance vacillated from pure innocence to sexy siren. Joshua suddenly felt dizzy. Her eyes and facial expressions conjured up a curiosity about how it would be to wake up in bed with her in his arms. Joshua was usually very calm and in control of every situation, but not now, his thoughts were verging on "out of control" and he knew it, he had to leave, soon. The "male predator" that lives inside of every man, overwhelmed him as he realized that he was staring at her with lust in his heart. He wasn't listening anymore.

Silently, his mind again repeated the poem that floated there every time he saw Charlotte. "She walks in beauty like the night, of cloudless climes and starry skies. And all that's best of dark and bright, meet in her aspect and her eyes. A heart whose love is innocent." A quick shake of his head tried to clear his cobwebs.

He had to leave now, his heart was pounding rapidly, sweat beaded on his forehead. He blushed as he quickly excused himself and escaped her overwhelming presence.

On his way back to his car he thought, "Who would want to shoot a baby doll like her? How could anyone dare to shoot her? There must have been an ulterior motive. Could it be that my buddy, Joe, was right? That she was shot to help her lose weight? What a crazy story that would be if it's true. That's never happened before."

The repeat interviews continued. The next day Richard Head was available for Joshua to review his brush with death, he still was a tad overweight, but not "Blimpy" like he once was. Richard, the show pig owner, looked healthy and happy.

They discussed any and all motives that would be behind why someone would entice him from his home and shoot him carefully in such a manner. Whoever shot him definitely didn't want to kill him or he would have done so when Richard attacked him.

Joshua disclosed that he had recovered the bullet casings from the small shed. Richard told him that his hospital stay and rehabilitation were all covered by his insurance company, 'Pink Cross Pink Shield', a company started by champion pig owners of America. Joshua laughed at his little joke.

Richard reiterated his gratitude for being alive and in much better shape than before the incident.

"Did you see a gray station wagon near the barn the day you were shot?"

"I briefly looked at the old station wagon, but I didn't have my glasses on, so I can't say that the one that I saw was gray, for sure. I didn't really study it when I saw it; I just thought that it was abandoned. I was more intent on meeting the guy with the money." He paused a few seconds with a serious look on his face.

"I have, another, new lease on life now. That's all that really matters to me at this moment in my life," his words drifted off as he smiled kindly and they said goodbye.

Last, but not least, on the second interview list, was Narvelle Phelps. Joshua's new nickname for Narvelle was Narvelle, the nervous. Actually, Narvelle was so nervous, he could barely make himself open the front door when the bell rang; after he did, he issued a half smile that smelled of fear. Vel had smoked a joint and swallowed half a fifth of Jack Daniels thirty minutes prior to their meeting, his eyes were bloodshot red and his breath reeked. Joshua backed up a little for some fresh air before he entered the house. He got a good whiff. Vel retold his story perfectly to the investigator without a hitch, reiterating that he was in the wrong place at the wrong time, then added that he had his medical treatments fully covered by insurance. When asked about ever owning a Ford station wagon, he pretended to think back, but it was pathetically obvious that he was not telling the truth.

He stuttered helplessly, "I-I-I have had a lot of vehicles in my life. I'm not sure if my old wagon was a fa-fa Ford." He looked pathetically guilty.

"Whatever it was I got rid of it a-a-a few years ago." His eyes looked up to his left as he spoke. A cold chill shivered Joshua's body as he stood still watching Mr. Phelps's sad performance. Joshua's eyes searched for the truth but it wasn't there, so he casually nodded as he decided that he wouldn't ask any more questions. Nothing else was needed from the meeting. He had read him like a book, enough was enough, it was over.

They both knew it, as he turned to leave.

Narvelle was now visibly sweating and his whole demeanor had suddenly changed, the desire to escape was written all over his face. Joshua politely let him go; he told him thanks and tried to act like nothing significant had happened, as he exited the house. Vel quickly closed the door and promptly headed for the booze closet.

Joshua herded his Cadillac towards the courthouse building downtown, which holds public records, he knew he was on to something significant.

As he drove along, calculating the end-game, he realized that the tough part of the case that still remained, was the lack of witnesses, and the fact that there was no believable motive that made any sense. His interview with Vel brought him back to the far fetched theory that Joe had come up with. The one about Narvelle shooting others. He repeated to himself, "If it was Narvelle that shot the others it will be the first time in my career that such a bizarre thing has happened."

Sometimes, the truth is stranger than fiction.

CHAPTER FORTY EIGHT
VEL WANTS TO ESCAPE

After Joshua left, the largest part of Narvelle was ready to go on the lam, he was scared, the cowboy was definitely on to him. Remembering back to when he was a teenager, running from the cop on his motorcycle, whipping the bully, raising hell in school, he wondered, could he do it again. "Things are different now, it's much more complicated," he told himself.

A small part of him wanted to apologize to the lady and her husband, and get it over with. It seemed like the right thing to do, and the easiest way out.

His mind kept twisting with answers to his problem, but none of them were convincing, none made enough sense, as he sat on the couch, sipping a whiskey and coke, watching television, his mind wandering uselessly.

When Linda came home an hour later, she smelled the booze. It was obvious from his erratic behavior, that his mind was scrambled eggs. He would start a sentence, then pause, then say nothing for twenty to thirty seconds, as he looked at the floor or the ceiling, thinking. She kept asking him to share what was happening to him, and why he seemed so irritable and mentally unclear. He slurred his speech and stuttered as he told her stories of horror from his war experience.

Linda believed that his mind was suddenly snapping, for no apparent reason.

Later that night as he sobered up, he again talked it over with himself. He tried to imagine what it would be like to actually confess that he had done this terrible deed, that it was just a terrible mistake and that he was actually trying to help. He imagined how angry he would be if someone shot his daughter, for any reason. A jury would surely give him an easy sentence if he admitted his wrong doing because his intention was good. He wondered if the lady would go completely crazy if she never found out what really happened. The paper said that her baby was eight and a half months along. His mind continued to jump from thought to thought without resolution.

Conversation with him became useless. Linda couldn't stand watching him space out any longer, so she called the psychologist again, this time at his home, got him out of bed.

She spoke strongly to the doctor on his answering machine, "This is Linda Phelps! Listen to me damn it! My husband needs to see you as soon as possible! He's acting very strange. I ask him questions and he won't respond in a normal fashion. He starts talking, then stops and looks around like he's thinking, then he may or may not continue having a conversation with me. I think that he is severely depressed. He keeps talking about not wanting to live anymore and about all that war mess that he lived through. I'm seriously worried that he might be suicidal! You need to get your shit together and talk to him soon!"

The doctor called back three minutes later, apologetically and professionally, he allowed himself to say, "I got your message, loud and clear. I'll call my secretary and have her set up a time for him tomorrow morning. She will call you within the next five minutes. I'll try my best to defuse him. Good night."

CHAPTER FORTY NINE
A BAG FULL OF NUTS

"What is irritating you so much Narvelle?" calmly came from the doctor.

"I have done some really bad things in my life; I don't know what to do about them. I shouldn't be here on this earth anymore, most of my war buddies are dead; I should be too." His body shivered like he was in forty below zero weather, his face pale, his eyes darting about, wildly searching. Nervous.

"What have you done that could eat at you so much?"

Narvelle looked perplexed for a few seconds, as he almost told him the truth. He wanted to tell him the truth and find a way out of his mess, but he didn't trust the doctor, never had.

"Have you killed or injured someone?" the doctor continued, cautiously probing.

"No," Narvelle lied as his hands began to tremble.

"I want to just go shoot myself or something," Vel said. "I keep seeing visions of body parts exploding. My life is so screwed up; I must be nuts. They're threatening to fire me from my job because I can't concentrate on what I'm doing, or where I'm going, I can't remember stuff."

The doctor looked a little surprised and asked him what it was that he was feeling inside. Vel refused to answer. The doctor tried to befriend him even more, tried to cajole him with light humor, as he tried to get a hint about what it was that was such a terrible secret. Next, he asked Narvelle if it was related to the war, no response came from Vel for a minute, then he absently replied, "What did you say?"

After the doctor carefully hounded him for another fifteen minutes, Vel suddenly got up and left the office without saying good by, go to hell, or anything else. He just suddenly jumped up and left. This was the first and only time that he had ever walked out on the psychologist, so the doctor knew that something really big was happening or had happened. He immediately called Linda. After he explained what had transpired during their meeting he said, "Can you give me anymore information that could help me defuse him?"

"Not really, not any more than I've told you already," Linda added. "Let me say this again just in case I haven't already, he keeps talking in riddles about his old war stories and the things that he sees in his mind like colors, explosions, body parts and so forth. He talks about wanting to die, says his job is in jeopardy. None of what he is saying is really new or unusual, to me, it's just mixed up crazier than I've heard it before."

The doctor finished with, "I am going to get him some stronger medication to help calm him down. He sounds and acts a bit suicidal, so I'll call his psychiatrist and we'll get stronger medicine, pronto. We also need him to make an appointment with the psychiatrist, I'll have my secretary do that. Call me if you come up with anything that can help us sort this out."

"Thank you for seeing him, I'm so worried that he might do something stupid."

CHAPTER FIFTY
JACKSON HOLE

Thoughts of Jackson Hole, Wyoming entered Vel's mind as he drove home from the meeting with the shrink.

As Narvelle neared his house, he decided to try to convince Linda to move away from California. His mind was frazzled with worry about being caught, moving made the most sense, for now. It was his best choice.

Narvelle's family had fond memories of Jackson Hole, Wyoming and the dude ranch that they stayed in, two years earlier. Linda had told him that if he ever wanted to move away from Southern California, that Jackson Hole would be her first pick of a place to live. He could get a job as a ranch hand or drive a truck or something. She could get a job as a nurse anywhere, and Olivia loved the horses and the Wild West attitude of the entire area. They could sell their house, and if they needed some quick money to move, he would tell her that he would let his beloved '55 Chevy be sold.

"Linda, my love, let me ask you a question," he asked her, later on that evening, as she combed her hair in the bathroom. "What would you say if I told you that I want to move away from this crowded, smoggy, rat race of a damn city?" He appeared to be lucid for the moment and very believable.

She stopped combing her hair and grinned like a little girl.

"And where would you like to move to, Mr. Phelps?"

"I was thinking back a few years, I remember how much you and Olivia loved Jackson Hole. Here's what I want to do, I want to sell our house and move there. It has been in the back of my mind for a really long time. The air is pure, the mountains are beautiful and there are four distinct seasons. We can go fishing in the summer, play in snow in the winter, and there is a hell of a lot less traffic.

We have a fair amount of equity in our house and I would be willing to sell my '55 Chevy, to rake up some quick cash. A man recently offered me twice what I paid for it. I have his phone number; he said to call him any time.

We could move there and get set up on the money from the Chevy, wait for the house to sell; the best part is that we could pull this off easily. I'm sure there are nursing jobs there, and I could find a job driving a truck, or something like that. It would be a dream come true."

"When would you want to move?" she asked. "I only need to give a two week notice at the hospital."

"I could also be ready to go in two weeks," he said.

"I like it," she replied. "We could get a small place with an acre of land, and a fence, and a horse for Olivia. I remember all those beautiful trees, and the rivers with the rocks, and the rodeo that we went to. Do you remember that huge stack on antlers in the downtown park in Jackson Hole?"

"I sure do," he answered with a grin. "Let's tell Olivia about it tonight at dinner."

That night they all sat around the evening meal and discussed what it would be like to live in Jackson Hole.

Olivia was excited as she got her scrap book out and showed her pictures of their Wyoming vacation. Linda retold the stories of the dude ranch and the rodeo they attended. Vel rehashed the account of the cattle drive they were allowed to be a part of. The excitement began to build as the evening wore down, and sleep became the next option.

CHAPTER FIFTY ONE
JOSHUA GETS IT

Joshua put the pieces to the puzzle together suddenly, when he checked public records and found that Narvelle Phelps had owned a 1960 Ford station wagon, gray in color, until recently. The final straw was that the records showed it was sold the day after Mrs. Manson was shot!

The cards were finally on the table.

He contacted the new owner and he went over and carefully inspected the vehicle. Big as life, it had a three and one half inch hole drilled in the tailgate. The body was dingy gray with primer spots on it. He methodically looked it over inside and out, the back seats had been removed. The floor was stripped to the metal and there were a few food particles, cigarette ashes, and one candy bar wrapper to be seen.

The police impounded the station wagon and searched it for finger prints, but none were found, other than the new owner's prints. The real thing of great value that the crime lab discovered was traces of gunpowder on the floor in the rear of the station wagon, which was enough for Joshua to reach a conclusion.

The next day Joshua sat in the easy chair in his room at the hotel, thinking, rehashing, contemplating. He had seriously mulled things over for an hour and had finally decided that he would call Mary Lynn and tell her of his findings.

He called her and drove over to her home to share with her the fruits of his labor. Mary Lynn answered the door and invited him into the kitchen. She got them both a cup of coffee, and then they migrated to the reading room where she sat down across from him, her eyes were anxious and begging information.

He began to unravel the mystery.

"I don't normally do what I going to do right now," he started slowly, "but you have been so terribly upset and so deeply wronged by this whole experience. I want you to know that I have discovered some very compelling information and evidence. Primarily, I've been investigating cases where people have been shot in the gut and not killed. Many pieces of this puzzle now fit together, so let me start with the first pieces. My investigation has disclosed a few related incidences where an old Ford station wagon was involved.

The first thing is that a neighbor of yours that you don't know, approximately three blocks from your house, noticed an unusual old Ford station wagon, the night of your shooting. Second, one of the other people who was apparently shot exactly like you were, identified an old Ford station wagon near a barn where he was shot. The third piece of evidence is that the old gray Ford station wagon has a hole in the rear door or tailgate.

Now the tricky part of the puzzle, where the evidence leads me. The first gut shot victim in my series of investigations owned an old gray Ford station wagon, and he lied to me about it! All of these other incidences imply that it was his Ford station wagon that was observed at the scene of some of the crimes. I have actually seen the car, can verify its condition and existence, it is a perfect piece of evidence."

"What are you telling me?" Mary Lynn asked cautiously.

"I am absolutely convinced that the man who shot you and three others, owned an old gray Ford station wagon!"

She looked perplexed.

"The strange part of my findings is that the first man who was gut shot was not targeted, he was hit in a "drive-by" shooting. The other four of you were apparently targeted by a sniper.

I pulled the records and did a ten year search of people in the metropolitan area, up to fifty miles in all directions, looking for people who were shot exactly like you were. The others that I found, and you, are all very rare cases due to the single shot to the side of the body."

He went on trying to explain it further as he reiterated. "Your pattern of a single shot to the stomach area, from the side, is unique and totally unusual.

There are only five of you with this exact pattern of being shot by a single bullet to the side of the body.

My bet is that the first victim, of you five, is the one who shot the rest of you. He seemingly has mimicked what happened to him. I think that he shot all of you on purpose. He was the only true accident victim. This guy's first target was an obese woman and then the others, before you, were obese men.

The point is this, all of these puzzle pieces now fit together nicely, and point the finger of guilt at the first gut shot victim of my investigation. His old gray station wagon is the confirming link to him, he quickly sold it the day after you were shot, then lied about owning it!

The only parts that are missing now are proof of motive, witnesses, and finally a confession."

"So, how do you know without a doubt that it was him who did it?" she asked. She still didn't understand it all, nor the significance of what he had just said to her.

Joshua began again, "He is as guilty as guilty can be, it was written all over his face, and in how he reacted when I interviewed him both times. He was so nervous that I might coin a new term to describe nervous people, in his honor. Trust me, if you were there with me, watching him talk to me, you would have known without a shadow of a doubt that he was lying. You know that old saying that says, actions speak louder than words, is true.

Like I just said, he lied to me about having an old Ford station wagon. After I left his house the second time I asked his neighbors if he had ever owned one. Three of them verified that he owned that exact description of a car for many years, and that he suddenly sold it the day after you were shot.

The final straw was when the crime lab discovered gun powder in the back of his vehicle. The bottom line is this, I will bet my reputation and my life, that he is the shooter."

"What's his name?" she asked quietly, still confused.

"Narvelle Phelps."

"So why would he want to shoot me?"

He paused. He knew that she was going to have to have it spelled out in its entirety. She still didn't understand the implications of his findings, it was time to tell her the cold hard truth. He had hoped that she would get it without having to be blatantly blunt about it, but this apparently was not going to happen.

"My old partner, Joe, and I think that this guy is some sort of a psycho case who is trying to help obese people by shooting them, so that they lose weight like he did. He shoots obese people, to force them to lose weight." There, he said it.

She looked at him strangely, like looking at a two headed dog.

"But I'm not overweight!" she said emphatically. "I have never been overweight. I still don't get it!"

Joshua stopped for a minute as he thought about what he was going to say next. The innocence of Mary's face was childlike and begging the truth.

Slowly he bowed his head and carefully began to unload the dreadful last dose of the truth, he spilled it out. "I know that you have never been overweight, but the theory is this, that from a distance, that night with your coat on, you appeared to be obese like all of the others that he shot. He thought that you were obese; he didn't know that you were pregnant."

He'd finally dropped the bomb.

It stopped her in her tracks.

"What did you say?" she croaked, as her eyes spoke of confusion and alarm.

A dreadful quiet settled throughout the room as a look of painful surprise continued to distort her face. All the color drained from her countenance as she repeatedly gasped for air.

Mary peered helplessly into his eyes as he nodded, "yes."

"Oh my God!" she barely whispered in slow motion.

"He, thought, that I was obese. He didn't know that I was pregnant. Oh my God!"

She was in shock as her eyes stared in disbelief at the wall, then she slowly shook her head, "No, no, no! How can this be true?"

Joshua remained silent, for once he was pathetically helpless. He didn't know what else to say, he had nothing else to say.

Finally she broke the silence and spoke quietly again in a little girl whisper, as her head hung on her chest, "Why would God allow this to happen?"

Tears clung to her eyes, and her lips began to quiver. Bravely she held back her tears as she hoarsely asked, "What are the police going to do about it?"

"I haven't told them all of my findings yet. They are still stumped worse than I was on day one. Luckily I have put together more pieces of the puzzle than they have. You know that the bottom line with them is that they probably won't arrest him without a confession, witnesses, and/or a motive. As far as I know, there are no witnesses, and certainly no confession.

Each of you, apparently, was very carefully targeted, and except for you, the others are thriving, and have lost tons of weight. This guy was very thorough and knew exactly what he was doing, very clever, very calculating, after all he was a Marine.

I'm afraid to say this, but a lot of unsolved crimes go without real justice in our country because of our messed up judicial system. Personally, I believe that truth serum and persuasive force could be of great benefit to our judicial system, especially in cases such as this one. Lie detectors aren't 100% reliable, as you may well know.

When I was in the Navy, we functioned under different rules. The war over there was different from the war that goes on here. Don't let anyone fool you, we extracted a lot of answers by forceful means. Personally, I believe there is a time and place to break rules, almost any rules. The Navy Seal part of me would love to twist this guy's arms until he confesses, the proper attorney part of me tells me not to do it."

"When are you going to tell the police about your evidence?"

"Not for a few days or maybe a couple of weeks from now. I want to keep digging around and see what else I can find that might put this guy in jail. I swear to you, this guy is totally bug running nuts, and I believe that he definitely is the one who shot you, and the others that I have been investigating."

The room was silent as Mary stared at the floor, Joshua could tell that it was time for him to stop talking, time to wait for the wheels to turn in her overloaded brain. He walked over to the kitchen sink and got himself a drink of water, slowly sipped it down, then returned to face his broken client. She stood up and put her hands on her forehead and closed her eyes for a few seconds. Then, she began to slowly walk around the room, back and forth like a caged lion, thinking of what to do about this new information that she had just been given. Suddenly she became cold, distant, and very businesslike.

As she paced the floor, she slyly spoke her mind.

"You know that my husband and I have a lot of money. I am sure that we will eventually be able to find someone who can bring that murderer to justice. But for the sake of expediency, let me ask you a straight, no bullshit, down and dirty question."

The cowboy was prepared for anything, but he knew what was coming.

Mary Lynn hesitated as she walked up to him and looked him squarely in the eyes, Joshua could feel the vibrations coming from her body and smell her foul coffee-breath. Anger, pain, and purpose painted her determined face, burning next to his. Her eyes coldly fixed on his, in a determined stare, as they demanded an honest answer from him.

"Do you know anyone who would dispose of that crazy bastard for me?" He had anticipated this desperate question.

The Navy Seal, didn't flinch. He stood tall, like a soldier at attention, waited a few seconds and honestly delivered his answer in military fashion, "Yes Madam, I do."

Silence let him think before he cautiously, thoughtfully, continued, "I promise that I will get back to you about this in a few months. I can't promise you anything right now, please understand that the case is too new. I think I know how you feel and I'm one hundred percent on your side. The only thing that I need to do for sure, right now, is keep searching. Let me see how information can be made available to you that will not entangle me. For a price and with a little hard work, anything can be done. Give me a few months and I'll get the necessary information into your hands."

"Thank you," Mary believed him as she answered in a quiet broken tone.

When she stood up to let him out, Joshua carefully leaned over and slowly, politely, respectfully, wrapped his arms around her, then carefully hugged her, as she remained stoic. Mary Lynn didn't hug him back, her arms remained pinned to her side. No tears fell as she stood there, wounded beyond belief, unable to cry anymore, angry beyond sanity.

Mrs. Manson had already cried more than a normal lifetime of tears.

CHAPTER FIFTY TWO
MOTHER MARY AND GOD

After Mr. Joshua Horlacher left, Mary Lynn could feel her heart begin to race, and the pumping and pounding of her blood vessels on her forehead, and down her neck. Her chest throbbed as her heart banged and thumped strongly, her brain began to ache behind her eyes. She tried to sort it all out but couldn't get past the fact that some crazy man had shot and killed her innocent baby, because he thought she was fat. Something had to be done to put it right.

"Vengeance is mine sayeth the Lord," haunted her from the Bible training that she had as a child, now she wanted it for herself.

Mary's mind rushed into a wild blur of thoughts. Dozens of solutions and questions sped through her head. "What will happen if they can't prove that he did it? Will this crazy man keep on doing what he has been doing? How many other babies or adults, will end up dying because the police can't or won't do anything about it? Some serial murderers are known to go on killing lots of people before they are finally caught. What will God do if I do the right thing to this killer and punish him? He deserves to die for what he has done to me and my baby. What will my husband do about this murderous man? Shall we go ahead and hire a hit man? What if the hit man misses and only injures this crazy man? How will I feel if I kill him myself, and get the right revenge? Maybe my brothers will kill him for me; no one would ever suspect them. What will a jury do to me for doing the right thing? I'll bet half of them would take the law into their own hands too, if it was their child. Can I just let it go, and forgive him? How could anyone forgive him? Can I just go on and act like all of this didn't really mean that much to me?"

She stopped for a second, her heart racing, about to explode.

"Oh, my God, my baby was killed for nothing! That crazy bastard thought I was fat!

What a terrible mistake this is, it is so unbelievable that it has me feeling half crazy. That crazy murderer is going to have to pay for his crime."

Her mind whirled as she discussed it again with herself. "I can do it, I know I can!"

"I need a good stiff drink." she said out loud as she reached the bar cabinet. "I can't stand this nightmare any longer. I'll kill that son-of-a-bitch, myself!"

She heard what she said. She said it again quietly, and then she said it out loud again as it finally sank in.

Mary Lynn stood there, numb. Her ears were rendered deaf by the thoughts that enveloped her head. Having said the words, she expected to feel guilt, but it didn't come. All of the normal feelings of guilt had floated away in the river of tears that had flowed from her eyes. Emotionless, unashamed, stripped of dignity, and with bitter resolve, she felt like a wild animal as she sipped her whiskey and stared blankly at the floor.

"That Narvelle Phelps, insane murderer of my child, better never let me see his face; I'll kill him just as sure as I'd swat a fly.

I never thought that I would really know how it feels to want to kill someone, but now I know. He killed my baby, and he could have killed me. He needs to be punished. By God! I'll do it myself!"

CHAPTER FIFTY THREE
WHAT TO DO, WHAT TO DO, WHAT TO DO

Narvelle walked around his backyard, smoking a cigarette and slowly sipping a beer. The sun was setting, the sky was spotted with clumps of beautiful orange and pink, above the horizon. Another beautiful California day was ending.

He went inside and took a long hot shower. After the shower he decided that he needed to get spiffed up, a bit, for the evening. On went a nice, blue, long sleeved shirt and his newest pair of Levi's. Linda had already left for a card game at the neighborhood ladies night-out party, Olivia was at the movies with her girlfriends.

As he continued to stare in the mirror, he looked deep into his eyes and wondered about the man in the mirror. How he got into this terrible mess. All he ever wanted to do was to help the people that he had shot. His intentions were good, he told himself.

As the full moon climbed up from the edge of the Earth, Narvelle felt like he had pulled himself together a little better. He needed to talk about it one more time with the only person that he truly trusted, his phone call asked Harold to meet him at his house.

A moment later, Fragile was on his way over to Narvelle's house.

When Fragile arrived, they headed for the garage, for a little privacy. By the time that they reached the garage, Narvelle looked a little shaken, as his demeanor changed. Fragile could tell that something serious was on his troubled mind as he quickly pulled out two beers from Narvelle's garage refrigerator. He handed one to Narvelle, then sat down patiently in front of him on a bar stool. Neither one of them said a word for a few long anxious seconds. Then, slowly, with much thought, and a few deep breaths, Narvelle calmed down enough to speak.

"I—I--I don't know if I can take all of this shit too much longer without going completely nuts." He half-cried as he shook his head, no. "The cops and that hotshot cowboy detective are all over my ass. I'm pretty sure that they know that I did it."

"Here's what I think I'm going to do." He grimaced and closed his eyes for a few seconds. "I'm going to go over to the ladies house tonight after you leave here, and tell her about me and how it was a big-assed mistake. I'm going to tell her about the other people that have done real good, after I popped them. I'm sure that she will be real surprised and I'm betting that she will be royally pissed. I'm going to say that I'm real sorry about her kid, because I am. I really do feel like shit about what happened to her kid and her. It was a bad mistake that I never figured on happening. I wish that I could undo it all.

If I ask for her forgiveness, she's got to forgive me because she was raised in the Mormon Church, like the Osmond's. So I'm going to tell her to call the cops while I'm over there at her house, that way she will sort of feel like she captured me. I'm thinking that it might help her some. If she wants to yell at me and even slap the hell out of me for a few minutes, I'll take that too. I've got to get past this all of this crap or I'm going to completely crack up. It's more than I can stand."

As patient as the Pope, Harold listened intently and didn't say a word until Narvelle had finished, then he spoke up. "It may be the best thing to do my brother."

Then Fragile added, "I've thought about it a lot and there really ain't no saner thing to do, cause if you hang on to it and keep it all stored up inside, it will eat a hole in your head big enough to where the wind will blow through. I've known you a long time, and we both know you ain't going to do well with worrying about this mess.

You know that I'm going to keep mum about it no matter what you do. You have my word on it, and my word is my bond. I'm sorry that this tragic shit happened to the lady, and that it happened to you, cause I know you were having a good time watching your folks losing weight, and you were getting all happy, and stuff."

He stopped for a second, then he continued, "Are you going to tell Linda about it before you go over there to get caught?"

An awkward silent veil separated them for a few long seconds, then Narvelle spoke up again, "She would pass out and die if I did tell her. I think the best thing to do, is just go get caught, and let her find out when the 'fuzz' call her to tell her the news."

Narvelle put his head down for a few seconds, and then he looked up and said. "Thanks for being here for me and being such a good friend, and for not judging me. You are my best bud. We've been through hell together."

Vel was obviously much more relaxed now. He grabbed Fragile with a bear-hug, said goodbye, and headed for his car.

Narvelle crawled into his beautiful, black, Chevrolet, lowered the roof to let the breeze and moon beams bath him as he headed out, seeking peace of mind. Calm dry hands, the result of a good decision, calmly gripped the steering wheel.

The sleek, black, '55 Chevy, entered the freeway with its top down, pipes a blazing. The wind was in his face, Narvelle was feeling better about his final decision. He was definitely more peaceful than when Fragile arrived at his home.

Steady, dry hands, good signs he thought, good luck for him.

The full moon continued to climb quickly up over the light smog haze of the California hills. It was big, beautiful and glowing like warm butternut pie, a golden globe appearing to be larger than normal. It reminded him that over a hundred years ago, Van Gogh painted this same moon perfectly in a state of insanity, just a few months before he cut his ear off, a few months before he shot himself in the stomach, and died.

As he cruised along the freeway, heading for Beverly Hills, he fired up a joint, turned the radio up, loud, and listened to Wolf Man Jack howl, as the next song came on. Oddly, "Bad Moon Rising" blared appropriately from his speakers, Narvelle smiled. He was cruising, styling, and profiling, finally he was right with the world. It felt good.

An infrequent, powerful, calm, drenched him from head to foot as he realized that he had made the right decision. Both hands continued to be steady and dry as he gently gripped the wheel.

The dual exhausts sang mellow and sweet as he bravely drove off to face his destiny.

CHAPTER FIFTY FOUR
BLOODY MARY

As the same moon rose over the hills that surround Beverly Hills, Mary Lynn Manson finished her fifth of vodka. She stumbled as she headed for her bed. Tomorrow was going to be a big day. Stephen was coming home on the 8:15 pm flight from Italy.

Tomorrow would be a day of revenge and justice, she told herself.

Mary Lynn had decided that she had to kill the killer of her child. It was the only way that justice would truly prevail, her mind was made up. She closed her eyes and asked God for His forgiveness, in a drunken prayer that she slurred, as she kneeled next to her bed.

She was ready to do what had to be done. Earlier that morning she spent an hour at the target practice range, shooting her husband's powerful pistol.

In her head, she tumbled her agenda and thoughts, one more time, as she talked to herself. After she got her revenge, she would tell her husband about it later at home. Stephen would be relieved, she was sure of it. Her doctors would verify that she was mentally disturbed and that she was suffering from major grief and depression. Her deer hunter brothers from Utah would be very proud of her for not being a wuss. The public would be on her side. Everyone that she knew had agreed that they would take justice into their own hands if someone murdered one of their children. All of her friends had agreed that the police and judicial system would do little or nothing to the killer of her child. There would be no jail time for her; their money would guarantee that.

The high powered cowboy detective had done his job in a very convincing manner and he was absolutely sure. God would have to forgive her for her crime, because it says in the Bible; "there is a time to live and a time to die, a time to kill, and a time to be killed." So, it was time for Narvelle Phelps to die.

Her plan was simple and straight to the point. Get up early and go to Narvelle's house before he leaves for work. Knock on the door, and if his wife answers, ask to speak to "Mr. Narvelle Phelps." If she asks why, tell her that he just won a thousand dollars, in a drawing. She would have the money in her left hand for Mrs. Phelps to see. If Narvelle answered the door, she would hand him the money, and then as he tried to ascertain the reason, she would pull the gun from her purse, and shoot him, pointblank. Her only words to him would be.

"This is from my son Stephen."

Mary locked all the doors to her room and turned off all the phones and intercoms. She needed quiet, and a night of peaceful sleep in order to be ready for the most exciting and daring day of her life. Within two minutes she was sound asleep.

CHAPTER FIFTY FIVE
BAD MOON RISING

Nearly everyone in Los Angeles goes a little nuts under a full moon. Emergency rooms are packed full of violently afflicted victims. Police get busier as gunshots explode by the hundreds all over town. Husbands and wives yell at each other as divorces are spoken of again, in earnest. Teenagers scream at their parents, while the parents scream back at them. Bouncers in the bars, throw hundreds of drunken men from their doors, all under the watch of the big round golden globe. Suicide rates nearly double, and child abuse intensifies during a full moon. Ask any shrink, he'll tell you it's so.

When one has lived a long time, alone, the exile they live in deepens. The world is almost lost to them. This was true for Charlotte's depressed brother, Mork.

This full moon, this night, would watch over the ending of certain people's lives.

The first one to go was Mork Johanson, obesity's sad child. He sat at his desk, still rotund, bloated looking, depressed, solitary, miserable, trying to finish a poem that he had been working on for a few weeks. He read it outloud.

THE WICK'D MAN

"There goes a man, a goodly woven wick, who lacking oil doth sputter and die out.

While all about, mere tufts of flax do spark and glim, as if lighted at both ends.

They waste away that precious oil of youth, with which but one small drop may light again, to burn on in truth to fame."

Mork set it down and pushed it away from him as he decided to write no more, it was good enough.

Charlotte's sad, obese, brother knew he was doomed, long before this particular evening arrived.

Mork looked out of his kitchen window at the moon as it peeked over the hills, and he realized that he had finally come to the end of his rope. He had half heartedly tried to kill himself twice before, the first time was with an overdose of sleeping pills. But, he survived because of the famous stomach pumping procedure. His second attempt was the wrist slitting technique that he drunkenly inflicted upon himself, a year or so ago. That time, his apartment-mate discovered him in the blood red bathtub water, passed out, but still very much alive. The ER doctor had written in his chart that it was merely a plea for attention, the cuts weren't deep enough.

He recently found out that his ex-wife, Dixie had married Robby the dancer, and that they were expecting a baby. She and Robby accidentally walked past him in front of the movie theater, six months ago, when he was at the mall. Dixie defiantly presented her watermelon belly as they passed each other without uttering a word. Robby, however, had done his best to torment Mork by loudly singing, "Away down south in Dixie," nice and loud as he danced around childishly. Then Robby had added more torment with one more verse, "Oh I wish I was, away down south, in Dixie."

Mork, rightly so, was pissed, he had whirled around and yelled, "You're both dead meat! One of these days I'm going to plant both of you shit-heads in the ground!"

His famous sister, Charlotte, was written about, again, recently in the newspapers, and recently had appeared, again, on another national news program. Her weight loss and new life made national news regularly now. She had announced six weeks ago, that she and her family were going to be moving to Australia, where her husband had been awarded a huge contract to build a sports arena and a massive shopping mall. All of this sent him into another dangerous dance with depression. He realized that soon he would be totally abandoned.

Down deep, he knew that he always had been alone, that no one ever really cared much, if he lived or died.

He stared at the moon as he began his last mental ramblings, justifying his need to exit the Earth, now.

Mork's life was a bitch, his weight was still slowly climbing, his present weight, nearly four hundred pounds. His body, now, was always in pain, somewhere. His blood pressure was dangerously high, his cholesterol was through the roof, and he had just been diagnosed with diabetes. He didn't have any real friends. Women in the bars wouldn't talk to him, and he had got his first hemorrhoids, two at one plop. Because of the diabetes, he now had to carefully watch what he ate.

Being alive wasn't fun any more.

He tried to think of the last time that he was truly happy, nothing came up.

It was time to go.

This time, he was going to do it for sure. His mind was made up, no more pussy-footing around. He told himself that death couldn't be anymore painful than living. He surmised that the universe and all of its laws were directed by the Infinite Integrity, the unknown and powerful thing that some people call God. He told himself that Christianity didn't make sense, any more. How could it be logical that people are born into sin? A huge percentage of the people who have ever lived on this Earth had never heard of such a strange concept. How could the powerful omnipotent God of the universe have chosen a goofy little bunch of people called Jews, to be his favorites from all of the civilizations that had ever existed? Every civilization that has existed has believed that they were the chosen ones. How could it be that the human body was a thing of shame and that nudity should be considered as lewd, or that we should be embarrassed by it? Who married Adam and Eve's children? Did they marry their sisters and brothers? He found holes in nearly everything Christian.

Mork liked the ideas of Buddha better. At least Buddha was straight up; his first premise was that life is a bitch. Five hundred years before Christ he had taught that people should never do anything to another person that they wouldn't want done to themselves. He had given ideas on how to get along peacefully and how to prosper. Way back then he taught the ancient wisdom that nothing could be created nor destroyed.

Mork liked the concept that our soul is never ending, has always existed, and always will exist. The soul just migrates from place to place and from form to form, that there was no real death to fear, life was just a continual transformation, an illusion.

Mork paused for a moment from his thoughts as he grinned a little, and imagined what it would be like to come back as a Great Dane, or a shark.

"Nothing can be created or destroyed," he said. "Einstein discovered the same thing nearly 2500 years after both Lao Tze and Buddha said it. No one knows where we came from, why we are here, and where we go after we die."

He fixed two large steak and cheese sandwiches smothered in hot sauce, and then wolfed them down after he gulped three shots of whiskey. Then he slowly savored a big bowl of chocolate ice cream, as his mind continued to release his mixed-up thoughts. He needed to confirm his decision that it was time for him to go.

With a satiated belly he sat down in his easy chair and read his final reading from his second most favorite book, the ancient Tao, by Lao Tze.

He read, "There is something formless yet complete that has existed before there was a heaven and an earth; without sound, without substance, eternal, dependent upon nothing, never changing, all pervading, unfailing. One may think of it as the Mother of all things under heaven. Its true name, I do not know, nor does anyone; some people use the word God. 'Tao' is the name I have chosen to given it.

The spirit in our life that came from the Tao never dies. It is the infinite gateway to the mysteries that lie within all other mysteries. It is the seed of yin, and the electric spark of yang. Male and Female. It is and has always been elusive, yet endlessly available, and never ceases to exist."

Mork closed the book and felt eased by its ancient wisdom.

"My life is not going to get any better! It's over for me."

Thoughts about writing some philosophical explanation about his painful life remained undone. No one had ever cared that he knocked up his girlfriend and ruined his chances as a professional wrestler, or that he had worked like a slave to make a living, or that his back pain was endless and severe, or that his wife and child left him, or that he was still dreadfully, painfully, grossly overweight. No one had ever really cared that he was depressed, or that he even existed.

After another moment of silence, he finally laid his pen to paper for the last time, and in a comically sarcastic and angry mode, wrote his final message: "Goodbye cruel world. I'm off to join the circus. I hate you one and all." Mork.

He placed his disturbed letter to the world on the dresser in his bedroom, and got into his car and headed for the bridge over the freeway. The moon lit up the sky in the cloudless starry milieu of eternity. The stars were as bright as he had ever seen them. The bridge was very large and was actually an overpass, over the six lanes of freeway that flowed like a river under it. He parked his car a block away, got out, and left the keys in the ignition. Then he reached into his back pocket, pulled out a fifth of whiskey and pressed it to his lips. He quickly chugged half of it so he wouldn't chicken-out. He was staggering noticeably when he finally made it to the walkway across the overpass.

The big bright Moon was rising far above houses and trees. Mork stopped for a minute and closed his eyes as he imagined his soul passing upward in a shaft of white light. When he opened his eyes and saw Venus, shining like a diamond, bright, much brighter than any of the other million stars, it was a good sign, he decided.

"No one has ever come back and said that it hurts to die," he said loudly to the man in the moon. The silent elegance of the moon agreed.

Mork looked at the long unending chain of lights passing under the bridge. The air was unusually crisp and clear. Three lanes in either direction of continuous cars, tractor trailers, and motorcycles passed below him. He decided to leap in front of a tractor trailer because it would surely solve his problems the quickest, a car would be too small. After he climbed on to the concrete guard rail, he waited for the right grouping of headlights. Then suddenly, there it was, three tractor trailers coming towards him, their dozens of yellow lights gave them away. He stood tall, his mind dulled, but determined. Mork Johanson leaned forward and fell head first, toward the freeway, landing two feet in front of the first tractor trailer. The truck driver didn't have a chance in hell of stopping, he hit Mork at around eighty miles an hour. There were teeth, hair, and eyeballs all over the road as his mangled body was thrown far from the trucks impact.

As the truck driver slammed on the brakes, he careened towards the side of the road, as the big rig slid, trying to stop. The tractor trailer behind him was way too close to him, the second truck hit the first trailer, squarely in the behind. The second driver over reacted when he hit his brakes, as he frantically twisted the steering wheel to the right. He skidded slightly and then suddenly his big rig flipped over on its side, into the famous jack-knife position. The driver was pinned inside due to the crushed cab doors, still alive, but unable to get out of his tractor.

The third big tractor was carrying a load of liquid, peanut cooking oil in a huge specially built stainless steel container. He was barely two hundred feet behind the second rig and he too was going very fast. He hit the second big rig as he slammed on his brakes, and his front tires exploded under the trailer in front of him. His tractor then went off the road and smashed into a concrete abutment that helps to hold up the overpass. In slow motion, his truck rolled over on its side and the engine compartment lazily caught fire, smoke began to twist up into the air overhead.

The truck driver was knocked unconscious. After five minutes he regained his wits, then he slowly gathered his composure and carefully crawled out of the cab with a small fire extinguisher in his hand. He was still in shock as he stood next to his tractor and watched the small fire. He just stood there holding the extinguisher watching it burn, totally unaware of the fact that he had been hit from behind while he was unconscious, and unaware of what had happened to the people behind him.

Actually, it all happened in the blink of an eye. Smack, crash, thud, pow, crunch, screech and skid. The pile up was a sudden enormous mess.

As the pile up was building, Narvelle was cruising down the highway in his black, shiny, convertible, top down. Quickly he approached the scene, happy as a lark, unaware of the impending danger.

Narvelle was casually admiring the dancing harbor lights to his left as "Are You Lonesome Tonight?" began to play solemnly on the radio, he smiled confidently and said out loud, the last word that he ever spoke, "No." Turning his head quickly to the right, he looked down and nonchalantly reached over to change the radio station.

He didn't see what was coming until it was too late.

Peripheral vision pulled his head up as something caught his eyes, then he looked up, just a couple of hundred feet before his car hit the third trailer. His foot instinctively hit the brake pedal, locking the brakes while his tires briefly belched smoke. Then Narvelle Phelps drove his rare, beautiful, black '55 Chevrolet, partially under the tail-end of the round tanker with the fluid in it. His steering column was partially impaled into his chest as he smashed his head through the front window, all the while gripping the steering wheel with a death grip. The convertible's hood collapsed as the motor flew from the car and landed near a light pole, fifty feet away.

The thud and explosion of the impact never made it to his ears, it happened way too fast. He instinctively pushed himself off of the steering column, and like an animal in ice water, blindly clawed his way towards the passenger side door. Blood covered his eyes from the gash in his skull, as he remained awake for a few more slow motion seconds. Then Narvelle passed out and fell forward with his head where the feet of a passenger would be, if they sat the front passenger seat.

As the scene settled, an unusual mechanical reaction began to happen. A large 8 inch diameter, loading and off loading hose, that was hooked to a huge pipe on the side of the big tank of oil, broke loose. It swung from the top side of the tank, like an aberrant elephant trunk. Suddenly it began to off load liquid, peanut cooking oil into the front seat of his smashed up car. It quickly and quietly filled his convertible, as if it was a bath tub.

Narvelle was unconscious when he drowned in the peanut cooking oil, a minute or so later.

As he laid there, lungs full of cooking oil, a big car skidded for over a hundred feet and plowed into him. The Chevrolet now looked like a broken accordion. The driver who hit him was an elderly woman. She was killed instantly from the impact when her face smashed into her dashboard, no seatbelt. A few seconds after that, another car skidded the same distance, bumping into the old lady who was already dead. The last car in the pile up was driven by a 17 year old girl, on the way to a movie with her "blind date."

Finally it was over. Silence wrapped them all in a cloak of death-shock, while the waves of reality vibrated around the bloody, oily, nightmare of a mess. The turn signal on the oil tanker continued to blink on and off faithfully, as the small engine fire on the third tractor continued to puff smoke.

Three souls floated, ethereally, from the scene. The old lady was dead, Mork was dead, and Narvelle was dead. Everyone else survived.

Luckily there was a long break in the flow of traffic behind the carnage, allowing distant drivers to slow down. They recognized the smoke, the odd arrangement of vehicles, and the blinking lights that accompany a pile up of such proportion. Traffic slowed to a standstill as a result of the "dreaded-onlooker-delay" that always occurs. A few long minutes passed, that seemed like forever, before the police, the fire truck, and the ambulances finally arrived. Each of them had to carefully weave their way through the hindering traffic.

When it was all over, the Earth continued to spin; it didn't give a damn. The Moon shined on, and a train in the distance whistled mournfully.

CHAPTER FIFTY SIX
BANG, BANG, YOU'RE DEAD!

Mary Lynn woke to the obnoxious ring of her alarm clock at 6 am, dizzy and fuzzy-headed, with a hangover. She staggered to the bathroom, where she peeped into the mirror at her puffed up face and bloodshot eyes, looking like "Tammy Faye in a rainstorm." After she took a long hot shower, she swallowed a couple of Aspirins.

The kitchen clock told her, "hurry."

Excitement filled the air as she fried bacon and eggs, and popped up some toast, to dip into her powerful, whiskey-laced coffee. The day beckoned her like a Shakespearean play, "get revenge, get revenge, get revenge!"

Unusual power from her "made up mind," created a childlike excitement, as she stared out of her kitchen window at the yard, without the faintest wisp of conscience.

"Everything is so unreal, I'm going to kill someone today, and it's going to be all right."

A few minutes after breakfast, she quickly downed four shots of vodka and a pain pill.

"God is going to have to sort all of this shit out," she said angrily, as she slammed the door and headed for the Mercedes in the driveway. Determined, like she had never been before, she was going to see that Mr. Phelps pays for his crime.

"That crazy son-of-a-bitch is going to die today!"

Mary had practiced, over and over, pulling the cocked pistol from her purse, while holding the handful of paper money with her left hand. She rehearsed it again in her mind as she neared her destination; drop the purse, aim the gun, drop the purse, aim the gun, drop the purse, aim the gun,--- pull the trigger.

"Aim for the heart," she said out loud as she neared Vel's house.

She pulled in Narvelle's driveway at 7:05 am just after the sun gave light to day.

Alcohol numbness dimmed her eyes like flickering lamps off in a fog. "I'm going to kill someone," she whispered.

A few deep breaths before she got out of the car seemed to help, a little, before she cautiously walked up to the front door. Wobbly legs carried her pounding heart, causing body vibrations; she was visibly shaking, her teeth chattering. She rang the bell and waited, her right hand in her purse, gripping the cannon-of-a-gun. It was cocked and ready to fire. Her left hand held a large wad of hundred dollar bills. The bell rang, but no one answered the door. She looked around, jittery, then noticed the car in the driveway. Rudely, she banged loudly on the door with her fistful of dollars, then pushed the doorbell, five times, rapidly. Another thirty seconds ticked away, still no answer. Strangely relieved and anxious at the same time, her mind raced, wondering what to do next. A few more, long drawn out seconds, passed slowly; Mary was still angry, and irritated. Her body shook from the internal rage that had brought her to this point in her life.

Then, suddenly, she decided to call it quits as she slowly turned to walk back to her car. A couple of seconds after she turned away from the door, she heard the door open with a slow, Halloween, creaking sound; she stopped and whirled around quickly, facing the door, nearly falling over, her balance amiss.

Mary was blinded with rage, and the sudden alcohol rush. She thought she saw a young child standing there, next to a woman, in the doorway. Blink, blink, blink, went her bloodshot eyes. A second look confirmed that it was true.

"A live child, there, in the doorway!-------- and hers was dead! It wasn't fair!" she explained it to herself in her stupor.

"An eye for an eye, a tooth for a tooth, it should be a child for a child!" her head pounded out the final solution.

"It's a law! I'm sure it's a law. It has to be a law, it is written, somewhere!---------God-damn-it!--- it's---it's—it's---Biblical!" her booze-brain explained.

Her world tumbled, as her feet stumbled once more, then she stabilized herself, with a jerk, awkwardly. Mary, in her high heels, ended up with her shoes four feet apart, unlady-like, gawky-looking, but somehow still standing, dangerously still there, ready to kill someone, anyone.

"A child for a child!" the devils in her brain screamed, then demanded of her, "Make them cry! ---like you have! ---do it now!"

Insanity overpowered her, controlled her for a moment.

Mary Lynn's purse landed on the concrete walkway as she suddenly pulled out the cocked pistol, aimed it at the Olivia's chest, and pulled the trigger. Smoothly, just like that, a lovely boom, as a foot-long burst of flame, belched from the end of the barrel.

Olivia was blown backwards from the blast, back into the living room, as if a powerful spring was attached to her small body. She literally disappeared, like magic, jet-blasted out of sight.

The explosion of the gun slammed Mary's eyes shut, her fuzzy head whirred as she almost fell over, again. Dizzy, disoriented, reeling, she struggled to maintain her balance.

A few teetering seconds later, she blinked a few more times, then squeezed her eyes, hard-shut, for a few seconds; her eyebrows hurt as she wrinkled them tightly, then cautiously she opened her eyes, again, and again, and again, trying to see more clearly each time. Looking at what she had done.

Reality slowly stared her in the face.

Linda's thin body was framed by the doorway, dressed in a pale yellow nightgown, she was squinting from the bright sunlight that nearly blinded her. She was crying, sobbing, as she held her arms across her stomach, as if she was in gut-wrenching pain. Her eyes were red and anguished, tears dripped freely from her nose and cheeks; her hair was a twisted, knotted, mess.

Olivia, her daughter, was standing by her side, holding a framed photograph in her hands, whimpering gently, eyes bloodshot and wet.

Fifteen feet, an ocean, separated them; they stared at each other for a few tenuous seconds, fellow passengers in pain. ·

The brave nurse raised her right hand over her eyebrows to see better, then she began, ever-so-quietly, "What are you doing?"

Mary Lynn gradually quit tripping as she stared curiously at Linda and her daughter. Unable to speak for a moment, she breathed deeply, trying again to sort reality from non-reality. She remained silent, then thought. "The child that I just shot is still standing next to that woman in the doorway."

Time passed slowly as they stood like statues, staring at each other, sorting things out.

Mary Lynn finally spoke, she uttered curiously, hesitatingly, kindly, "Uhm, -- ahh, ahh, ----- uhm, ---- are, --- are you all right?"

"No, I'm not," Linda whimpered tearfully. "My husband has been killed in an auto accident, I just found out about it a few hours ago."

Silence held them lonely in their means, separated them while they stared at each other, frozen, unable to speak, confused, still trying to figure out what was happening.

Then, Linda regained her composure a little more, and boldly asked, "Why are you pointing a gun at me?"

The enraged, would be killer, Mrs. Mary Lynn Manson, held her tongue for a few more deliberate seconds, allowing the new information gradually to register in her inebriated brain. "The lady just said that her husband is dead!" -----pause---- "He just died, last night!"

Still aiming the pistol, waving it around dangerously, and searching for the right thing to say, Mary finally let curious slow-motion-movie words tumble from her lips, "Is your husband Narvelle Phelps?"

"Yes, he is. How did you know?" Linda looked surprised as she questioned with her eyes, "Do you know him? ----- Did you know him?

Compassion, somehow, from somewhere, filled Mary Lynn; she could feel a little of Linda's pain and loss. Tears of understanding quickly filled Mary's eyes, blurring her vision even more. She stood motionless and silent, still holding the gun, trying to figure out what to say next, what to do next. She didn't want to make things worse than they already were.

Then, confidently, from out of nowhere, Mary Lynn suddenly blurted out, "I heard about it on the morning news!" She lowered the pistol to her side and continued thoughtfully, "Ah—uhm---I don't know you, and I didn't know him, and, --but, --well,----ah--ah--I came here to tell you that I'm sorry." Mrs. Manson stopped as she listened and analyzed what she had just said. Her expression changed, now she looked as puzzled and mentally unstable as when she had arrived at Linda's doorstep a few minutes earlier.

An awkward wall of silence separated them.

Linda looked puzzled too. "What did you say?"

Mary Lynn didn't say another word. Numbed, nearly drunk and still befuddled, her left hand released its grip on the fistful of hundred dollar bills; they floated quickly to the sidewalk. She ignored the money, and like a robot, slowly turned around and marched back to her car, sixty feet away.

Linda stood there, confused, surprised, not knowing what to say or do, she looked curiously at the money on the sidewalk for a few seconds, and then slowly stepped forward to pick it up.

As she approached the money, in a bent-forward position, she heard Mary Lynn's car door slam shut, then, the sound of a loud explosion. BANG! It stopped Linda dead in her tracks. She looked up to see what had happened, but she couldn't see through the darkened windows of the Mercedes.

"Oh my God!" came from Linda's lips.

As Mary Lynn reached for the glove compartment with her right hand, with the gun in it, she accidentally touched the cocked, hair-trigger, and it went off. A DEAFENING, THUNDEROUS EXPLOSION! BOOM! It was real this time! It was a powerful, terrifying, sound!

The bullet passed through the passenger door, hit the nearby concrete steps and ricocheted towards a mail-box, close by. Oddly, the chunk of lead came to rest inside the neighbor's mail-box.

Mary Lynn dropped the gun on the seat as she covered her ears and screamed.

Realizing that she was deaf, she began to cry.

She cried quietly most of the way home, for her lost baby, and the terrible experience that she had just lived through. The relief from not having to shoot Narvelle, didn't register with her for a few days.

When she got home, she swallowed an anti-depressant, and a sleeping pill, before she sought shelter in the safety of her bedroom. She desperately needed to get some good sleep before Stephen got home that evening.

Just before going to bed she sat at her elegant hand carved French writing desk, pen in hand. "God works in mysterious ways," Mary Lynn quoted while she sat, calmly writing out a check. It was written to, Linda Phelps, for one hundred thousand dollars, cash. A beautiful, scented and flowered, unsigned note, accompanied the check, it read, "To help you raise your daughter." Signed, stamped and sealed, she placed the letter in the mail-box.

The pillow and the bed beckoned her, as the sleeping pill and the anti-depressant sang her into a whispering spell, "It's time to sleep."

Later that evening, after some good drugged sleep, a wake-up pill, and a dab of expensive makeup, put her back together again.

Before she left for the airport, Mary Lynn called Joshua to tell him the news. Joshua told her that he had read all about it in the newspaper that morning. She thanked him and praised his good work. Their goodbyes were brief.

As night fell, she arrived at the airport terminal, waiting her husband's return. Mary Lynn was dressed nicely, as if nothing had happened that day, but blue skies.

Stephen's airplane from Italy arrived, right on time. Down the ramp he came, looking like a millionaire, confident, smiling.

Suddenly, he peered into the dazed, anxious eyes of his wife. She gazed at him, and for a minute, escaped the distress that had surrounded her earlier that day.

Her kindest smile returned, when her anxious loving arms wrapped him warmly. A desperate hug, then a loving kiss quickly found its way to his cheek.

He had a wonderful surprise for Mary Lynn. While he was in Italy, working on business deals, he had secretly processed some important papers, and pulled a few strings that were attached to his American green-backs. He smiled widely as he told her the good news, they had been officially accepted to adopt a child. He handed her the adoption papers and a photograph as they stood together at the bottom of the ramp. Mary Lynn was surprised, and speechless. He hugged her tenderly again as they allowed happy tears to flow once more.

A moment of calm, peace, and solitude finally returned to their world of woe. He informed her that they would be returning to Italy in two months, to accept their baby girl, who had been born just four months ago.

"I named her Gabriella," he whispered. "She looks a lot like you, life is going to be good for us again." A quiet prayer of thanks whispered up from her lips, "Thank you sweetheart, I love you more than dirt." She grinned, little-girl like.

Stephen smiled kindly at their private joke, then kissed her again, tenderly, lovingly.

CHAPTER FIFTY SEVEN
A WOOD BOX

Clouds threatened to rain, as a cool breeze made the tall grass along the edge of the road, wave in glitters of light. It was high noon, and flashlight beams of light shone down on Narvelle Phelps's grave site. Suddenly, serious dark clouds threatened to crowd out the cool blue sky. A police car with lights blinking and flashing, led the parade of cars from the main highway up the winding road of the cemetery, to the designated spot. Slowly, the mourners gathered around the hole in the dirt and the beautiful simple wooden box that lay next to it. They were all appropriately dressed in black. A beautiful, large wreath of purple and yellow flowers graced the spot next to the casket.

Narvelle's funeral was attended by six of his military buddies, his wife and child, three UPS drivers, and a few girl friends of his daughter, a total of sixteen people showed up. His military buddies were all stoic except for Harold Glasscock, his eyes were ripe with tears that wouldn't flow. He stood at the rear of the group, analyzing the situation, his best friend was gone. Memories floated through his mind in a whirlwind of thought.

The funeral was cut and dried. The preacher did his thing and it was over. It didn't last long, no great oratory, no grandeur. It was as non-emotional as any paid preacher could make it.

Few tears were shed, everyone had their own private story of who Narvelle Phelps was, to them.

Linda cried alone.

Those that had gone to the funeral home earlier commented on how nice a job the mortician had done on Narvelle, he finally looked at peace with the world. The only comment that they whispered among themselves that was unusual, was about how all of his finger nails and thumb nails were absent. The wavy scar tissue, where they had been, was apparent when they peered into his casket earlier.

Narvelle had methodically chewed all of his fingernails, and thumbnails, off, down to the quick, during the last ten years of his life, nervous to the bone.

After the service, standing near the casket, Linda's face became a streaked mess as her wet mascara ran down her pretty cheeks. Olivia stood next to her, quiet, overwhelmed with it all. She loved her father even though he was distant, at times. She knew that the war had damaged his mind, but she remembered that he had always been polite, kind, loving, and generous to her and her mother. She hugged her Mother and closed her eyes as baby tears slowly slid down her cheeks.

Linda looked distant and painfully withdrawn, as if she was in outer-space, while the misty rain that had held off gradually began to rain harder; thunder and lightning suddenly cracked nearby signaling that it was time to go. She moved forward and lovingly placed a kiss on the casket, then she paused and placed both hands on the beautiful wood box for a few seconds.

"Good by my love," she whispered, and then slowly walked across the grass to the black sedan that waited for them, her arm wrapped tightly around Olivia. Just before they entered the black sedan, Olivia turned and looked back at the grave site to remember exactly where her father was buried. She studied the trees nearby and the lay of the land, memorizing it all, for the future.

Olivia issued a message across the wet grass, "I'll always bring you flowers, I love you, Daddy."

The head stone that was to be put in place later, simply read: Beloved Husband and Father. Narvelle Sherrington Phelps. 1948-1985. USMC

CHAPTER FIFTY EIGHT
JOHNNY CAKE

Two weeks after Narvelle was buried, his two best friends, Johnny Anderson and Harold "Fragile" Glasscock, got together at their favorite pool hall, to talk about what had happened to their good buddy. Fragile released a slow grin when he noticed the straggly hair cascading six inches from Johnny's chin. Round metal glasses, with "hot pink" lenses, hung on John's nose. His skinny frame was draped with an old faded green GI shirt, that had a yellow lightning bolt embroidered on the sleeve, and Levi's with holes in the knees. A homemade cigarette hung from Johnny lips, it looked like a joint, rolled with papers from a convenience store, filled with Bull Durham tobacco.

Harold and Johnny sat at a table, facing each other.

"Have you ever heard it said that everyone is a moon, and that we have a dark side that we never show to anyone?" Fragile asked. His friend replied, "Yeah, I believe it was Mark Twain that coined that phrase."

Fragile started their conversation, "Well, I ain't talking out of school, but I have some really weird shit that I would like to tell you about Narvelle. As we both know, the boy was up to doing things that normal folks wouldn't easily do, remember that time in Nam, when Vel jumped up and sprayed the Cong with his machine gun, all by himself? That boy was never afraid of risky business."

He added, "And then, later on, he was man enough to tell us that he crapped his pants during that little escapade!" they both laughed.

Fragile, told Johnny that he had been instructed by Narvelle to write about him after he was dead. Narvelle wanted to be known as the famous serial shooter, who helped scare the fat off of the people of America.

Fragile explained that he needed to share the secret life that Narvelle had lived, because it was so bizarre. As Fragile told the beginning part of it, Johnny stared at him through his pink colored lenses, and never said a word. He was all ears, unmoved, mentally tough. He had been through hell, literally.

Johnny, in Viet Nam, had survived a death march of fifty miles, witnessed his friends being killed around him. Spent ten months in a prison camp, where the enemy soldiers beat him daily. The Viet Cong nearly starved him to death; during his incarceration, he ate cockroaches, roots, mice, and a handful of rice a day. Johnny had witnessed two Marines brutally hacked to death with machetes, by a group of angry Vietnamese women. Nothing, after all of that, seemed to faze or shock him.

What most people didn't know about Johnny was that he seldom used drugs, he merely sold them for a living.

A perfect, restored, black, 1947 Indian motorcycle, was securely protected with chains and an alarm, in his two car garage. His car was a sleeper, a turquoise colored 1954 Chevrolet panel truck, it had a few dents, some rust on the body, and a hot Corvette motor. His secret 43 foot sailboat was always ready for him and his girl friend, to sail peacefully, from the pier at Long Beach.

Harold continued to unload his information while Johnny listened, "So brother, that's most of the story on Narvelle, I was asked by him to write it all down and let the newspapers know that he was the one who 'dun' the shooting. He said that he wanted to be famous, for what he thought was a series of good deeds.

For the last two weeks, I've been researching this whole mess, about Narvelle's targets, and how they have responded, just in case I decide to give the information to the newspaper. So, listen to this, the rest of the story is pretty damned interesting!

The FAT FOX, you remember her, Charlotte was her name, just moved to Australia, is pregnant with her second child, married a rich guy, still is super gorgeous, and is no longer fat! She had a really fat brother named Mork, he's the one who jumped off the bridge, causing the big wreck that killed Narvelle. Mork was divorced. I heard that his ex-wife, Dixie, left him because he wouldn't lose weight."

Fragile stopped talking for a few seconds to let it soak in, before he continued. "The two obese men that Narvelle shot, Richard and Andy, both lost a lot of weight and appear to be happy and doing well. The rich lady, Mrs. Manson, is doing pretty good, she and her husband, have adopted a baby and she is going to a psychiatrist regularly. So----maybe----well-------perhaps, I might venture to say that, mostly good things happened, because of Vel's 'crazy hobby.' The loss of the baby, or course, was the only really bad thing."

Fragile stopped talking again, to let his barrage of words register. Then he added slowly, "That's the whole nine yards! What do you think we, or should I say, I, should do about it?"

Pensive seconds passed, then Johnny slowly pushed his "John Lennon" glasses farther up on his nose, and squinted his eyes almost shut before he spoke thoughtfully, and quietly.

"You know what," he hesitated, "there are a lot of crazy people in this world." Johnny waited again. "I read about the rich lady losing her baby, that truly was some seriously sad shit." He looked away, then back at Fragile. His moist eyes looked pained, hurt, like it had happened to him. Johnny's teeth bit his lower lip, thoughtfully, then he went on.

"Here's the thing, my friend, I'll bet that some sick bastard, somewhere, would want to 'copycat' this crazy-crap that Narvelle did. Personally, I think that it would turn out really bad if anyone found out about all of this wacko stuff. What Vel did, ain't right by no ones book, he went way across the line of sanity. Think about it, what good would it do to publish any information about what he did?"

They both remained silent as his words slowly sank in.

Johnny, carefully continued, "I think that the story you just told me about him is very interesting, and that it might make a cool movie or book, someday. It actually makes me think of some fat-asses that I know, that would benefit from a therapeutically administered bullet to the belly. I think the right thing to do, mostly because of the poor rich lady, is to just let it fade into history."

He waited again, then forced a half smile, allowing a quiet whisper, "We both knew that our good buddy, was nuttier than a popcorn fart." Fragile smiled his agreement.

Johnny ended with, "My advice, old friend, ------ just let it be."

Fragile listened carefully to what Johnny said, he closed his eyes for a few seconds, and then nodded, and respectfully said, "OK, my brother,---- mum's the word."

Silence sealed their pact.

Then, when it was all over, Fragile grinned and said, "Hey John, let's play a couple of games.....come on, quick man, our table's open! Grab the beer and I'll go order up some pizza!"

THE END

Contact: Jan Franklin Tooke at
haska131313@yahoo.com

A few of my favorite books about diet are: Habits of Health by Wayne Scott Anderson MD, The China Study by T. Colin Campbell PhD, The South Beach Diet by Arthur Agatston MD, and Common Sense Nutrition by John McDougall MD.

By the way, my previous book, BACKFIRE: The Untold Secrets for Self Treatment of Neck and Back Pain, published in 1993, Taylor Publishing, is my only other published work. I am a Physical Therapist, with twenty eight years of clinical experience. Yes, it is available for purchase. See above.

Now, the three true stories, that prompted me to write this book.

1. The first true story. One day in 2008 as my wife and I walked around the state fair of Indiana, we were shocked as we saw, literally, hundreds of grossly obese men, women, and children! They weren't just overweight, they were seriously obese. Most of them were distorted in shape. Each of the adults must have weighed three, or four hundred pounds. Smiling, they happily munched on fried cheese, fried Twinkies, fried pickles, and fried everything, while they drank their diet drinks and waddled around like nothing was wrong.

2. The second true story. A precious young girl was shot and killed in Charlotte, North Carolina ten years or so ago. Some young men were target practicing with high powered rifles nearly a mile away from where she was killed. One of their "horsing around" shots was aimed up into the air, randomly fired, with no evil intention. That stray bullet, hit the pretty sixteen year old young lady in the head, in front of her friends, at an amusement park. It was horrible! It is still unforgettable!

3. The third true story. As we walked around the Indiana state fair in 2008, appalled by the obesity parade, a bizarre and somewhat alarming thought, crossed my mind. It stopped me in my tracks! I thought, wouldn't it be a strange blessing if a stray bullet came from "somewhere/nowhere" and hit one of these obese people in the stomach, in a therapeutic way. They might be forced to lose weight!

I smiled at the thought of it, I know I did. Hence the book.

Thanks for reading it, and remember, it's best to be a TRIM FOX!

Jan Franklin Tooke M.A, P.T.